R. G. Adams is a former social worker with thirty years of experience across all areas of social services. She lives in Wales with her family. *The Last House* is the second novel in a series that began with *Allegation*.

Praise for *The Last House*

'I'm completely hooked. Adams is a skilled and engaging writer, confident in her knowledge – and it shows. Social worker Kit is a fascinating protagonist, burdened by a troubled youth and equipped, because of it, to show us a fresh perspective on the world of crime and the "clients" she endeavours to help'

Alex Marwood, author of *The Island of Lost Girls*

'Social workers often get a bad press but this thoughtful and moving novel, written by someone with plenty of experience of the profession, shows how impossibly difficult their job is'

Literary Review

T0349920

Praise for *Allegation*

'This searing debut from a retired social worker of thirty years could not be more timely – nor more true . . . Harrowing, moving and written with a fearsome authenticity, the story forces the reader to question where the truth lies'

Daily Mail

'*Allegation*'s subject of historical abuse could not be more timely or alarming in this smashing debut from R G Adams. Social worker Kit Goddard is an utterly convincing character negotiating an obstacle course of prejudice, gossip and false truths. I hope we see more of her'

Christopher Fowler, author of *The Book of Forgotten Authors*

'Thought provoking and page turning at the same time. Kit Goddard is a fantastically drawn character and I look forward to reading more in the series'

Jenny Blackhurst, author of *Someone is Lying*

Also by R. G. Adams

Allegation

THE
LAST
HOUSE

R. G. ADAMS

riverrun

First published in Great Britain in 2022

This paperback edition published in 2023 by

riverrun

an imprint of

Quercus Editions Ltd
Carmelite House
50 Victoria Embankment
London EC4Y 0DZ

An Hachette UK company

A CIP catalogue record for this book is available
from the British Library.

Paperback ISBN 978 1 52940 472 2
Ebook 978 1 52940 473 9

10 9 8 7 6 5 4 3 2 1

Typeset by CC Book Production
Printed and bound in Great Britain by Clays Ltd, Elcograf S.p.A.

Papers used by riverrun are from well-managed forests and other responsible sources.

For my husband and children with all my love,
and in memory of my friend Richard

The dogs sensed it coming. They played invisible, breathing in the air as it rose icy from the tiles, biting their noses. By this time, they should be curled up on scratchy blankets, spines to the wood burner, the two old boys sleeping off the stiffness in their back legs. But not tonight. There was nothing for them to do now, nothing but keep alert and lie low.

It was the same as usual, to start with. The arguing, the shouting, on and on it went. Bella was the one who would get in the way. Young, bursting with devotion, she hadn't yet learnt that any move to protect him would bring a sharp tug to her collar, claws scraping across the floor, head snapping backwards. Griff and Tomos knew better. They would wait it out then slink into their corner and sleep until the house stirred in the rising light and they recognised their humans again.

This time, though, something new. A sudden tumbling out into the frigid night. A fast walk, the dogs hanging their heads, tails low. The voice commanding, directing the search, the boy soothing but losing the battle this time. The pressure building and building until it boiled over, bursting out into the bleak night, all control lost. He took flight, his pack chasing after him and circling as he stumbled and was caught. They saw the moment of the strike and the fast-changing shape of his eyes as shock gave way to rage. He hung in the balance for a stretched second, straining to subdue his retaliation, somehow bringing it under control. The world was restored, for now, but something still simmered and it would erupt again.

CHAPTER 1

'Totally psychotic, if you ask me.' Georgia Pritchard's mean, grating voice sounded from her office, filling the team room. 'Why can't you guys deal with it, Tim? It says right here the mother's weird and the boy sounds abnormal too.'

Everyone in the First Response Team stopped what they were doing and waited, gripped. No one ever got the better of Georgia. Apart from Tim Page.

'Weird doesn't mean mentally ill, of course. We'd have three-quarters of the population of Sandbeach on our books if that was the case.' There was light amusement in his tone. 'Look, Georgia, the bottom line is this: we have no records on the mum or the boy in psychiatric services. It's not one for us.'

'But someone in this family is known to mental health services. It's right there in the background checks.' Georgia was on the ropes now, disarmed by Tim's mild banter in a way she never would have been by a direct attack.

'That was the grandmother, actually, if you read it closely. She died in Penlan psychiatric hospital in 2012. She'd been there for years.'

'Oh well, if the gran was mad, I expect her daughter inherited it. Maybe the boy has whatever it is too. Isn't that how it works?'

'With respect, it's a little more complex than that. But I appreciate mental health is not your area. Anyway, I have a proposal. What I'm hearing from you is that you don't want this case. We don't want it either. Why don't we just agree to close it down? It doesn't sound like the boy's badly hurt. This doesn't need to go above our pay grade, surely?'

'Fine by me.'

'Great stuff. Leave it with me, then, I'll get it closed off on the system. Thanks for your cooperation, Georgia.'

Everyone dropped their eyes as Tim emerged from Georgia's office. Crossing the team room, he a threw a glance towards the desk area, which seemed at first to be coming Kit's way but then passed by her as if she were invisible and settled on Maisie at the desk immediately behind hers. He paused as if he had been brought up short by what he saw, smiled, appeared to gather himself, and went on his way.

Once the door had closed on Tim's retreating back, Kit and the others exchanged glances of amazement. This was unheard of. A turf war over a referral had never been resolved before without angry recourse to several tiers of higher management. Kit turned the conversation over in her mind, alighting on Tim's comment about an injured boy. Not badly hurt, he'd said. But that still meant hurt. It didn't sound like something that should be closed to her. She was on her feet and cracking

Georgia's door open within seconds, her knuckles giving no more than a cursory rap as she went.

'Georgia?'

'What now?' Georgia looked up from her paperwork, her eyes narrowing in the way they always did at Kit's approach, as if she might need close monitoring.

'I couldn't help overhearing that conversation with Tim. Do you think maybe we ought to just take a quick look – seeing as a child's been hurt, I mean?'

Georgia's bony face was particularly sour. 'Number one, you shouldn't have been listening, and number two, no, I don't. Some lunatic woman and her grandson or son – whatever, the boy sounds a bit inadequate to me. But he's seventeen, I'm sure he can look after himself. I've spoken to Tim, he's refused it, I'm recording that conversation, so if it goes kaput, it's down to him. We don't need any extra problems in this team right now, not while the inspectors are in. Anything else?'

'Do you mind if I take a look at the referral?'

'And why would you want to do that?'

'Well, it sounds like you made a good call there. It might be useful for my development to understand your thinking.' In reality, Kit knew Georgia had been outmanoeuvred. She'd planned to divert the case to the Mental Health Team, she'd failed, and she didn't like having lost, even though it made no odds to her since her team hadn't ended up with it either. In all those machinations, Georgia had totally lost sight of the boy at the heart of it all. Kit worried that Sandbeach Child

Services had already let him down. The same department that had let her brothers down just ten years ago. She couldn't let that happen again.

'Sure. Be my guest.' Georgia passed the referral over and began burrowing in her handbag. Her brows must be due another refresh. Kit imagined all that powder and wax must build up into quite a crust by the end of the day. She wondered how Georgia managed to prise it off. Perhaps she kept a sand-blaster in her bathroom cabinet.

Kit took the referral back to her desk before Georgia could change her mind. Easing off her boots, she reached into her drawer for her wine gums, selected two red ones and started to read. An anonymous referrer had rung the police to say that seventeen-year-old Dylan Meredith had been hurt, that he lived with his 'weird' mother and that their house was 'falling down'. Nothing to say how he'd been injured, or how severely, and no clue as to how the referrer knew about it. Then the next line jumped out at her, the tiny hairs on her arms rippling with anxiety. 'Referrer says the boy is too frightened to tell anyone what's going on, in case it makes things worse.'

There it was, the hammer blow. In the fifteen months she'd been in the job, Kit had already seen so many versions of it. *Your father will go to prison, the police will come, they'll put you into care, no one will believe you over me.* This referral had to have come from someone who knew Dylan, who understood what he felt. And if it seemed strange that a boy of seventeen could be silenced, that only made her more worried about exactly how it was being done.

She scanned the first page again, noting with a jolt that the address given for Dylan and his mother was in Craig Uchel. Deep down her stomach tensed, but whether in happiness or in upset, she couldn't immediately say. She hadn't been to Rock in almost ten years, hadn't even set foot in the valley if she could avoid it. After exhaling to regain some calm, she pushed on, following the referral's journey.

After getting the call, the police had made a welfare visit before sending the referral on to Child Services. They hadn't got further than the doorstep; the officer had described the house as very isolated and marked down a concern over the home conditions, which he said were 'basic', from the little he could see. A Ms Meredith had met them at the door and denied any problems; the officers had found her behaviour 'defensive' and 'odd' but polite and that had been good enough for them. They hadn't even asked to see Dylan. The most basic of errors, right there. Anything could be going on in that house, and no one would know.

The referral had been taken from the police by Frankie Freeman in the Intake Team, where it had been marked under the heading of physical abuse and neglect. Kit could see from the file that Frankie had looked into it a bit further before passing it on. She'd spoken to the pastoral teacher at Sandbeach High School, taking a guess that Dylan might still be a pupil. The teacher had confirmed that he'd stopped turning up for his

A-level lessons a few weeks after the Christmas break. He'd let slip to a teaching assistant that people in his home area were talking about him and his mum. She had pressed for more details and Dylan had become aggressive, overturning a desk, walking out of school, and never returning. The school's summary of concerns sounded a clanging alarm bell: *Staff report feeling intimidated by Dylan on occasion. At other times he was very quiet. No friends in school. Family not seen in recent years, no attendance at parents' evenings. Known to be very isolated in Rock.* No one had a clue what was happening with this boy, or what state he might be in.

Kit slipped her feet back into her ankle boots, slipped out and ran downstairs to the Intake Team's office. As she pushed through the swing doors, the noise level hit her ears so hard that she flinched. Rows of social workers wearing headsets were taking call after call from anxious, desperate people and attempting to re-route them to overloaded teams. The buzz of it was electric; she'd thought about applying to work in the team herself when she'd finished uni. But the repeated sifting and passing on of referrals would have driven her nuts, not being able to work with families properly, never following anything through. It was a job that clocked up a lot of brownie points if you could hack it, though, not least because one tiny mistake could mean something catastrophic happening to a child. The Intake staff were experts at knowing when to delve deeper. Frankie Freeman's extra bit of care in checking out the Meredith referral could only mean that she, too, was worried about what might be going on with the silenced boy in the dilapidated house at the top of the valley.

Kit found Frankie in her cubicle taking a break, her headset lying on her desk. She was a tall, rangy type with long chestnut hair, which she wore tied back in a tight ponytail, ready for action. She was usually dressed in sportswear, as if at any minute she might be asked to jump into a netball match and bring the cup home to Wales.

'Frankie, hi.'

'Kit. You good?' Frankie didn't waste words. She didn't have the time.

'Yeah. Can I ask you about a referral you took?'

Kit handed the referral to her and she glanced at it. 'Yep, I remember this.' She raised just the one eyebrow, indicating a willingness to accept questioning, so long as it was kept brief.

'Great. I knew you would. Can you recall anything else about it? Did the police give any clues as to who the referrer might have been? Male, female, age?'

'Male. Young. Low confidence, never done this type of thing before, dead anxious.'

'The control room said all that?'

'Nope. Rang him back myself. Had a quick word, confirmed what he'd already said to the police, then he lost his nerve and ended it. Tried him again, no answer, number unobtainable after that. I've rung it every day since.'

'Really?'

'Yeah. It bothered me. That's why I sent it on to Georgia for allocation. You get an instinct, you know?'

'Sure. What was it exactly that bothered you about this one?'

'The referrer could barely speak. Sounded like he was very scared. I thought maybe there was something seriously bad going on there, but I couldn't get a handle on it. Didn't like the bit about the kid not being able to tell anyone. Red flag, that, always.'

'Yeah, I thought so too. OK, thanks, Frankie.'

'No problem. How come you guys have it, anyway? Thought Georgia was going to bounce it. Someone mentally unwell in the family, wasn't there? Gran, I think? *"Let Tim deal with it,"* were Georgia's exact words, tbh.'

'Yeah, the gran was ill, apparently. But she's dead, and she'd been in psychiatric hospital for years anyway, so she isn't relevant.'

Frankie frowned. 'No. She was in a care home.'

'She was a long-term hospital patient.'

'Nope. Deffo. I had a quick scan of her file. Just in case there was anything relevant. Fflur, Welsh spelling, btw. Saw the placement paperwork myself. It didn't make much sense to me, adult services stuff, you know? But she was in a home, right up until she died, on Valentine's Day 2012 as a matter of fact. Daffodil Towers, or some stupid name like that, over in Hafod. Who told you otherwise?'

'Well, it was Tim Page who said it actually, just now.'

'That's strange.'

'Why?'

'Not like Tim to make a mistake, that's all. He's usually all over the cases, making sure he picks out the best stuff, you know?'

'Best stuff?'

'I mean the high-profile ones, anything a bit risky, anything complex. As long as it can make his team look good, Tim's on it.'

'You don't rate him, then, by the sound of it.'

'It's not that. He's impressive when he wants to be. But we've had a few run-ins. Tim hasn't got any interest in the more routine stuff. Trust me, if it's all legwork and no drama, he doesn't want to know.'

'This one does look like drama, though, that's the thing. I mean, there's an injury of some kind and there's quite a bit going on besides that. But nothing about it is clear. I think it's really concerning.'

'Yeah, you're right there, actually. I'm surprised Tim didn't spot the potential for the Community Mental Health Team to do something heroic. As I said, it's not like him to get a detail wrong either. I'd check that out about the gran, then, if I were you. You'll learn to pick up on these things yourself in time.'

'Yeah, thanks. Probably doesn't matter much where the gran died, though, does it?' Kit took the referral back with a touch more force than was strictly necessary and turned on her heel.

'Detail is important, though, Kit.' Frankie's tone said that Kit would never get picked for her team. Pretending not to hear her, Kit reached the door and slipped out into the corridor.

Back in the team room, she found Maisie, Nazia and Ricky still at their desks. Raising her eyebrows, she tipped her head towards Georgia's office door. Maisie answered with a nod and a warning finger to her lips. Disappointed, Kit threw the Meredith referral onto her desk and flopped into her chair. She'd been hoping for a chat with Nazia about it. Resting her chin on her hands, she stared at the front page, trying to figure out where to start.

'You're going to get yourself involved in that, aren't you?' Nazia's kind face appeared at Kit's shoulder as she leant over to read the referral.

'I'm really worried about him. He's been hurt, it sounds like the home's half-derelict, the police didn't even get a look at him and he's not turned up at school. Where is he? Anything could have happened. And Frankie said the referrer was in a bad way, really upset.'

'Well, maybe, but much as I hate to agree with Georgia, it's a little bit vague and he is seventeen.'

'That's not what Vernon would have said. He'd have said to go and check on the boy, just in case.'

'Yes. You're right.' Nazia fell silent and Kit immediately felt bad for bringing it up. They all missed Vernon, their old team manager who had been off sick since the previous summer, but Nazia was struggling the most. As the senior social worker, it fell to her to limit all forms of Georgia-related damage. Cases rejected without assessment; others started up but then closed too quickly with complete disregard of the social worker's judgement. Vernon had been the grumpiest, most politically incorrect manager in the building, but he'd been far and away the most competent too, and the entire team had total faith in him. Nazia was cool-headed and her sharp judgement was second only to Vernon's, but Kit knew she was starting to feel the strain of keeping disaster at bay. All of the First Response Team's cases were high risk and they couldn't afford to drop the ball for a single second on any one of them.

'Come on then, Naz. I really think I should check on him. I don't understand how Tim and Georgia thought any differently. They've never once agreed on anything else.'

Maisie sidled over. 'Well, if Tim thought it could be closed, I'm sure he was right. His judgement's impeccable.'

'If you say so.' She wasn't getting involved in Maisie's pursuit of Tim, that was for sure. Especially after the way he'd finally seemed to notice her existence that morning. She probably wouldn't shut up about it for weeks. 'But he's not thinking about the child and neither is Georgia. Look at this bit – the boy won't tell anyone what's going on because he's scared. It doesn't feel right. At least let me go and speak to him.'

Nazia sighed. 'Yes, OK, I agree. But you've got to get it allocated to our team first. That's above my level. You'd have to go to Georgia.'

Kit stood. 'I'll cross that bridge later. I need to get up there and see him first, make sure he's OK.'

'You're going right now? On your own?' Ricky had managed to contain himself so far but his agonising fear of what Kit might do next always got the better of him in the end.

'Yes, I am. If Georgia asks, tell her I've gone to take nappies to one of my young mums or something.' With that, she scribbled her name and a couple of vague destinations in the signing-out book, snagged a couple of bags of nappies from the cupboard, and made tracks for Rock before anyone could insist on coming along to get under her feet.

CHAPTER 2

After making a couple of flying visits en route so as to set up her alibi, Kit took the main road northwards into Cwm Hir, her mood darkening further with each and every mile. 'Beats Italy any day,' her grandfather had been fond of saying, having honeymooned in the Apennine mountains in 1967 and not having been unduly impressed. But while Kit could just about grant her grandfather's comparison in summer, the landscape didn't bear it out today. Ribbons of terraced houses hung along this flank of the Hir; as she drove, she glanced through the gaps between the rows but could only see a thick blanket of cloud, hanging so low that it completely obscured the valley floor. She found herself marking off the sites of the collieries in her mind as she went. Some were commemorated by plaques and sculptures, but most were simply gone and forgotten. She knew the names of them all, ingrained by her grandad, who had been destined for a lifetime in one himself until he'd escaped by marrying the only child of the Alessi family and taking over their chain of Italian cafés along the south Wales coast. His family had been delighted, the greatest ambition of every father in the valley being that their own sons would not follow them down the mines. Her grandad had refused to live anywhere but Rock, though, and he'd worked hard at knowing the history of Cwm Hir. It had been his penance for having escaped a couple of decades of working underground plus at least another spent slowly suffocating to death. 'He had the dust,' her grandfather would say of some dead schoolfriend or acquaintance, his face full of survivor guilt. Kit had been the only audience to this, no one else being in the slightest bit interested, including her father.

A couple of miles after the last colliery site she entered the lower end of the High Street, then turned left at the old Top Rank, which now housed a welfare rights advice service and a food bank behind its peeling Art Deco façade. The cinema had finally closed overnight back in the mid-eighties after years of struggling to stay open, just like almost every other business in the area. The once thriving little town of Craig Uchel, known affectionately as Rock by all native south Walians, had staggered back to half-life in the thirty or so years since the final pit closures, but its vitality was gone for good. Kit's sympathy for Dylan deepened. With no friends to hang around with, no school to fill his days, and little to do in Rock, his life already had to be pretty grim, let alone what might be happening at home.

At the same time, her own low mood was now tipping right over into foreboding. Should she have thought twice about the possibility of someone in this household being violent before she set out? It didn't help that she knew not the first thing about mental illness, apart from the little she had been forced to learn at university. She'd focussed on the modules about working with children, since this had been the only thing she had ever wanted to do. She had managed to grit her teeth through a few lectures about alcohol and drug abuse, anxiety and depression, all of which felt like a return visit to her childhood that she would rather not have made. It had been necessary; if she wanted to work with children, she needed to understand what affected their parents, of course she did. But as for terms like schizophrenia, bipolar disorder and psychosis, she'd never seen the point in looking too far into those. Children didn't get those conditions, on the whole, and she'd vaguely thought that any adults who had them probably didn't end up having kids themselves. Now she wondered if she'd miscalculated that one. And here she was, right out of her depth once again. But at the same time, it felt good to be there.

After turning left again into the top end of Sunnyside, Kit started looking out for the Merediths' house, which the referral told her was called Ty Olaf. She saw at once that all the stone-fronted houses lining the street had names rather than numbers. After driving down and then slowly back up again, checking every house, she'd drawn a blank. She pulled over close to where the street ended in a dank patch of bushes and brambles, under the looming Mynydd Oer. Cold Mountain. It was certainly living up to its name today. Bending her neck to look up through the drizzly windscreen, she remembered her grandfather's words: 'Cwm Hir is an unusual valley, Krystal. It's not like anywhere else. Only the one road in and out at the bottom end, no exit at the top. It can affect people, the feeling that it's hard to leave.' Rock was the last town in the Hir, sitting at the head of the valley, and Sunnyside was the last street in Rock before the mountain blocked the way. Kit felt more and more suffocated on Dylan's behalf. She hadn't missed the movement of curtains at several windows as she passed, either. No doubt a few pairs of eyes were fixed on her right now.

Glancing back at the referral form, she reread the address. Ty Olaf, off Sunnyside. She'd missed the 'off'. Exasperated, she got out of the car to have a look around, standing for a moment outside the last house in the street, a neat end-of-terrace with a dark-red front door and a tiny front garden edged with a brightly painted white fence. Someone was clearly very proud of that house. After lighting a cigarette, she surveyed the length of the road but still couldn't grasp what the 'off' might signify. The terraces were unbroken; there was no opening on either side that might give access to another property.

The red door swung open and a man appeared on the doorstep, where he stood examining her while drawing an e-cigarette out of his pocket.

'Lost, are you?'

'Yeah, I am a bit.' A sweet scent drifted over, hitting Kit's nostrils so that she had to rub her nose hard to stop a sneeze.

'Sorry. Pink lemonade. Tastes like hell but I'm trying to give up the fags.' He was in his early fifties, well-built and wearing a crisp navy-blue shirt and black trousers with sharp creases. He was immaculately dressed, in fact, for standing about on his doorstep having a vape and a good old nose. His thick brown hair had only a few strands of grey and he had vivid blue eyes, which had already clocked her ID badge and lanyard, recognisable at fifty paces due to the council's lurid purple and yellow corporate colours.

'Looking for Dylan?'

Kit didn't know what to say. She didn't want to be rude, the man seemed pleasant enough, but she couldn't breach confidentiality. At the same time, she wasn't going to find Dylan at all if she didn't ask for help.

'Don't worry,' the man said. 'I know you can't tell me anything. But I can tell you. Turn in there and follow the lane. It's a bumpy ride, mind.' He was using his vape to indicate the patch of brambles just past his house.

'Really?'

'Yeah, I know it's pretty overgrown. They don't leave the house much. I try to help out where I can, but you're needed up there urgently, I can tell you that. I'm John, by the way. John Ellis. If I can do anything at all, just give me a knock.'

'Thanks.' She saw that he was waiting for something more. It couldn't hurt. 'I'm Kit.'

'Good to meet you, Kit. And you're welcome.'

She was glad of this ray of warmth, which stayed with her as she locked her car and nipped up to the top of the street to take a look. It occurred to her that John might be the anony-mous referrer. Frankie could have misjudged the age. She wasn't infallible, after all. But then again, he didn't seem the type to get upset and he certainly didn't lack in confidence.

Standing in the spot he'd indicated, she made out a narrow path burrowing through the centre of a murky tangle of bushes and trees. She started back for her car but upon reaching it, changed her mind, not liking the thought of those brambles scraping her shiny black bodywork. After retrieving her ruck-sack from the back seat, she threw several green and white wine gums into her mouth, leaving a satisfying amount of red and black in the bag for later. She pulled her hoody out too, wriggled into it, and then locked the car and started towards the tunnel of damp foliage. As she went, she tried to trans-late 'Ty Olaf', finally remembering that it meant: 'Last House'. She was chuffed to have retrieved a little of her Welsh. So, it was Last House, High Rock, Long Valley. And under the Cold Mountain, to boot. Perhaps the council had named the street 'Sunnyside' in an attempt to cheer the residents up.

As she turned into the lane, the stony path took her breath at once and she realised that it didn't run flat behind the terrace of houses as she'd thought it would but climbed towards the lower reaches of the mountain. She ploughed on for another few minutes and was seriously considering giving up when the path turned sharply to the left and emerged into a narrow clearing. A steep pile of rocks stood ahead of her, blocking the way, and the Oer towered to her right, its sheer elevation bare of foliage and blackened by the rain. An ugly breeze-block wall stood to the left of the clearing, reaching well above her head and topped with a thick tangle of barbed wire. She walked alongside it for a few feet until she found a rusty iron gate, the latch secured with a heavy brass padlock.

Behind the gate sat a small grey house with lawns to the front and a path running up the middle to the front door. For a moment, she wondered if it was inhabited. There were four windows to the front and the curtains were closed tight at all of them, giving the house a blank, eyeless look. There were no personal touches anywhere; no bedraggled winter pots or hanging baskets waiting to be filled come spring, no trellises or garden ornaments, no dog toys, no muddy boots or wellies left out on the step to dry. None of the clues that usually gave her the first inkling as to what life might be like behind the closed doors of a family home. But then again, the lawns were tidy and the path was free of weeds. Someone lived here, but did so very quietly, attracting no attention, barely making a mark on the outside world. She hesitated, unsure what might lie inside this house, and whether she should disturb it. It wasn't too late to walk away.

But there might be a boy inside, someone who was being hurt and threatened. She followed the wall further along, until it met the pile of boulders at the dead end of the clearing. Chicken wire had been pushed into the gap between the wall and the rocks, but it was sagging down on one side. Pulling at it, she managed to open up a gap of a few inches, just enough to squeeze through if she breathed in hard and moved very carefully. The wire snagged on her clothes as she inched her way into the gap but she tugged and pulled herself free, tumbling through into the garden. It occurred to her far too late that it was not going to be easy to get back out again, and especially not to do it quickly. From this side, the block wall and the barbed wire turned the little garden into a prison yard.

She pushed herself across the grass and marched smartly up the path to the door, hoping to look authoritative. As she did so, she took in for the first time the panoramic view of Rock that lay to either side of the house. The property must stand on a ledge, a kind of half-way point between the town and the start of the mountain proper, just behind John's house but higher up, overlooking his roof and those of his immediate neighbours. In the distance to the left of the house lay the eastern side of Rock. The sight brought a stinging pang of grief; she averted her eyes before they could autopilot their way to what used to be her grandparents' red-brick villa. No time for that now.

Pausing to gather herself on the doorstep of Ty Olaf, she could detect no noise whatsoever from within. Perhaps they were out. That would be a relief; she could leave a visit card and call back tomorrow, bringing someone with her next time. But hadn't John just told her that they hardly went anywhere? She lifted the tarnished knocker, breathed deeply to steady herself, and after rapping it smartly onto its brass plate three times, put her ear close to the door, listening for the sound of movement.

After a long pause, and just as she was about to try again, light footsteps emerged from the silence and padded towards the door. They reached it then stopped; whoever was on the other side must be looking at her through the spyhole. She stood back, allowing herself to be evaluated by someone unknown and unfathomed. Perhaps the very person who had hurt Dylan Meredith. It came to her that the house was so isolated that no one could know what was going on there. There was not a living soul within earshot and the only person who knew exactly where she was right now was John Ellis, who had no reason to be monitoring when she got back to her car, and perhaps wouldn't notice for hours or even more if she didn't arrive back at all. All things considered, this had been a very bad idea, and she was turning to go when a creak from behind her announced that the door was opening. She turned back to see that a narrow gap had appeared, with a short, thick security chain hanging across it.

'Can I help you?' A faint voice came from someone who stood well back, cowering in the shadows of the hall. A chill ran across Kit's shoulders and up the back of her neck as she tried to get a proper look. Why was this person so reluctant to be seen? As her eyes adjusted to the lack of light in the house, she made out a tiny figure with very dark hair. Tensing, Kit picked through possible ways to start, unsure what reaction might come flying at her from the gloom. She couldn't even make out whether the figure was male or female, an adult or a child.

'My name's Kit.' She kept her voice quiet, trying to soothe. 'I'm from Children's Services. I'm looking for Dylan Meredith.'

'What do you mean?' The voice was tremulous now. Definitely female, probably adult. What mental state was the woman in, and how much could she understand?

'I'm a social worker.'

'What do you want with Dylan?'

'I'd just like to know he's OK. After he dropped out of school, you know? Nothing to worry about, just a check.'

'Am I forced to let you in?'

'No, of course not. But it is hard to talk properly with the door nearly shut. I don't want to say it too loud, in case any-one's listening, you know?'

There was not another soul within earshot, but for some reason it worked. The door closed for a few seconds, then the chain clanked and it reopened, a few inches wider this time. The figure stayed partly behind the door, using it as a shield and a barrier. But enough of her was visible now for Kit to see that it was a tiny woman, thin to the point of emaciation. She wore a washed-out navy blouse with a tie neck and a matching fitted skirt streaked with the chalky lines of repeated ironing. Her jet-black hair was pulled up into a tight bun at the back of her head, emphasising high cheekbones and even features. Her face was handsome, and her dark eyes were alert as they quickly scanned Kit's face before dropping to gaze fixedly at the floor. But her skin was pallid, almost grey, and she was as fearful as a cornered animal.

'Are you Dylan's mother?'

'Yes. How can I help you, please?'

'We've had some concerns raised about Dylan. As I said, I just need to check he's OK.'

'Who's been talking about us? I don't understand why you're here. Why are you here?' The woman was moving her body slightly now, using it to block Kit's every attempt to look past her. Nothing but darkness was visible in the gaps anyway; there must not be a single light on in the entire house. A stale, musty smell slipped out and circulated into the cold air every time the woman adjusted her position, catching in Kit's throat and making her feel nauseous. What the hell was it?

'To be honest, we don't know who. We had a referral; someone rang in to say they were worried about his welfare.' She knew at once that she'd put that badly. The hurt on the woman's face stood out a mile.

'I look after Dylan.'

Kit felt terrible. Whatever else was going on here, this woman was surely very unwell, and she desperately wanted to extend some warmth to her, make her feel safe. Instead, she'd done the opposite. 'I'm sure you do look after him. It was probably a mistake of some kind, but this is just routine. What's your name?'

The woman hesitated but she gave in. 'Rhian.'

'The thing is, Rhian, we also spoke to the school and they

said Dylan stopped turning up for his A-level lessons. I wondered why?'

'They were hounding him in that school. Hounding him, you see.'

'The other kids?'

'The teachers too.'

'That's hard for him, has he got any friends around here?'

'No, they're not good people. That's why we have to keep the chain on. We always keep the chain on.' Rhian's eyes were scanning the air over Kit's shoulder now, and she had shrunk back a little more into the house.

'Can I say hello to Dylan?'

'No. You can't, no.'

'Why not?'

'He's out with the dogs, up the mountain.'

'Right.' After all that. 'So, when will he be back?'

Rhian shrugged. 'Collies they are, they need a lot of exercise.'

Kit tucked this information away for later use. Glancing at her watch, she saw it was only 2.15. Ideally, she'd wanted to speak to the lad without his mother getting in first, but on the other hand, she didn't want to hang around for hours on the off-chance that he'd turn up. 'Can I pop back tomorrow?'

Rhian considered for a few seconds. 'Not here, no, that won't suit. Dylan will meet you at the bottom of the lane.' The voice she brought out for this was surprisingly firm. Entry to the house was clearly non-negotiable.

'OK, then, if that's what you want.'

Rhian cringed back into the hall a little. 'I didn't mean to be rude to you. It's just, we don't need any help. We're fine as we are. But you've got to do your job, haven't you? You've got to do it. I didn't mean to be rude.'

'All right. Can I come about two thirty tomorrow?'

Rhian's eyes went back to the floor, as if she was working out a complex sum. Then she nodded without looking up. 'He will meet you then.'

'Thank you, Rhian. Can I ask you one more thing?'

Rhian was already edging the door shut. 'Yes?'

'Am I right that services have been involved with your family before? Social work or psychiatry maybe? Only, we have a record for your mother on our system. Fflur, was it?'

The door flew open and Rhian was revealed in full, her posture poker-straight and all her cringing, apologetic behaviour fallen away. 'My mother has been dead these four years.' She rubbed hard at her mouth with clenched knuckles. 'How *dare* you bring her into this. How dare you? That has nothing to do with you. You go away and you leave us alone.' Her words were coming faster now, and her voice growing louder. She moved forward into the doorway, making little jabs of her body in Kit's direction, her chin jutting out with each one. Kit stumbled on the edge of the step as she moved backwards, landing awkwardly on the path, going over on her ankle and only just managing not to hit the ground. Still Rhian advanced, out on the doorstep herself now, her foot poised to go further, her voice reaching a near-scream. '*Go away, go away, go away!*' A blast of cold wind blew into the garden and hit her, whipping a few stray strands of hair across her face. She stopped and drew the hair back, her eyes darting around as if she had just woken up and didn't know how she had got there. She looked to Kit as if for help or explanation, then turned and slipped back into the house, swallowed up at once by the gloom of the hallway, the door slamming behind her and the sounds of locking up beginning at once.

Kit shivered and swore as she half ran and half slid her way back across the grass, struggled through the gap, and walked off quickly down the lane, her ankle tingling and pains throbbing in her calves where the chicken wire had stabbed her flesh through her thin leggings on her way out. She was thoroughly chilled, but more than that she was thrown by the changes in Rhian, as if she had been several entirely different people in the space of no more than a few minutes. But any doubt about the need for her to be here was gone. She had seen first-hand that there was one version of this woman that might easily be capable of hurting someone.

A volley of barking came from somewhere above her as she reached the end of the path, making her frayed nerves jump like firecrackers in her chest and upper arms. Glancing upwards, she located the source: three Border collies looping around a figure in dark clothes that was making its way down the side of the mountain. She hesitated, wondering whether to wait and talk to him now, but the figure turned slightly in her direction and after seeming to take her in, immediately ducked into the bushes, disappearing from sight. She waited a few minutes but he didn't reappear. A hood obscured most of the face, but it must be Dylan. Was he so wary of strangers that he'd avoided even walking past her? He'd looked much taller and bigger-framed than she'd expected. She had imagined him as a boy. Now the whole picture had flipped again. Even with that furious temper, could birdlike Rhian have hurt this sturdy young man? And if she had, what would it have taken to silence him afterwards?

CHAPTER 3

The following day, Kit made sure that she recorded the previous afternoon's nappy-dispensing visits as soon as she got to the office. She extended the time each one had taken by a good margin so that they more or less covered her whole afternoon, obscuring the period she had spent in Rock. Georgia had an unnerving habit of going into the system to check that the team's visits matched up with both the signing out book and the timesheets. It was the type of thing that Vernon had lacked both the time and the inclination for, regarding it as spying and caring only that his team got the job done in whatever way worked best for them. Georgia's view was quite different, and Kit didn't want her getting wind of any gaps in her schedule, just in case she decided to probe further. Having spent the whole of the previous evening drinking beer to calm her nerves and thinking about the Merediths, Kit already knew she was not going to give this case up. She hadn't even met Dylan and she had no idea what was going on with him. There were too many questions and she couldn't close it without making sure he was OK. She had slept uneasily, the memory of

Rhian's aggressive outburst tangling itself into dreams of her grandfather's funeral, which in turn flowed over into Danny's funeral, waking her with a jolt of tears and adrenaline that had become all too familiar in the six years since her older brother had committed suicide.

As she sat at her desk updating her other records, she could not stop returning to the thought of Dylan, alone in that house with his mother. Pushing her mind back to the moment before Rhian lost control, she recalled the woman's reluctance to move into the light and the way she had kept checking the outside world over Kit's shoulder as if for imminent danger. She must live in an agony of fear, something of a type and depth that Kit could not fathom. It made Kit want to help her, but she was afraid of her, that was the truth. Afraid that whatever it was that tormented Rhian might seize control of her again, overwhelming her boundaries this time and causing her to do something terrible. Exactly what that might be, Kit found she couldn't say. She could only nail down that there had been something watchful, something tensing under that polite reserve. The mention of her mother had obviously triggered whatever it was, and although Rhian had got hold of herself at the last minute, it had only been the shock of finding herself outside that had interrupted her trajectory. Kit's usual toolkit of charm and communication skills would have been of no use to her whatsoever if that had not been the case. God only knew what might have happened. What was it about this grandmother? Maybe she'd do a quick scan of Fflur Meredith's file while she had a minute, just to clear up what Frankie was banging on about.

She entered Fflur's name in the search box, noting as her basic details came up that she had indeed died on Valentine's Day 2012, then she clicked to open the file. It was a very small one, but it didn't open straight away. The system must be running slow. Staring at the wheel as it spun, she thought about Dylan, looking after his mother at the age of seventeen, and already well on the way to giving up his own life. How long had that been going on? It would explain him standing out in the village and at school; he was teased and bullied because of her, no doubt. Kit googled some information about young carers and bookmarked a few websites and articles to go through later. She was dying to talk it over with her team-mates, to have a big shouty debate like they used to do in Vernon's day, all of them vying to show off their knowledge and come up with an answer as to how a child could be saved from harm. But Georgia's presence exuded from her office, hanging over the team room like a noxious cloud. They couldn't risk so much as a passing chat.

At 9.40 a.m., Georgia emerged. 'I'm going to meet the inspectors.' She waited, but no one was two-faced enough to wish her luck, even though they all knew something big was at stake. Sandbeach Social Services was on the brink of special measures and the inspectorate had been in since the new year, conducting a review which would decide the department's fate one way or the other.

'Tools down, guys.' Maisie dropped her pen the second the

door closed. Several conversations started at once and a few people jumped up and made for the kitchenette. Ricky got there first and put the kettle on. Kit's computer screen flashed up a message. *Incorrect permissions.* She had no clue what it meant; she'd have to try another time. She joined Ricky, snagging a loaf of bread from the cupboard on the way.

'Georgia's particularly on edge today.' Ricky was carefully lining up a mug for each member of the team, frowning over the task as if getting it wrong might be an actual catastrophe.

'I don't get it. What will happen if we go into special measures anyway?' Kit fed four slices of bread into the toaster and rooted about in the fridge for the butter and jam.

'Search me.' Ricky looked over the room to Nazia, the only one still sitting at her desk, head down. 'Naz?' he called out. 'What does special measures mean?'

Nazia dragged her eyes away from her work with a huge sigh, her knockout smile nowhere to be seen. 'Well, obviously it means we'd get taken over by an outside management team.'

'What, no more Cole Jackson?'

'He might or might not survive it, but even if he did, he'd be under a lot of pressure. He'd have to answer to the team on everything, do exactly what they said to try and dig us back out of trouble. The same for Gail and the rest of the senior management group. Plus, the elected members.'

'Why? What difference does it make to them?' Kit held out a plate of toast for Maisie, who took it and started munching greedily right by Kit's left ear.

'Sandbeach is developing, isn't it?' Maisie said. 'Going places, attracting investment, making itself the place to live in south Wales. Special measures would be an embarrassment.'

'No, that's not it,' Nazia snapped. 'It's far worse than that. Being in special measures makes headlines. It reminds people that our department exists. It would suit Sandbeach council to pretend we didn't, keep us low profile, focus on the sexy stuff, the regeneration and planning strategies, all the lovely new shops and restaurants. Having a social services department that's crumbling because it can't keep up with the demand, can't do anything about the poverty and the misery and the generations of disadvantage – well, it doesn't look good. Not such a coastal idyll then, is it? Would you relocate to that, eh? I bloody wouldn't, if I wasn't stuck in the place to start off with, which unfortunately I am.' With that, her head went back down to her notepad, leaving everyone standing around looking at each other awkwardly.

'She's having another flip-out,' Maisie whispered.

Kit nodded. She could guess at some of what was making Nazia so upset. In the scenario she had just described, no one was going to allow Vernon Griffiths to come blundering back into his job, gob permanently open and primed for straight-talking. The team would be stuck with Georgia, pandering to the consultants' every whim, bolstering her own career, angling for a job in Cardiff or London no doubt. Even so, the strength of Nazia's reaction was a surprise. Her lovely face was more and more lined these days, Kit had noticed. She decided

34

that she'd make sure to talk to Nazia alone later. For now, it was time to change the subject.

'So, I made that visit yesterday,' she told Ricky, instantly regretting the taking of that particular tack as his eyebrows shot high on his forehead and he glanced nervously around the room.

'It's all right, Ricky,' Maisie said. 'Georgia hasn't got the office bugged, you know. Yet.'

Ricky ignored her. 'How did the visit go? Are you closing it down today?' His fine-boned face was always particularly handsome when he was tense. He really was very attractive, with a slim athletic frame, flawless dark-brown skin, and huge eyes that were fixed on Kit now, trying to read her. Not for the first time, Kit wondered if she'd made the right decision about not getting involved with Ricky back in the days when they'd first bonded as the two newcomers in the team. It was nice, the way he hovered about, trying to look after her. Well, if she was honest with herself, it was nice now and again. The rest of the time it was bloody annoying. No, of course she'd made the right decision; beautiful he might be, but how the hell did his girlfriend put up with his constant flapping? To make matters worse, Meg was a paramedic, which must provide him with endless room for anxiety.

'I think I'm going to keep it a bit longer.'

'What? Why?'

'I didn't even see Dylan. I think he might be a young carer. His mother's really ill. I think she loves him, but Ricky, she's mad – I mean, proper mad now. Scary. And I think they are being harassed or something too – probably because of her.'

Maisie threw the last piece of toast into her mouth. 'You'd better keep that away from the inspectors, then. Tim mentioned to me that they're very tough on boundaries between teams.'

As one, Kit and Ricky looked at Maisie, trying not to catch each other's eye. 'Been chatting to Tim, have you, Maze?' Kit giggled.

'Don't be childish. The point is, the Merediths are not our case and it's not really your area either, is it?'

'Sorry, say it again? Being a young carer isn't my area?'

'No offence. But personal experience doesn't necessarily make you an expert.' Maisie was unperturbed, packing her wicker basket now, ready to go off on her visits.

'I think it does.' Kit thought back to her family. The way the five of them had looked after their mother. Picking Christine up off the floor when they came in from school, sobering her up and putting her to bed, taking money from her purse first thing on benefits day to put on the electricity card before she could spend it on booze.

'Never mind about her.' Ricky watched Maisie waddling out of the office in her all-enveloping winter outfit of purple puffa coat and matching bobble hat. 'She only says that kind of thing to wind you up.'

'I know.' Kit wondered what it must be like to be at the end of your tether and then to open the front door and find Maisie standing there, your last hope.

'So, what exactly happened yesterday?'

'The place gave me the creeps, and at first she wouldn't let me in. She wasn't hostile at first, she seemed scared.'

'Scared of what? Of you?'

'Yes, but not just me. Scared generally. The house is all locked up, all the curtains closed, huge wall round it and she's got this massive chain on the door. She was terrified one minute. Then she warmed up a bit. Next thing I knew, she'd completely flipped: I backed off so fast I nearly broke my neck right there on the garden path. Then she was back to being terrified again.'

'What do you reckon is going on?'

'I don't know, but the way I saw her she could hurt someone for sure. She needs treatment of some kind. I'm going to go back today and see if I can get to talk to the boy.'

'Should I come with you?'

'No, you're all right. I won't drag you into it. I still owe you for that time last summer with the Coopers. I feel a bit bad about it, if I'm honest. I should have said before.' The Cooper family had been Kit's first big case, during which she'd managed to bring down a child abuse ring that had preyed on numerous children on her home patch of the Coed estate, including her own brothers. She'd stepped beyond procedure once or twice in the process, and what was worse, she'd taken Ricky over the boundary with her.

'That's fine, but just be careful. Please.' One of the best things about Ricky was that he knew an implicit apology when he heard one. And the other was that he knew not to make a thing of it.

'You all right, Naz?' Kit slid onto the desk next to Nazia's, fully prepared to get her head bitten off.

Nazia barely glanced up from her screen. 'Yeah. Tired, that's all.'

'Any news on Vernon?'

'No. Last time I tried to speak to him Nell was protecting him like a guard dog. I can't see him coming back to work, though, can you?'

'I can't see him giving it up either.'

'He may not have a choice in the matter. Anyway, look, are you around Thursday of next week? The inspectors want to see some actual social workers and I've pencilled you in for nine thirty.'

'Me? I mean, that's great, but why me?'

'You're a new member of the team. I thought it might be useful for you to speak to them about your induction, what it's been like settling in, how we've helped you to gain all the basic skills, you know?'

'Oh, OK.' Suitably crushed by the news that she was apparently only meeting the inspectors to talk about her own lack of experience, Kit immediately lost interest.

'Nine thirty it is, then. And please be careful what you say. No moaning about Georgia – it won't do any good, it looks unprofessional and if it gets back to the senior management group you will not be popular.'

'I don't think I need to worry about that, do I?' Kit said, regretting it even before Nazia's face told her it had been the wrong thing to say.

'I know you did well with that one case last year. But don't get above yourself. You're still new and you've got a lot to learn. I don't want to sound harsh, but it's dangerous to get too complacent.'

'So you keep saying.'

'Take note then, missy. Don't overreach yourself. And what are you going to do about this Meredith case? You're running about on it and it's not even ours.'

'Just on my way to sort that now.' She had catapulted back off the desk and was on her way to the door before Nazia could open her mouth to question her. No need to get into the whys and wherefores of what she was about to do. It would only cause upset.

As Kit took the stairs to the fifth floor, she wished Georgia hadn't agreed to close the case. Normally, a dispute like that would have ended in a row somewhere higher up the building. Occasionally, it got to head of service level. When that happened, everyone knew Child Services had already lost the argument; Cole Jackson was no match for his redoubtable counterpart Gail Wilson, Head of Adult Services. But Tim and Georgia's unexpected collusion had derailed that and now she was left with the job of persuading Cole to accept it into his department. Even if he did, he'd stand on his head to avoid allocating it to Georgia's team. Cole liked to keep Georgia happy; rumours abounded as to exactly how happy.

Arriving at the heads of service office suite, Kit realised she had better pause and get her argument together before she went any further. She leant the fronts of her thighs against the radiator under the window to warm her flesh, which was still somehow chilly under her thick tights and woolly skirt. Gazing out over Sandbeach, she saw with disappointment that it looked grey and ugly in the February rain. Summer felt too far away in both directions. Even the sea was flat and unappealing today. She'd managed to keep swimming in her wetsuit well into November, but then the choppy waves had got the better of her and she'd had to give it up. Since then, her life had consisted of going to work every day, falling asleep on the sofa every evening and spending weekends watching Netflix and eating takeaways with her brother, occasionally summoning up the energy to visit her nieces and nephews or even her mother if she was feeling particularly generous.

She'd taken a few days off at Christmas to stay with her former foster carers, Huw and Menna, out west at Cliffside. She'd whiled away the time by walking the cliff paths above the beach with her collie, Jess, torturing herself with the sight of the Bayside Café, all shut up for the winter now while Alex made his way across Europe. There had been an occasional text or Snapchat from him but otherwise no sign that he thought about her at all. A few days ago, he'd texted her a single kiss. It had been lunchtime before she'd remembered the date, and then she'd fallen down a rabbit hole for the rest of the day, trying to work out whether Alex would even be aware that it was Valentine's Day, whether the kiss meant anything, and if so, what. She'd fretted herself into a state of irritation with him. But she had no right to feel angry at all, of course. She'd had the chance over and over again to tell him how she felt. She hadn't realised it herself for a long time. She'd started working in Alex's café while she was in uni. His interest in her had been obvious from the start, but she hadn't been in a position to start anything with him, or even to give it more than a passing thought. Her head had been full of nothing but Jem and his dramas. Jem had been her first boyfriend, a relationship formed when they had both been in the children's home and hung onto long after she moved into foster care. It had gone on far beyond the point where it was good for either of them, in fact. Only once Jem was out of the picture, safely in hospital being treated and with no prospect of a return any time soon, had she realised how comfortable it was between her and Alex, and how kind and shrewd he'd been throughout all the madness, always ready to help her. Danny had come to like Alex too, confiding in him a lot towards the end. Danny didn't trust easily, so that had stood as a pretty important recommendation. She should have told Alex how she felt about him last summer, the very minute it had all come together in her mind and her heart. If she'd just been clear that she was interested, something would have started between them right there and then. But she hadn't done it, for reasons she now couldn't quite pin down. Perhaps she'd been wary after her relationship with Jem, the way he'd always called the tune; she wasn't about to risk getting back into anything like that again. Time had passed while she dithered and, in the end, the runes had suggested that Alex might enjoy a trip to the sun while the café was shut for the winter. He'd been gone within two days. But he'd be back, she reassured herself. In the meantime, the important thing now was that she must not under any circumstances come across as desperate.

'Ah, Kit. I was just . . . are you all right?' Cole Jackson hovered behind her, exuding social anxiety and sandalwood in equal measure.

'Yes, sorry, I was miles away.'

'Good, good. I was just on my way down to your room. Is Georgia there at all?'

'I'm pretty sure she's out all day,' Kit lied fluently. 'Have you got a minute?' She held the referral out to him. He shied away, presumably fearing he might have to get involved in some actual social work.

'Is it a referral issue? Because as you know, I don't get embroiled in those.'

'I know. But it's a bit of a tricky one. The police have been but they didn't see the boy and there's a suggestion he's at risk, he may already have been harmed. I popped up yesterday just to take a look, but I didn't get to see the boy. I just feel someone needs to clear it up, make sure there's no comeback if something's wrong up there.'

'What's Georgia's view?'

She was all ready for this one. 'Tim Page and Georgia were thinking of closing it. With all due respect to Georgia, she's pretty busy with the inspection, and I thought maybe I could sort it without bothering her. I'm afraid this one might blow up in our faces.'

Cole might as well have heard only the last sentence. He scanned the referral. 'I see what you mean. And I can definitely see that it's not Adult Services' role to sort this.' Cole's background was in admin, so he could see no such thing, but Gail Wilson's strident tones could be heard reverberating through his every word, an echo of their previous altercations. He rubbed at the back of his neck, working at the tension knots that had no doubt sprung up out of nowhere in the last thirty seconds. 'At the same time, Kit, I know how busy you are in the First Response Team and I'm thinking it doesn't meet the criteria for you guys either. Perhaps it would be better if I gave it to case management.' He was back to thinking what Georgia was going to say now, and he was in quite a pickle.

'Case management will want it assessed first to rule out the suggestion of violence. I can sort that easily, Cole. It sounds like the school overreacted and made the referral and didn't even want to put their name to it. I'm up that way later today, so I could pop in and have a chat with the boy and get it closed tomorrow. I'll bring it up to you to sign the closure if you like.' She hadn't said the words 'and Georgia will never know'. But they hung in the air, nonetheless.

'That really would be most helpful, if you feel you can manage it. We need to make sure everything's running smoothly during this inspection. And you'd be my first choice to tidy this up, of course.'

'Thanks.' In truth, Kit had been struggling to find her work interesting in recent months. Everything felt too easy, a bit of an anticlimax. Nazia protected her constantly, kindly but firmly pointing out her lack of experience, and diverting Georgia into allocating the more difficult cases to other team members. Vernon had never made her feel like she couldn't manage the more difficult stuff; he'd thrown anything and everything at her right from the start and just expected her to rise to the challenge. She always had. But he'd been off sick since the previous summer and the team had been in a different place since Cole had parachuted Georgia into the manager's post.

Cole shifted his weight from one leg to the other, stuck for a way to close things. 'Anyway, thanks for your help, Kit,' he managed, eventually. Having ticked the box for today's five minutes of interaction with the lower orders, he took his relieved expression and retreated into the safety of the senior management suite, the swing of the heavy wooden doors wafting undertones of vanilla and cherry in Kit's direction. She took the stairs two at a time, planning to get her bag and leave before Nazia could find her something less interesting to do.

In the team room, Ricky and Maisie were leaning back in their chairs, chatting in a way that told her Georgia must have minced off to the lunch area to nibble on her cloud bread. If Maisie was banging on about Tim for the millionth time, she was just going to turn right round and go back out again.

'Where have you been?' Maisie demanded.

Kit looked around. 'Where's Nazia?'

'Lunchtime Zumba. Why, what are you up to?'

'I've been to see Cole.'

'How's his aftershave today?'

Kit struggled as to how to sum up the olfactory horror. 'Like someone threw up birthday cake in the Body Shop,' she said, finally.

'Oh, yuk. What did you want him for anyway?'

'I got him to allocate me the Meredith case.'

'What's Georgia going to say about that? You're not her favourite to start off with, I'm not sure if you're aware?'

'Thanks, Maze, it hadn't passed me by. But so what? Anyway, she won't know. All I've got to do is see the boy, talk him round and find out what's going on up there. It should be easy enough to sort.'

'Well, it's your funeral. Now, we've been talking about how I can get Tim to move things along. I think he's interested, he's been really quite charming whenever I've run into him the last couple of days. Why don't you sit down? I could do with a female perspective.'

'Sorry, Maze, gotta run. See you guys later.' She pretended not to notice that Ricky was using his eyes to signal for help.

On her way across the car park, she pulled out her phone

and brought up Vernon's numbers. Nazia hadn't got through to him, but surely if she used his personal mobile rather than his landline, Nell wouldn't answer that? It rang out for a long time and she was about to give up when he finally answered.

'What's up with you, now? You do realise I'm off sick?'

'Well, it had come to my attention, yes. I fancied a chat.'

'You're lucky Nell's not in. She's monitoring all my communications, it's like being in prison.'

'I'd heard that too. I suppose she just doesn't want you getting stressed.'

'Yeah, well she had a fright, what with me being snatched back from the brink of death.'

'Chill out, Vern. You had a mild heart attack.'

'Have you rung up specially for an argument? Or has something gone wrong? Ricky again? Or Maisie? It's gotta be one of those two.'

'No, nothing like that. I'm just wondering when you'll be back.'

'Missing me, are you?'

'No, but Georgia's obnoxious. And she doesn't know what she's doing. Something's going to blow up, she's closing cases too soon just to get our numbers down.'

'Well, sorry to disappoint you but I haven't had any news either way. There's an ominous silence, in fact. I've got a suspicion Cole's not that keen to have me back at all.'

'He can't do that, surely?'

'He seems to pretty much do what he likes. Look, I've got to go, Nell will be here any minute. But if you're worried about any of your cases, drop me a text and I'll call you for a quick supervision when she's not around, OK? I'm not liking the sound of what you're telling me one bit.'

'That would be great. Thanks, Vern.' She wouldn't do it, though, not if she could possibly avoid it. She couldn't bring herself to worry him anymore than she already had. She said her goodbyes and got into the car, worrying over what he'd said and the prospect of Georgia becoming a permanent fixture.

CHAPTER 4

Kit's spirits lifted as she turned onto the valley road. The weather was much better today and the sight of winter sun falling on the deep green expanse of fir trees on the far side of the valley brought back good memories of long walks with her grandad, who'd always been at pains to squeeze in a bit of history, explaining that the forest had been planted to provide props to support the roofs of the local collieries.

Her grandad had loved her and her brothers and sisters, and he'd done his best to help them, she knew that. When their parents' marriage had ended and her mother had fallen apart, her grandparents had had all five of them to stay. She didn't remember that too well, she'd been small. But she knew that after her gran had died he'd found it hard to manage them all turning up without notice, often brought by the emergency social worker in the middle of the night after Christine had lost the plot yet again. Not to mention the inevitable backlash when she changed her mind and got abusive, demanding her children back. Their grandad had been a gentle man, and he didn't cope with Christine once Nana Martina wasn't around to stand up to her. Even the social workers had seen that it was too much for him and so the cycle of foster placements and residential homes had started for the Goddard kids. But Kit had always kept in touch with her grandad. She'd get the bus up to Rock most weekends, glad to escape Redbridge House for a few hours, and they'd spend whole days wandering about in the forest or up on the Oer. He'd died just after she moved to Cliffside, so he'd never seen how happy she'd become with Huw and Menna, or how her life had turned out.

Now that she'd allowed herself to start remembering it was hard to close the floodgates, but as she drew closer to Sunnyside, Kit forced her attention onto Dylan. How could she approach him, and what would draw him out? There had to be a way to get him to tell her what was going on. Kit was ace at handling teenagers, so provided she kept her focus and didn't get diverted into the deranged mother or the dead gran, it should be straightforward enough.

As she turned past the Top Rank, she reached into the door pocket for her fags but her fingers met an empty packet. Spotting an orange and yellow sign a few yards past the turning for Sunnyside, she drove towards it and pulled up outside the Valleys Local One Stop Shop.

The shop was quiet inside and it smelt of warm bread and cheap pastry. It was fantastic and it made Kit's stomach growl. She followed her nose to the back where she spotted a small bakery counter. A skinny, middle-aged woman stood behind it, gloves on her hands, taking fresh pasties from a metal tray with a pair of tongs and lining them up one by one behind their respective labels in the glass cabinet.

She looked up at Kit's approach. 'What can I get you, love? They're nice and hot.'

'Cheese and onion, please.'

'There you go.' She dropped a pasty into a paper bag and scribbled on it, then held it out, taking the opportunity to examine Kit from head to toe. Kit instinctively reached for her ID badge, intending to push it into her coat, but it was too late.

'From the council, are you?'

'Me? No. Just visiting.'

'Got family up here?'

'What do I owe you for the pasty?'

'Pay at the front, love. Price is on the bag.'

A younger, even thinner version of the first woman stood behind the till, not attempting to hide that she had been listening. Sisters, Kit reckoned, and they were clearly unnaturally close, because they'd recently shared a shade of Nice'n Easy that was way too harsh for both of them. Blue-black, by the look of it. It emphasised the pinched look to their faces, not unkind exactly, but ready to peck into everyone's business. Kit paid the younger woman, avoiding eye contact with difficulty, and was outside the shop and almost into her car before she realised she'd forgotten her fags. She hesitated on the pavement; she really didn't want to have to stop again on the way back to the office. But the two women would be talking about her for sure, and she was embarrassed at the thought of walking in on them. She wasn't keen to know what they were saying, either. She waited a little longer, then propelled herself back to the door, still wary but calculating that they must have finished by now. She wasn't interesting enough to merit more than a couple of minutes of chat, surely? She pushed the door open a couple of inches and immediately picked up the sound of voices from the back of the shop.

'That's the girl's been seen in Sunnyside. Only one place she'd be going up there.'

'Well, it is about time the authorities did something, Rowena. It's not right, the way they live.'

'You don't need to tell me, Cath. I was in school with her, remember? Something bad happened. How else did her mother disappear like that? Then she comes out with some tale that she died in hospital, years and years later that was. It's never been gone into, no, not at all. All that time and finally some-one's turned up. It's a case of shutting the stable door, if you ask me.'

'Some people say they've seen the ghost of Fflur wandering on the Oer, looking to be reunited with Owen.'

'Some people are bloody tapped.'

'True enough. Mind, you'd have thought the council could have sent someone proper to do it. She's not long out of school, that one.'

Kit let the door swing shut, totally unneedled by the refer-ence to her age, which she was well used to, but so fascinated by the rest that she forgot about her cigarettes all over again.

As she drove the few yards to Sunnyside, she turned it over in her mind, wondering how she could find a way to penetrate the swirl of rumour that surrounded Fflur Meredith and her family.

This time John didn't appear when she pulled up in front of his house, which could only mean that he wasn't in. After locking her car, she made her way to the end of the lane where Rhian had indicated she should meet Dylan. There was no sign of him, and she wondered after the scene the day before whether Rhian would have changed her mind about sending Dylan to meet her. But she was a few minutes early. So she'd hang on and see if he turned up. She was longing for a fag now; she tried to distract herself, turning her face up towards the weak rays of sun, drinking in the hope of summer, of Alex being back and a second chance.

She became aware of shouting over to her left, coming from the next street. After a few seconds, a figure turned into Sunnyside, on the opposite side to Kit, walking fast and then breaking into an ungainly trot, a loaded carrier bag in each hand. The same figure she had seen with the dogs up on the mountain the day before. The shouting continued behind him and the reason for it became clear a couple of seconds later when a tatty silver Fiesta came careering around the corner, two teenage boys shouting and jeering at Dylan from the front windows. Time for some direct intervention.

She crossed the road to the opposite pavement and waited as Dylan barrelled towards her, half running now but hampered by the carrier bags banging against his knees. As the car drew nearer, she made out what the boys were shouting.

'Where's your psycho nan, Dylan Meredith?'

Dylan was about to pass her but Kit stepped forward and caught him by the arm.

'I'm Kit,' she told him. 'I spoke to your mother yesterday. When I give you the nod, go over the road and wait outside John's. I'll sort these two out.'

He looked at her with surprise, but then his eyes showed relief. She pushed him behind her and turned back to see that the car had pulled in against the kerb and the two boys were scrambling out of it. She appraised them quickly; the driver was about her own height, the other much taller, almost equal to Dylan and equally big in frame. As they came towards her, their eyes were fixed over her shoulder, intent upon Dylan. She was invisible to them. She stood square in the middle of the pavement and spread her arms out straight from her sides. They could have squeezed past her easily, but it was a challenge, and from a female at that. They would be incapable of ignoring it. Having grown up with two brothers, Kit knew the mentality of boys inside out.

'Get out of the fucking way,' the taller one spat, still advancing.

'No, I don't think so.' She flashed them her sweetest smile, knowing it would wind them up even more.

They stopped, brought up short by her refusal to do as she was told. She watched the silent exchange in their eyes carefully, and it told her that the smaller one with straggly hair was in charge; the bigger one was looking to him to see what they should do next. Armed with this knowledge, she stood firm. In spite of the fags and the takeaways, she was reasonably fit from her years of swimming, and more importantly, she was unafraid. That was enough to throw most boys right off balance.

'Move, bitch.'

'I'm going nowhere.' She resisted adding 'dickhead' on the grounds that it would be unprofessional.

The smaller one stepped up close to her and started shoving and barging. She did the same back for a few seconds, getting her shoulder in firmly against the sharp bones of his chest, breathing through her mouth to offset the combination of body odour and weed that clung to his clothes. When she could see he was absorbed in his furious determination to win the tussle, she slipped her hand around the back of his neck and grabbed a long hank of his greasy hair, winding it in her fingers and holding it downwards firmly. She was careful not to hurt him, but if he tried to move, he'd hurt himself. His mate stood rooted to the ground, mouth hanging open, rendered incapable of action by shock and the absence of instructions. Total amateurs, the pair of them.

'Right, you two can leave Dylan alone from now on.' She turned and gave Dylan the promised nod, and after a second's hesitation, he took off across the road.

'Let go of him, you fat cow.' The taller one had come to

life now and was making a token move to edge in closer to Kit. She turned to face him, still holding the handful of his mate's hair.

'I wouldn't if I were you. One scream from me and you'll have twenty people out on the street. Two boys on one girl. Wouldn't look good at all, would it? You'd be banged up for a very long time with a bunch of lads a hell of a lot harder than you two. So, are you going to do as I say and piss off, or am I going to start screaming?'

She opened her mouth wide in readiness and then let go of the boy's hair, giving him a slight shove as she did so. He stumbled backwards against his mate then straightened up quickly, embarrassed, and turned and walked off towards the car, trying to retain some swagger. The other boy followed him. She watched them get into the car, feeling very pleased with herself until she saw that the small one was grinning and dangling something purple and yellow out of the window. Her ID badge. He must have grabbed the lanyard when they were struggling and the safety catch must have snapped open without her even noticing.

'Want it back, do you, bitch?' he crowed. Kit launched herself at the car window and just had time to see fear cross his face before the car shot past her, banged its wheels loudly against one kerb and then the other in a clumsy three-point turn and then disappeared down the street and around the corner. She doubled up with laughter at the sight of their desperation to get away from the mad girl.

As she crossed the road, Kit was panting slightly from a combination of exertion and irritation at having let her ID badge go. She'd have to think about how she was going to get that back. She could go to HR for a new one, but that would take a few days. Besides, she'd already got through three badges since she'd started the job, and they'd threatened to charge her if she lost another one. She wasn't keen on the idea of leaving it in the boy's hands, either. God knows what fun and games the little sod might get up to with it. Still, other than that, she reckoned she'd done well. She would text Tyler later and tell him about it. She'd used the hair trick on him once during a fight, but he wasn't the type to give in anymore than she was and she'd ended up with a handful of hair and a nasty bruise from falling backwards onto a concrete floor, while he'd had to go around with a bald patch for six weeks.

Dylan was waiting for her outside John's house. He was pale-skinned, like his mother, and he had the same thick black hair, falling across his upper face in an untidy fringe. His smile was a surprise, though; it flared brief but warm, lighting up his dark slate eyes and softening his square, heavy features. But as soon as it had gone, she saw his teeth biting down into his lower lip. It was an odd tic, vulnerable and boyish and totally at odds with his physical appearance. She wondered why he hadn't turned on the two boys. He was capable of giving them a hiding if he wanted to, physically at least.

'You OK?' she asked him.

'Yeah, I guess so.'

'You worried they'll be back?'

'Yeah. They don't leave me alone.'

'They might think twice now they've met me, eh?'

'I doubt it.'

'Come on,' she told him. 'I'll walk back up to the house with you. We can talk on the way.'

They started walking together, and she could see that he didn't know what to say next. 'I saw you with your dogs, yesterday. You should take one of them with you when you go to the shop. A collie will see those idiots off, no trouble. I've got one too – look, her name's Jess.' Kit pulled out her phone and scrolled to a photo she'd taken out on the cliffs at Christmas. Dylan peered at it and that beautiful smile flashed across his face again.

'She's stunning.'

'She is, and she'd do anything to protect me. I'm sure any of yours would do the same.'

'I'm afraid, though, see. Joe Pavey put a screwdriver in a dog's neck once.'

'So, it's Joe Pavey – which one is he?'

'The tall one.'

'And who's his mate?'

'Aled Simms.'

'Were they in your school?'

'Aled's still there. Joe's left.'

Kit made a mental note. Maybe it was time someone spoke

to the school about Aled and his antics, see if they could get his parents involved. And perhaps then she could get her ID badge back too. For now, though, she needed to get a conversation going with Dylan.

'So, is he the reason you gave up going?'

He shrugged. 'Yeah, I guess so. I didn't see the point anyway, though.'

'Well, I guess the point is to study something you like. What A-levels were you doing?'

'Maths, Physics and English. I liked English best.'

'Me too. Who are your favourite authors?'

'I like poetry. We were doing Wordsworth.' He was looking at her sideways. 'I know loads off by heart.'

'Go on then, let's hear some.'

'Nah.'

'OK then. So would you have gone on with the English? Gone to uni maybe?'

'I'd have loved that. But it's safer at home.'

'How do you mean, safer?'

He stared straight ahead, as if she hadn't spoken.

'Dylan, what do you mean, safer? What's not safe about being away from home?'

His lip blanched as his teeth burrowed into it. 'It's just better at home.'

'Is that what your mum says?'

He nodded. 'Yeah. She says I can read my books there anyway. My neighbour gets them from the library for me.

Anyway, thanks again for helping me.' They'd reached the gate of Ty Olaf now. He lingered awkwardly, pushing his hair out of his eyes. The movement exposed his right cheekbone, which bore a small patch of yellowed skin. A fading bruise. She scanned it for fingertip marks as subtly as she could, but he caught her at it and immediately combed his hair back down with the flat of his hand. She saw in his eyes that he didn't want her to ask. She couldn't let him go yet, though; she hadn't made enough of a connection to be sure that he'd see her again. Keeping well back from the gate, she leant her side against the forbidding breeze block wall.

'Why don't you stay here for a couple of minutes, so we can finish talking?'

He mirrored her posture. 'OK then. But I can't be long.'

'So, have you got any mates up here?'

'Not really.'

'What do you do with your time?'

'I walk the dogs, go to the shop. I do stuff around the house for my mother, chop wood and that. I built this wall last summer, took the fence down and put this up instead. It's really strong.' He smacked it twice with an open palm.

'Wow, that's impressive.'

'Yeah, it was really hard work, it took me, like, weeks. I did it on my own.'

'That's great. Sounds like you did well at school too. Any chance of hearing a bit of that Wordsworth now?'

He shook his head. 'Nah. It's stupid.'

'It's not, but no problem. Maybe next time, if I come and see you again?'

'I dunno. My mam said only once, then you'd leave us alone.'

'But I haven't had the chance to explain what I'm here for yet. I'm a social worker, my job is to help you.'

'Who said we need help? Was it school?'

'It might have been. Honestly, we don't know. But someone was worried about you.'

He shrugged. 'We're fine as we are.'

'I'm just here to check that out. I'll come and have a word with your mum about it now if you like?'

'No, don't do that. You could meet me on the Oer. Do you know the viewing point?'

Kit nodded. 'Sure.'

'I go up every day about this time with the dogs, after I get back from the shop. Come up if you want to find me.'

'Thursday?'

'Yeah, OK. I need to go now.' He threw a glance at the gate.

'All right, but I need to ask you something first. One more question and then I'll let you go.'

'You're annoying.' He grinned, watching her face to monitor her reaction.

'Yeah, I know. So, one question?'

'Go on.'

'You're coming across like everything's fine but I think it might not be. I need an honest answer, because if you do need

60

help, I will find a way to do it. You're right, I don't give up. So do I keep coming back to see you or not?'

His guard was down and as her words landed, his face crumpled. His hand came up to cover his mouth, and he stayed that way for a few seconds. When he finally spoke, he was struggling against tears. 'Please come back. Even if my mother says not to, or if I say in front of her, it's only because I have to. Please just come back.' She reached out to touch his shoulder but he shook her off, turned away to the gate and fiddled with the lock for a few seconds before disappearing into the garden, securing the gate behind him. She edged closer to the gate, peering through the fretwork. Halfway up the path he stopped dead in his tracks, bending to the ground. He made a small circuit, bending again to look at the same spot from three different directions, then picked something up, turned it over and over, and cupped it in his two hands as he scanned the garden, peering into every corner.

'I see your signs. I know you've been here,' he shouted. 'That's the last time. You won't get in again.' Behind him the front door swung open and Rhian stood on the threshold, her arms crossed over her upper body, her mouth and eyes huge with alarm.

'They've been here again. It was pointing at the house this time.' He held the object up to show her, then turned, stretched his powerful arm into the air and flung it with such force that it shot over the garden wall and hit the ground a few feet away from Kit. She kept well back from the gate, keeping her eye on the spot where it had fallen, and after hearing the front door slam, she crossed to where the object lay. It was nothing but a large pebble, almost triangular in shape and with a pronounced apex. It was quite striking, with several thick white veins running across it, but nothing out of the ordinary. She put it in her pocket, planning to have a proper look later and see if she could decipher what he'd meant.

Back in her car, she sat for a while, dithering about what to do. There was no way she could go back to the office and pretend to be interested in something other than this case. The sheer desperation of Dylan's pleas for help haunted her, and she was bewildered and unsettled by the episode with the pebble. But there was no point in storming up to the house and forcing the issue with Rhian either; she needed to be more strategic than that. In the meantime, there was the mystery over Fflur Meredith and the impact she'd had on the community in Rock. What the hell had happened that could have caused them to be gossiping about her all these years later? Whatever it was, it had stuck to Dylan, because even Aled had known about it, shouting at him about his psycho nan. She couldn't get into the social services file to find anything out, but there was another way to clear it up quite easily. She started her car and drove quickly through Rock, stopping only to pick up fags at the petrol station on the main road to Hafod.

CHAPTER 5

Hafod lay just outside the boundaries of Sandbeach, on the outskirts of Dinas, and Kit knew the town well from her very occasional trips to see her father. But she didn't know the suburbs at all, and as she drew near, she realised that she had no idea where she was going. Daffodil Towers didn't ring a bell either. But then, Frankie had been pretty vague about the name. She pulled over as soon as she spotted a lay-by and googled it, but nothing came up. *Daffodil Towers or some stupid name like that*, Frankie had said. She brought up the short list of care homes in the Hafod area, rejected several, including the horrific-sounding Eventide Rest, and finally took a bet on Snowdrop Court Residential Home for the Elderly Mentally Ill. Maps told her it was just three minutes away.

Snowdrop Court turned out to be housed in a modern building on a trading estate just off the coast road. No snow-drops or any other type of flora in sight. Perhaps there had been once, before someone dropped a vast concrete residential home on top of them. After parking in the underground car park, Kit found the lift and pressed the button for reception, emerging a few seconds later into a light, airy lobby. It smelt far nicer than she had anticipated and had a thick beige carpet rather than the cheap lino she'd been expecting. There was a plush taupe sofa positioned on each side of the reception desk. An elderly man sat on one of them, his walking stick gripped between his knees and his hands clasped over its top. He was greeting everyone who passed. She said hello in return while feeling around inside her coat for her ID badge, only remembering at the last minute that she didn't have it.

'Could I have a word with the officer in charge?' Leaning her elbow on the highly polished wooden front desk, she attempted to look as if she had every right to be here. The receptionist swivelled in her chair to attract the attention of a middle-aged woman who was leafing through some files in a cabinet at the back of the room. 'Jane? Someone for you?'

'Can I help you? I'm Jane Stanley, I'm the officer in charge here.' She had mid-brown hair styled in a sharp bob and was dressed in a beige woollen suit with a silky cream-coloured blouse. Approachable but efficient, that was the overall tone of her. And of the whole place, actually.

'I'm Kit Goddard. I'm a social worker.' Hope was already fading. This woman didn't seem the type to fall for just anything. Like outright fibs, for instance, or unauthorised attempts to get access to confidential records.

'I don't think we've met before have we, Kit? Which team are you from?'

'I'm from Child Services. You had a resident here a few years ago. Fflur Meredith. I'd like to have a chat with any staff who remember her. Or failing that, would you still have her records in your archives? She died in 2012.'

'And you're a Child Services social worker? That's certainly an unusual request for us here.'

'Yes, it's for a genogram I'm doing, on her family.'

'I see. Well, I'm sorry to tell you this. I would love to help you, I really would. But I'd require a little more from you first. I can't just release records to anyone, I'll need your manager to speak to my manager to get that authorised.'

'That's going to cause an issue for me, Jane, I'll be honest with you. I need to have the genogram in front of the judge first thing tomorrow morning. I may have to explain to her that you wouldn't give me access.' The elderly man straightened up in his seat, his interest snagged by the change in tone.

'I see your dilemma. I'm happy to come to court and explain to the judge if need be. Or perhaps the judge would like to issue a direction to my company to disclose any information? That might be the best way forward.'

Bollocks. Kit was still clearing her throat to buy time when the old man appeared next to her, wheezing heavily with the effort of getting to his feet.

'Fflur was here, mind,' he managed, flopping the upper half of his body onto the counter for support. 'She was a good friend of mine. But she disappeared.'

Jane Stanley nodded. 'Thank you, Deri, for that. It's very

helpful. I'm not sure whether it can be *quite* right, though. Could you give us two minutes?'

He grunted but ambled off without argument, leaving Kit to weigh up whether to try again. But even she could see it wasn't worth it.

'Can I help you with anything else? Or would you like to take my business card and you can pass it on to the judge?'

'Yes, that might be best.' Kit tucked the card into her pocket to be disposed of later.

'That's lovely. No doubt we will speak further, then.' Jane was already returning to her filing cabinet, leaving Kit to pad back across the thick pile carpet to the lift, feeling told off. She found Deri lurking just out of Jane's line of vision, his finger on the lift door button, holding it open. He beckoned and waved her into the lift ahead of him. Once they were both in, he pressed for the sixth floor and then leant his weight onto his walking stick with a wheezy gasp. He looked to be in his early eighties and was very overweight and perspiring heavily.

'This'll give us time,' he said, once he got his breath back. 'I can tell you all about Fflur.'

Kit wondered whether she should have got herself into this situation. It was all the information she was going to get, but was it reliable? Deri's suggestion that Fflur had somehow disappeared was one indication to the contrary, not to mention the fact that he was himself currently resident in a home for the mentally infirm.

'I'm not nuts, if that's what you're worried about. I'm as

sane as you are, but I gets depressed, been like it all my life and I'm better off here, they look after me. I used to neglect myself so bad I'd nearly starve. Not wash for weeks. They don't let that happen to me here. What it is, I go down, see,' he demonstrated with a swooping motion of one hand towards the floor that threatened to unbalance him altogether. 'They say to me, Deri, you're going down you are, boy, and they pop me in to see the doc and he sends me for some ECT and I'm all sorted.'

The button for the sixth floor lit up and he immediately stabbed out a fat finger, pressed the bottom button and sent the lift heading straight back down to the car-park level.

'That's good then.' She'd have to get control of those buttons or she'd be going up and down in here for the entire day with sweaty Deri for company.

'Yes, it's a better place now, Jane's new and she's most efficient. It wasn't so good back then, very sloppy. No one cared when Fflur went.'

'Where did she go, do you reckon?' She'd better not say that Fflur had died. Perhaps the staff had protected him from the loss of his friend, what with him being so prone to depression. Patronising, but understandable, to a degree.

He shrugged. 'Search me. I'm not a conspiracy theorist, you know. I don't think the earth is flat or the moon landing was faked or any of that rubbish. I'm a rational man, when I'm not depressed. But I don't understand how she was here one day, gone the next. She always wanted to go, always on about it, and her beautiful daughter and that lovely grandson coming to see her every weekend like clockwork. The kid's got a smile would light up the world, if he didn't have such a weight on his shoulders most of the time. Of course Fflur wanted to go home to them. But she wasn't well enough. She had a few funny ideas about the boy's father, always saying she couldn't tell anyone who it was, it wasn't safe to say. They live by the Oer, and she was obsessed with going up there. Well, she was fit as a flea for her age but it can be dangerous up the mountain on times, you know? So the one place Fflur Meredith could not go was home. I keep my ears open and my eyes peeled, see, I know what goes on in here, and no way would they have discharged her. It's the law, it's called mental capacity. Would you like me to explain it to you?'

'No, don't worry.' She saw the car-park level approaching and hastily moved towards the control panel, managing to block his way so he couldn't send them both shooting back up to the sixth floor again. She saw his face fall as the doors slid open and she moved towards them. 'Thank you, Deri, it's been very helpful. I'm Kit, by the way.'

'I hope you'll call in again, Kit. It's nice to have a chat. I don't get a lot of visitors. Bring me some Turkish Delight, I love that.'

She teetered, but she couldn't commit and she didn't want to promise and then let him down. 'Well, thanks again, Deri. Goodbye now.' The lift doors closed on his dejected face.

*

Kit texted Tyler on the way to her last visit, hoping he'd fancy a takeaway later. It was only Thursday but she was knackered already and couldn't face cooking. He didn't answer straight away and then she was preoccupied for a bit, dealing with a stroppy twelve-year-old. By the time she'd calmed Ella's foster carers down and extracted an agreement from her that she wouldn't climb out of her bedroom window at 4 a.m. for tonight, this being Ella's best offer, she'd almost forgotten about him. She felt even more tired by the time her phone buzzed, and half hoped he might be texting to say he was busy. She knew deep down this was unlikely and he'd probably be dead keen.

come up Josies with me

This was even worse. The last thing she needed now was an evening with either of her sisters, especially Josette. Jasmine was by far the easier one of the two. She'd been the eldest and had mothered Kit and Tyler a bit. It had, however, only been a bit, and all the older three had done their part. Jazz seemed unaware of this, though, and tension fizzed in the gulf between how grateful the twins were for it and how grateful Jazz thought they ought to be. But still, all that said, Jazz was basically sound enough. Josie was a different matter. Of the five Goddard children, Josie had grown up to be the most like Christine, in both personality and temperament. Unfortunately, their parenting styles bore marked similarities, too. Kit spent too much of her time in Josie's presence trying to weigh up whether she ought to make a referral to

Child Services about her nephews and nieces. She wasn't in the mood for any of that. The more she thought about it, the more appealing an evening home alone was becoming. Her fingers hovered over her phone as she tried to work out how she was going to wriggle out of this one.

doubt she wants to see me

It was worth a try.

she's out Im babysitting

At least it would give Kit a chance to see whether Amber and Tom were OK without Josie getting in the way. She'd likely come home trolleyed, though, so Kit would have to get out of the house before that happened. Tyler could kip on the sofa and make sure the kids got to school in the morning.

order chicken for me c u bout 7

sure

After finishing her visit, Kit drove home full of plans for a deep bath and a good book before she had to set off for Josie's. But once installed in the bubbles with the latest Susie Steiner, she found she couldn't relax. The Meredith case was biting at her mind. The latest mystery about the grandmother, with all the tittle-tattle in Rock, had only added to her muddle over what could be going on. Dropping her book onto the bathroom floor she slid her shoulders down into the warm water, only to feel the same old question bubbling up that had been troubling her for days. It could only be a matter of time before Georgia's snooping revealed that Kit had a mystery child lurking on her caseload, and her chance to help Dylan would expire at that point. Georgia could wind Cole Jackson around her little finger, everyone knew it, and she'd have the case closed at once. Was it time to give up on Dylan and get Cole to hand it over to mental health? She'd rarely felt so flatly defeated. Working for Georgia was totally miserable, and it didn't look likely to end any time soon; it had been nine months since Vernon's heart attack had given Cole the chance to slot Georgia into his job. If Vernon was going to come back to work, there surely would have been some sign of it by now?

She was about to submerge her head too, in an attempt to stifle the thought of having to work in a different team, away from the front line, safe but boring, when the buzz of her phone caught her attention. Wondering if Tyler was cancelling after all, she grabbed it from its precarious position on the side of the bath and blinked to get the water out of her eyes. Alex. As if her head wasn't messed-up enough already.

hi

hi – where r u?

lanzarote

She paused for a minute. It was the first time she'd heard from him since Valentine's Day.

when u back?

His reply told her March. In the interests of not appearing double-desperate, she resisted asking whether that would be the start or the end of the month. Either way, it felt like forever. She texted a neutral *OK* and then got out of the bath and dressed quickly, trying not to think about how she might have come across. She distracted herself some more by choosing a couple of bags of sweets from her kitchen cupboard for the kids, and after throwing them into her rucksack, pulled on her boots and instructed herself firmly to set off for Josie's, wondering what reception she might be about to get from her least favourite sibling.

Josie lived three streets up the hill from Christine. As she passed the end of her mother's road, Kit did a quick mental calculation as to when she had last seen her. It had been about two weeks. So, she could probably get away with another week. She asked herself why she felt she ought to keep checking on Christine anyway. Maybe it was her increasingly poor health, which Kit alone seemed to recognise as meaning that her time was running out. And she had to admit that while good memories of Christine were few and far between, they weren't totally non-existent. Like most care leavers, Kit could forgive her mother for an awful lot. Far more than someone who hadn't been in the care system would ever comprehend. It was the way it worked; it was what made twelve-year-old Ella climb out of the window of her lovely foster carers' house every night to run back to her parents' cold, chaotic home. Personally, Kit wouldn't have swapped Huw and Menna for Christine, but she took Ella's point. The pull of biological family could be irresistible, no matter how little it was deserved.

As she approached her sister's house, Kit could see Josie and her mates heading off in the other direction, tottering in their high heels, their legs bare and glowing orange in patches from the drunken application of fake tan. Judging by Josie's particularly unsteady gait, she was already well on her way to trouble. Kit pulled into the kerb and waited until they'd gone, then got out of the car, waving at Amber who was in the window, bouncing up and down with excitement.

'Glad you're here.' Tyler had appeared at the front door. 'Tom's got homework. I told him – you need to see your auntie, boy, she got the brains, I got the looks.'

'Cocky fucker,' she whispered, pushing past him rather hard.

'Nice to see you, too. What's wrong with you now?'

'Nothing. Hi there, you two.' She turned to hug Tom and Amber who immediately started vying for her attention. She knew Tyler was joking, or even if he wasn't, it was just his usual high opinion of himself at work. It wasn't so much that he thought she was unattractive; it was more that he knew he was gorgeous. It was inarguable, and she didn't mind it. But she had arrived with a head full of anxious Dylan, absent Alex and ill Christine, and the combination was making her snappy.

'Better have some chicken. Put a smile on your miserable chops.' Tyler held out a slightly greasy box towards her. He was right; she was starving, now she thought about it. She took the box of chicken wings, found some garlic and herb dip on the coffee table and settled down on the floor with the kids, sharing her attention between her food, Tom's English homework and Amber's Lego. Tyler stretched out on the sofa behind them, preoccupied with his phone in a manner suggestive of a new female interest. It would be best not even to think about that until she felt less spiky.

After she'd eaten, she started to feel a bit better. She managed to get the kids settled with the TV, then gathered up her food containers and stood, indicating to Tyler that he should follow her into the kitchen.

'What's up?'

'Have you been to see Christine?'

'What would I want to do that for?'

'I'm worried. She looked terrible last time I saw her.'

Tyler laughed. 'Well, there you go. She can rot for all I care.'

'Ty . . .'

'Don't bother, Krystal. You know why, so leave it.'

She did know and she left it. She didn't blame him for the way he felt. But at the same time, nobody had ever denied that she was her mother's least favourite child and it didn't feel fair that she should have to shoulder the responsibility for Christine's declining years. Or more likely, months. But Danny was dead, Tyler was angry, and Josie was irresponsible. So, it was down to Kit and Jazz, who didn't have any excuse, now Kit thought about it.

'Right. I'll ask Jazz to go up with me.'

'Yeah, that's it, you land her with it if you like. Keep me out of it.'

'OK.'

'Sorry. I'm not trying to be an arse, but I just can't, you know?'

'Yeah, I know.' She didn't have much of a leg to stand on. Tyler held Christine responsible for the abuse that he and Danny had suffered, and for Danny having committed suicide as a result of it, too. If she'd been a better mother to them all, if she hadn't let the boys get out of control, the two of them wouldn't have been running about the estate and they wouldn't have fallen into the hands of their abusers. It was undeniably true. But although she felt spiteful just thinking it, Kit wondered for the first time whether it wasn't also a rather convenient ace card, closing the argument down and allowing Tyler to wriggle off the hook of taking any responsibility for Christine. Kit hadn't had much parenting from her mother either, and she missed Danny just as much as he did, after all. She was hardly ever angry with Tyler, and she didn't like the feeling or the way it was making her think. The best thing to do right now was to move on. 'By the way, are you staying here tonight?'

'Yeah, I'll see to them.'

'Thanks.'

'No worries. She was already wasted when I got here.'

'No surprise there, then. Who were you messaging earlier?'

'No one. What do you mean? Messaging who? When?'

Kit eyed him. 'Five minutes ago, when you were on the sofa.'

'You're a nosy beggar, you are.'

'I am, yes. Who was it?'

'No one.'

'Ty? It's not your probation officer again, is it?'

His eye roll said this was by far the most ridiculous suggestion he'd ever heard. 'Technically, she's not my probation officer anymore,' he snapped, somewhat undermining his own dramatics. 'The order ended, remember?'

'Well, it would still be totally unprofessional for her to . . .'

'Funnily enough, that's what she said.'

'*What?*'

He laughed. 'Calm down, misery guts. Fuss about nothing if you ask me, but that's what she said, so no, it's not her. I'm considering my options on Tinder, that's all. Nothing for you to worry over at all.'

'What happened to Catrin?'

He shrugged. 'Didn't work out.'

'That's a shame. I liked her.'

'Soz. The heart wants what it wants.'

'You are making me sick.'

'Well, at least I'm out there. You're not still hanging around hoping Jem's gonna sort himself out, are you?'

'Hardly.'

'Cos the last I heard he had a drug-related psychosis. Doesn't seem like he's the settling down type.'

'Yes, I am aware.'

Thankfully, they were interrupted by a loud scream and the sound of a scuffle in the living room, where Kit soon found that trouble had broken out over the TV remote and Tom was attempting to throttle Amber.

'Right, that's enough of that.' She used her firmest tone but Tom took no notice whatsoever. She got hold of him under his arms and lifted him off his sister's chest, handing him over to Tyler, who held him tight, his flailing legs making no impact on his uncle's muscular bulk.

'I'll take him into his bedroom for a bit.'

'Thanks. Come here, sweetie.' Kit sat down on the floor with Amber, who was looking thoroughly miserable.

'He hurt me. He's always doing it.'

Kit put an arm around her. 'If you remind me later, I'll show you a trick with his hair that'll put a stop to that.'

'OK.' Amber snuggled up closer to Kit and rested her head on her shoulder. Amber must have started straightening her hair; it hung down her back in a gleaming chestnut stream. Josie was going to have to cope with a pre-teen soon. Dear God, was she going to be bad at that.

'Kit?'

'What?'

'Is Nana going to die?'

Kit looked into Amber's wide grey-green eyes. 'Why do you ask that?'

'We saw her at the shops yesterday. She looked ill.'

'Did she? Maybe she just had a cold or something.'

'You are such a bad liar. Her stomach was big, and she looked a funny colour. I told my mother she needs to go and see her, but she said she won't.'

Kit sighed. If things had got so bad that even a child could see it, Christine's liver must be getting close to packing up altogether.

'I tell you what – I'll go and see her, shall I? Check she's OK?'

Amber nodded. 'I know she's not very nice. But she's my nana and I don't want her to be ill on her own.'

'No. Quite right. I'll go at the weekend. Right, how about those cookies now?'

As she led Amber into the kitchen, Kit knew that now she'd have to face her mother, like it or not. Bugger. The problems of work were beginning to feel like light relief.

CHAPTER 6

The following day, Kit made tracks for Rock straight after lunch. There had been no sign of Georgia all morning. She was busy with the inspectors, which suited Kit's purposes very well, but it couldn't last; pretty soon they'd be finished, and Georgia's fault-finding searchlight would be back in full operation.

As Kit parked outside John's house, she saw him swiping the curtain aside. He was out on the doorstep within seconds.

'Hi, John. How are you?'

'Very well. Still missing the fags, though. Got time for a cuppa?'

'Not now, sorry, no.' His face fell. 'Maybe after my visit?'

'I'll keep an eye out. I'll make sure not to miss you.' He was clearly not going to shift one inch from the window until she came back, so there was little chance of her being missed. She couldn't work out whether he was lonely, nosy or both.

She gave him a wave and set off for the lower slopes of the mountain. She knew where to head for; her grandfather had taken her up to the viewing point many times. Sitting about halfway up the mountain, it consisted of a narrow ledge with a bench, and gave a spectacular view down the entire length of the valley, over Rock, all the way down to Sandbeach and on out to sea. The ledge could be dangerous, hanging over a steep drop to a bed of rocks below. The path up to it was hazardous, too, subject to strong winds and sudden changes in temperature and visibility. A couple of tourists would get stuck on the viewing point every year, managing to get themselves up but then too afraid to risk the trip back down. Only locals knew about the other rocky path, known locally as the stairway. Sitting on the less windy south-western face, it led from the viewing point to the lower ledges and from there to safety. Kit's grandfather had shown her how to find it. Even back then it had been badly overgrown, and she'd never known a tourist to spot it amongst the bushes and trees. Or perhaps, to the eye of an outsider, it didn't look a much better prospect than the mountain path, dropping vertiginous, uneven and slippery in anything but the height of summer. It was either that or fight against the capricious weather and sudden-dropping cloud on the mountain path, and with that being the choice, the tourists didn't usually get themselves down at all and would be stranded until the mountain rescue got there. The whole thing would cause Kit's grandad to mumble under his breath on a regular basis about the waste of resources and the stupidity of grockles. He'd taken her for many walks down the stairway, pointing out all the twists and turns so that she'd be safe if she ever needed to use it.

Pushing the thought of him away, she checked her watch; she had forty minutes to make it up to meet Dylan. She passed the opening of the lane to Ty Olaf and walked the opposite way, picking up the narrow path that rounded the base of the mountain for a few yards then climbed up the steep side towards the viewing point. The weather was dry today and the bitter chill had dropped out of the air. As she walked, she started to enjoy the comforting familiarity of the path. She loved the coast so much that she had almost forgotten that she loved mountains and forests, too. She should come here more often, but she'd found it hard after her grandfather died.

Arriving at the point, Kit could see Dylan sitting on the bench. Two black-and-white dogs snuffled around in the undergrowth behind him and the third, a smooth-coated tricolour, sat tight by his side. He was fiddling with a small bunch of crocuses, which was tied to the arm of the bench. The sight stirred a memory in Kit's mind. The flower seat, that was what she'd called it when she'd been small. She'd sat on this bench with her grandfather so many times but hadn't given it a thought in years. Every time they'd come, there had been a different bunch of flowers. She remembered the daffodils in spring, replaced by sweet peas and miniature roses in summer. Once or twice, they'd come in December, if the weather wasn't too harsh, and found holly sprigs and mistletoe. She'd loved to see what was on the bench each time. It had fascinated her. She'd asked her grandfather about it once, when she was a bit older, curious to know why someone was leaving the flowers. He'd told her quickly that it was a way for someone to remember a loved one who had passed away. All these years later, she understood that they were something to do with Dylan's family.

He'd finished with the flowers now and was bending down to stroke the dog, murmuring to it gently. As she approached, she faked a gentle cough, not wanting to make him jump by just appearing out of nowhere. He looked up with a start all the same but gave her a shy smile.

'Hiya. You OK?' He'd put himself on the far end of the bench; she had to sit to his left and couldn't get a surreptitious look at the right side of his face to see whether the bruise was still there.

'Yeah.'

'What are the dogs called?'

He indicated the two black-and-white collies. 'That's Griff and that's Tomos.'

'And what about this one?'

'Bella.'

Kit leant forward and held her hand out to Bella, who snuffled against it, interested enough to stretch a bit from her seated position but not willing to move an inch away from Dylan.

'She's your girl, isn't she?'

'Yeah, she is. They all are but . . .' He shrugged.

'She's special?'

'Yeah.'

'I get you. So, what have you been doing today?' It was the type of lame question she didn't normally bother kids with, but this boy's awkwardness was transmitting itself to her and tying her tongue.

He shrugged again. 'I've been to the shop.'

'The one around the corner? I bet they don't have much there. Don't you ever get the bus down to Asda? Or what about an Internet shop?'

'My mother knows Rowena – she owns the shop.'

'So?'

'So – we trust Rowena.'

There was a snap in his tone, a finality. He must have registered Kit's glance, but he kept his face away from her, staring fixedly out towards the sea, refusing to meet her eye.

'Why is it important that you trust her, Dylan?'

His mouth started moving but she couldn't tell whether he was struggling to find the words or whether it was just his lip-chewing tic kicking in again. She waited, although she desperately wanted to fill the gap. But if she did, he'd be able to avoid answering her.

'It's hard to explain,' he said, finally.

'Try me.'

'No. It doesn't matter.'

'OK.' Based on Kit's visit to the corner shop, any trust in Rowena was pretty misplaced, but she left it. She wouldn't push him for anymore details yet either. She had met some difficult teenagers, variously sullen, withdrawn and aggressive, but she had never met one this wary. But even as she thought it, she questioned herself. Was he anymore guarded than most teenage boys, or was she nervous of him? It was an unfamiliar thought and she turned it over in her mind. He was an unusual mix; physically he was powerful, but he was also fearful and vulnerable. Then there was something else surfacing, just now and again. A tension, a feeling that he was holding himself in check. The occasional irritability, like a dog drawing back its lips.

They sat in silence for a few more seconds while she pondered how to break the tension. She thought it was probably best to move about. 'Shall we walk back down a bit?'

Dylan stood at once, relieved. As they went, she managed to get him chatting about the dogs by asking him about their temperaments and habits. She wasn't surprised that it seemed to be working. With teenagers, it was always best to walk, or drive around, or just do something alongside them – being in parallel gave them the space to open up, whereas they felt cornered by any head-on attempt at a heart-to-heart. She was enjoying the chat anyway; he was articulate and alive when talking about his dogs and she didn't need to feign an interest. She told him a few stories about Jess and the other dogs at Huw and Menna's in return. Now he was more relaxed, throwing a tatty tennis ball for Bella and letting his guard down without even realising it, Kit could see what Dylan might be like if he were free of the weight sitting on his life.

After a while Kit's chest began to catch a little.

'Need a sit-down?'

'All right, chopsy. No, I don't. I bet I've walked this mountain more times than you have.'

'Not recently, I reckon, judging by the state of you.'

'I guess not. OK, let's have a break, shall we?'

They found a couple of boulders on the side of the path and took one each, perching on the top.

'How come you've been up here before? Where do you live?'

'I live in Sandbeach. But my dad is from Rock. I used to walk up here with my grandad. I loved it as a kid.'

'Yeah, me too.' He turned away from her to face the view out to Sandbeach again and started murmuring quietly to himself. She couldn't catch the words but she picked up the cadence.

'Come on then, be brave. I'd really like to hear it.'

'*A hundred hills their dusty backs upheaved / All over this still ocean and beyond / Far, far beyond, the vapours shot themselves / In headlands, tongues, and promontory shapes / Into the sea, the real sea.* That's about climbing Snowdon.'

'Yes, I remember. You're good at learning poetry. Do you write it too?'

'Sometimes.' He was beaming now.

'Chances of me seeing it?'

'Absolutely zero.'

'Fair enough. I still think it's a shame you had to give up school.'

'I tried, I kept going for ages after my mother said not to, but it caused so much trouble. She needs me home, see.'

'Do you always do as she says?'

'Yeah, cos she gets upset otherwise.'

'Well, at that rate, you're never going to get away from home at all, are you?'

'No. I'll be like John, living in my mother's house when I'm fifty. He keeps it all exactly the same as when she was there. It's weird.'

'Really? Does he use her tea towels? Maybe he wears her pinny.'

'Please stop.' His chuckle was deep and satisfying to hear.

'So have you got anyone to stick up for you? Where's your dad?'

'Never met him.'

'No? How come?'

'My mother says he was no good. He never bothered with me, anyway.'

He bent to pick up the ball and threw it with sudden force ahead of them. The path was uneven here and the ball bounced on the jagged stones, shot up into the air and veered off to the right. The dogs chased after it, Bella nearly flattening the other two, but it had sailed over the top of the bushes and dropped down on the other side. Bella immediately threw herself at the bushes and started trying to paw and scrape her way through at the bottom. Kit got hold of her collar and dragged her back.

'Hang on, girl, let's see what's over there first.' The Oer was unpredictable, with changes in level where you'd least expect them; she didn't want Bella going over a ledge. She peered through the bushes, carefully pulling the thorny limbs to one side. But it wasn't as dangerous as she'd thought. The ground fell away on the other side, but only by a few inches and then it levelled out. The ball must have gone into the dip.

'All right, all right,' she said to the frantic Bella. 'I'll get it.' She squeezed through, pushing the gap wider, brambles catching at her hands and wrists, and jumped down onto the flat ground, where she spotted the ball lying on the grass. She picked it up and was about to turn back to the hedge when something caught her eye in a small copse of trees ten feet or so further on.

'What are you looking at?' Dylan's face had appeared in the gap.

'There's something over there. The sun caught it; it looks like metal. I'm going to have a quick look.' Within a few paces she could see that it was just a pile of rubbish. It seemed to be mainly beer cans, but once she got close enough to give it a good kick with the toe of her boot, a couple of discarded Rizla packets and a Bic lighter told her more of the story. A fire had been lit in the centre of the copse, and looking around, she could see that the trees provided both shelter and cover. She saw that Dylan was struggling through the bushes himself now, displacing considerably more of them with his bulk than she had.

'It's OK, I've got the ball, let's go.' She felt a sudden urge to protect him, because it seemed unlikely that he'd know the first thing about weed-smoking dens and she didn't want him to find out.

He pulled back through the hedge and she followed him. As they walked on, he started throwing the ball again, but less furiously. 'Thanks for getting it for her.'

'It's OK. They get a bit obsessed, don't they? I didn't want her to have to leave it behind.'

'Yeah, they do.'

Maybe she could chance another gentle nudge. 'So, you mentioned your father, but what about other family, then? Grandparents?'

'My grandad died before I was born.'

'That would be your mum's father, would it?'

'Yeah.'

'So, what about your gran?'

'She died too.' He looked at his watch. 'I need to get home now.' He quickened his pace.

Kit hurried after him. 'What's the rush?'

'My mam worries.' The set of his face told her that his guard was back up. Why would Rhian be concerned about a seven-teen-year-old being out in broad daylight with three large dogs for protection? But it wasn't that. She'd pushed too hard, too soon. She'd got nowhere near asking him about his bruise or his mother's behaviour and she'd managed to scare him off already.

'I'll walk down with you.'

He didn't object but he didn't speak again, and his pace

picked up even more. They walked in silence and when they reached the bottom of the mountain, Dylan gave a cursory wave and disappeared into the bushes in the lane, the dogs running ahead of him.

'I'll call up Monday,' she shouted after him. No reply came.

Remembering John's offer of coffee, Kit was tempted. She probably shouldn't, but she was chilly now and she really fancied it. She wondered if he would have any cake. Or a few chocolate biscuits, maybe.

John smiled with delight as he opened the door before she'd even knocked on it and stood back to let her into his neat magnolia-painted hallway.

'I was watching out for you.'

'I thought you might be.'

'You must be freezing, come with me.' She followed him along the corridor, noticing for the first time that he walked with a slight limp. After showing her into his warm living room, John went into the kitchen. She took the opportunity to have a good look round. The room was small but furnished simply with a two-seater sofa and one matching armchair, so that it didn't feel overcrowded. The colour scheme was warm red and rich cream and the whole place was spotlessly clean and tidy. Numerous photos of John crowded the mantelpiece, school and sports ones, and some of him as a young adult, including two in which he wore a dark-blue uniform, both displayed in ornate gold frames.

'Here you go.' Mrs Ellis's pride and joy had reappeared with two mugs of milky coffee, one of which he handed to Kit before placing a plate piled high with biscuits on the arm of her chair. Her chilly toes had uncurled inside her boots as the heat from the fire soaked into them. She wondered whether she could get away with staying here until the end of the day. Her own flat suddenly seemed boxy and unappealing in comparison.

'Your house is lovely, John.' She selected a bourbon and dipped it in her coffee.

'Oh, thank you. It was my mother's house, though, see, so I just moved myself back into my old bedroom and kept it all pretty much as it was. It would have confused her if I'd changed it and after she'd gone, well, I couldn't bear to do it.'

'When did you move back?'

'About two years ago. She had dementia, and I looked after her until she died. It was the least I could do, after all that time away in London.'

'What were you doing there?' She had him pegged for the police, based on the uniform in the photo.

'I was a prison officer.' That fitted. He certainly had the posture and build. But there was a firmness and confidence to his manner too. He was warm and at ease, but you wouldn't mess with him. She liked him very much.

'Why didn't you go back after your mother died?'

'I found I didn't miss London like I expected to. I'd got divorced, then taken early retirement – medical grounds, I'd been assaulted one too many times. Hence the dodgy leg.

Anyway, once I wasn't working, London turned out to be a lonely old place. So, I sold my flat down there and that was that. It's good being back, there's still a fair few people who remember me from school. What about you, Kit? Where are you from?'

'I grew up in Sandbeach,' she said, giving him the edited version. 'My grandparents were from around here, though.'

'Really? Would I know them? What was their surname?'

'Goddard.'

'You're Ceri Goddard's granddaughter? Ceri and Martina? You must be Gino's girl, then?'

'Yes, that's it.'

'I knew your grandfather well. I used to go in his café in Sandbeach for a frothy coffee every Saturday when I was younger. Now, your dad had a few daughters, from what I remember. So, which one are you?'

'The youngest. There were three of us girls. Plus two boys. One of the boys is my twin.'

'Yes, I remember now. What's Gino up to these days?'

'He's in Dinas. He's got a bar there.'

'Ah yes – Ceri's cafés all got sold off, didn't they?'

'They did. My dad ran the Sandbeach one for a bit, it was the last in the chain to go but he closed it in the nineties and bought the bar.'

'Well, he was lucky to keep it open that long, really. Most of the Italian cafés were long gone by then. Is your dad doing well?'

'Yes, very well.' In truth, Kit hadn't seen her father for six months. He'd texted out of the blue to invite her to spend Christmas with him and Mal, she'd declined, he'd sent her some money and that had been the end of it. The same had happened with Tyler, Jazz and Josie. None of them knew what to do with Gino. They'd grown up understanding him to be the worst person in the world and then after Danny died, he'd suddenly wanted to make amends. It was impossible to fathom. None of them believed a word that emanated from Christine's mouth as a rule, but Gino hadn't made so much as a guest appearance throughout all their years in care. If Christine had been lying all along, if he wasn't that bad after all, why hadn't their father ever stepped up when they'd needed him?

'Well, it's good to hear that Gino is doing well. You must know all around here like the back of your hand then, if your grandfather had anything to do with it. No one knew the Hir like Ceri Goddard.'

'I was only thirteen when he died. But yes, I do remember a lot.'

'And remind me now, who did your dad marry? A girl from town, wasn't it?'

'Yes.' She dropped eye contact and reached for another biscuit.

'Sorry. I know I'm nosy. I'm a bit of an amateur psychologist, I'm afraid, it's a hobby with me now. I've had a lifetime of trying to understand the mentality of criminals, wanting to figure out what makes them tick. Suddenly that's over and I haven't quite managed to switch it off yet. Ignore me, I know you aren't here to talk about yourself. Now, can I tell you anything about Dylan?'

'Maybe. He's very hard to get to know, isn't he?'

'Yes, he is. And Rhian's the same. I try to look after them a bit, see. I go up to cut the grass and tidy the garden and I've shown Dylan how to pay their bills at the post office in the corner shop. But that's all she'll let me do. The kids round here torment them, just won't leave them alone, and I think it's affected the boy, you know? Rhian never was the outgoing type but she's withdrawing even more and she's taking him with her. He's stopped going to school and that does bother me. He only sets foot outside to walk the dogs and go to the shop now.'

'Was it you rang in to social services about them, John?'

'Me, love? No. Maybe I should have but it didn't occur to me if I'm honest.' He looked sad, as if she'd criticised him.

'How long have you known them?'

'Well, we grew up together, me and Rhian. Same class right through school. As I said, I went away in my thirties, married a girl from London. I hardly ever came home and after a bit I lost touch with Rhian completely. She stayed living with her mother at first, but in the end, Fflur had a breakdown and she was in Penlan hospital for fourteen years. She was gone before Dylan was born, never came home, died there a couple of years before I moved back.'

'God, how awful.' Kit meant it, but she wanted him to move

on, before Fflur crept into the picture again, muddying the waters with irrelevancies about where she'd died.

'Yes, it was very sad. Not many people know about that, mind, at least officially, the party line was that Fflur had a chronic illness, needed skilled nursing care, but my mother knew a bit more. The gossip up here was terrible, you wouldn't believe it.'

'I would.'

John chuckled. 'Of course, I'd forgotten, you know the place. There were all kinds of rumours about where Fflur went to, you know the kind of thing, some saying she got taken away in a straitjacket by a white van in the middle of the night, others insisting Rhian had bumped her off. Mad stuff. Some people even reckoned they'd seen Fflur walking the Oer at night, crying, looking for her dead husband. Load of old rubbish, she was on a ward in Penlan, safe and sound, watched over 24/7. But people had picked up that something was funny about the situation, and they knew Fflur's mental health wasn't good; the human mind fills in the blanks, doesn't it? Anyway, she didn't get better, whatever was wrong with her, and she never came back to Rock. When I moved back in here, I found Rhian living up at the house with Dylan. I didn't even know she'd had a child. Well, perhaps my mother did tell me, but I wasn't that interested, to be honest. Too busy living my own life to bother about Rock gossip.'

This was a bit rich, given how much John himself had just divulged about the Merediths. The smart and controlled ex-prison officer had been quick to give way to a square-miler with a love of village tittle-tattle. Still, it suited her purposes very well.

'What happened to Dylan's father?'

'He's long gone. Rhian did tell me that much, though none of the details. There were always boys chasing after Rhian when she was young, she was a good-looking girl, the prettiest girl in Rock, actually. But her mother wouldn't tolerate any of them. She was quite a personality, Fflur. She ran her husband, by all accounts, and she certainly ran Rhian. I thought that girl was headed for the single life but it seems she finally met someone late on, in her thirties. Fflur was off in hospital by that time so Rhian had the opportunity to spread her wings. Don't know where the fella went to, mind, he's never shown up to see his own son. Anyway, I think Rhian trusts me a little bit, you know? Because she's known me all her life. Even I can't get inside the house anymore, though. I've tried all ways, but she won't have it.'

Kit selected a jammie dodger and started nibbling the top layer of biscuit off to get at the jam. 'Why do you think she won't she let you in?'

'No idea. Her mum didn't bother with anyone outside the family much either. I don't think Fflur was ever the same after Rhian's father died, that's where it started with her. He was in the accident at the Oer colliery, the explosion. I expect your grandfather told you all about that. Owen Meredith was the pit deputy. He was very young for the job, promoted a bit too quick, perhaps, some thought. Not that it was his fault, it was the firedamp caused it.'

Kit hadn't given the accident a thought for years. The story came flooding back to her now, along with the pain that always deepened the lines on her grandfather's face, no matter how many times he told it. Four men had died when firedamp ignited in the pit, setting off a blast that travelled several hundred feet. The cause of the ignition had never been established, but the pit had not been properly ventilated, allowing the lethal methane to build up. It was a common enough story, of a type that never got much attention. Everyone knew about the big pit disasters, the ones that had been on the national news, bringing forth platitudes about the price of coal. But her grandfather had told her about the others – the small day-to-day accidents, part and parcel of life in the valleys. The women always got up to see their husbands off for their shifts, he had told her, because every goodbye kiss might be the last.

'Is that why there's flowers on the bench at the viewing point?'

John nodded. 'They scattered Owen's ashes up there. Well, there wasn't much left of him to bury, you see. Owen and Fflur did their courting on the viewing point so it was there she could find him, I suppose. Dylan never even knew him, but Rhian's got the poor boy doing the flowers now. It's not healthy, if you ask me. Well, as I say, Fflur never recovered. The community looked after her, and she had her compensation from the Coal Board, so she managed to keep the house.

She kept herself to herself and brought Rhian up to be the same and no one minded. But then when Rhian and I were about turning twenty-one, the pit closures came. You and I both know what that did to the valleys. But Fflur felt differently – she believed it was better they were gone, after what had happened to her husband, you know? She hated the pits with a passion.'

Kit nodded. 'Yes, I can see that.'

'Anyway, you can imagine how that set her aside when the strike started. Fflur wouldn't join in with the other women. People resented that, they felt like they'd given the family the benefit of the doubt over whether the accident had been Owen's fault, they'd helped her out all those years and now she wouldn't repay them. She was in a different place to the other women and it all added up to make her even more isolated. Though my mam used to say she was a right funny bugger before any of it happened, to be honest.'

John's mother sounded like the kind of woman Kit would have got along with. But even as she laughed, she was feeling sad for Fflur. Not only had she been left alone to bring up her child, she'd stood to one side through the strike that had brought the women of the valleys together and changed their lives. Kit knew all about how the women had developed confidence and gone on afterwards to work or education, some standing as local councillors and even becoming MPs. She knew, too, how high feelings had run in the valleys during the strike, and how those who did not support it were ostracised.

Some of the rifts created back then had still not healed after thirty years. Poor Fflur, and poor Rhian.

'It must have been lonely for Rhian, growing up with all that going on.'

'I think it was. But she did all right for quite a long time.' John smiled fondly. 'She's a clever lady and she got herself a good job. She was a doctor's receptionist. But as I say, always very private, and once Fflur died in Penlan she went right downhill. That's when the not leaving the house started, about four years ago. Well, Rhian had a difficult start in life, and in the end, it came out on her. It always does, doesn't it?'

'It does.' That all fitted together with a satisfying click. There was a touch of the doctor's receptionist about Rhian. A remnant of who she'd been. No wonder she was so good at fending people off. Perhaps that explained the formal-looking clothes too; the straight skirt and the matching blouse. Old and worn out, but she was still wearing them. It must have mattered to her, that she had a good job. And she'd brought up a child on her own. 'Sounds like Rhian was quite strong, too.'

'Yes, she was, in a way. Always lovely with it, mind. She did manage to win a few people over, even those who hated her mother because of the strike. She had a way with her.'

He kept qualifying his comments about Rhian like this, as if he just could not speak about her without mentioning how fantastic she was. But it was hard to relate John's image of Rhian to the haunted waif Kit had seen cowering in the doorway of Ty Olaf, let alone to what had come next. 'What do people round here think of her now?'

'Ah, well, that's it, you see. Unfortunately, Rock is a different place nowadays. People used to give them a wide berth, leave them to it and in time, the rumours died down a bit. But now we've got people moving in who don't know the family history and they find Rhian and Dylan unusual. That's at the bottom of the problems they're having in the community, I think. Plus, you've got the old guard still here too, there's a new audience for their nonsense and the rumour mill's started up again, recycling the stories about Fflur, saying there's always been something funny in the Meredith family and Rhian's going the same way. Trying to scare the incomers, if you ask me.'

'Yes, I get you.' She'd seen for herself what was happening with Dylan. Even Aled and Joe had known about Fflur, she realised – that's what they had been shouting at Dylan, something to do with his 'psycho nan'. The picture was coming together now, forming the backdrop to Dylan's situation. He was not in the throes of early psychosis at all. He was looking after his mother, the two of them were outcasts in Rock, and he had no one to run to, no one to tell. Even as she fretted about what to do, a tiny puff of pride expanded in her chest. She'd got it sussed.

'Mind you, that's not all of it. It's a bit of the old chicken and egg, isn't it?' John was clearly keen to prolong this.

'How do you mean?' Kit got up and reached for her coat, hoping to give him the hint.

'Well, people are funny with them, and that drives them further inwards. That's one way of looking at it. But on the other hand, is it being on their own so much that is the problem? Have the two of them both got a bit strange?'

Kit paused in the zipping-up of her coat. 'Sorry, I'm not with you.' Admittedly, she'd only been half listening, but it didn't sound like he was making any sense whatsoever.

'Being on your own with someone, not seeing another face or interacting with anyone else – it can drive you a bit mad in the end, you know. I can tell you that from experience, with my mother.'

He wasn't kidding. He'd taken on his mother's house, her possessions and her furniture and no doubt the interest in everyone else's business had emanated from Mrs Ellis, too. But Kit couldn't for the life of her see what all this had to do with anything. John had already said his mother had dementia; that was a totally different scenario to Dylan and Rhian. 'I'm sure you can. I should be making a move now.'

'All right then, love. Before you go, let me give you something I've been reading. I've got a bit of a pet theory about all this and it might help you out.'

She waited while John ambled off into another room. A printer whirred for a few minutes and then he came back with a sheaf of pages. She glanced at it as he pressed it into her hands. A journal of psychiatry. She looked at him for explanation as she rolled it up and pushed it down into her rucksack.

'I picked something up, that's all I'm saying. Have a read

and see whether you spot it, too. I'm going to do some more research, I'll keep you updated.'

'OK, will do. I've really got to run.'

He walked her to the door where she said her goodbyes and slipped out before he could shoot off on another tangent. Within seconds she was trudging up the lane to Ty Olaf, fired up with renewed energy. If she could get this case formally allocated to her, she'd have the chance to show what she could do, and then maybe Georgia and Nazia would start giving her some more interesting work. But all this nonsense of not being able to go inside the house had to stop. She'd go up there right now, insist on a proper discussion about their problems, and then she could crack on. Rhian was not going to scare her away a second time.

It was gone four o'clock and the light was dropping already, the lane darkening by the minute, but she only vaguely registered that. She sorted her strategy as she went. Perhaps she'd have a word with Tim Page about Rhian, see what the Mental Health Team could do for her, and then that would free up her own time to concentrate on Dylan.

Arriving at Ty Olaf, Kit saw that there was a dim light showing through the curtains of one of the upstairs rooms. All the other windows were dark, their curtains closed as tightly as they had been last time she'd come, not a chink of light to be seen. After squeezing through the gap at the end of the wall, she crossed the garden quickly and paused to listen at the front door. Not a sound from inside the house. She lifted the brass knocker and rapped firmly, so as to indicate that she meant business.

There was a brief moment of silence then the murmur of voices, deep in the house but just loud enough for Kit to pick up that one of them was urgent, beseeching. Was Rhian trying to stop Dylan from answering the door? She lifted the knocker again and slammed it down hard, to let them know that she was taking charge and was not going away. Instantly, a shrill scream rang out from the direction of the upstairs window, continuing for several long seconds. Forcing herself to stay where she was, she huddled against the door as the scream died down into a repetitious wail. A loud bang from above sent another jolt through her; she stepped out onto the path and looking upwards saw Dylan at the open sash window. As soon as their eyes met, he started waving at her frantically, using his hands to usher her away, his face a picture of panic. His insistence gave her all the excuse she needed. She was across the garden and out through the gap in seconds, sinking into the depths of the lane, not even stopping to fumble for her phone and switch on the torch until she was more than halfway down. She knew she needed to do something but Dylan's face told her that it was her very presence that was the problem. She was the cause of whatever was going on in that room and she'd need to clear the area first and then decide what to do.

CHAPTER 7

As soon as she got out of sight, Kit pulled out her phone and called Dai Davies, using his personal mobile rather than his work line in the Public Protection Unit. She didn't much fancy her clueless panic being permanently captured on the police recording system.

'Hello, lovely. We haven't heard from you in a while.' He sounded really delighted and she knew he must be at home because his partner Martin was audible in the background, noisily instructing Dai to invite her over for dinner.

'Dai, I need your help, it's urgent.'

'Are you all right? You do sound in a bit of a state actually, now you mention it.'

She gave Dai a quick summary of the situation. As she did so, she heard a door closing at his end. He must have moved into a different room. Dai took his professional responsibilities very seriously and no doubt Martin was all ears.

'So, you've never managed to get inside the house?'

'It's only the second time I've tried. But no, the first time she just wouldn't let me and then I went again just now, and this happened.'

'Hmm. It does sound a bit odd. Would you like me to organise a couple of officers to make a welfare call?'

'I doubt they'll get in there either.'

'They might. People react differently to a uniform sometimes. But even if they don't, maybe they can get someone to the door, have a chat and check they're both in one piece. They don't need to say it's come from you; they can just say they had an anonymous call reporting a concern.'

'They'll know it's me, though. I'll never stand a chance of getting in myself then.'

'I don't think that's the main worry right now, Kit, do you?'

She sighed. 'No. I guess not.'

'OK. Leave it with me, I'll speak to the local station and they can call up. I'll tell them to have a report on your desk Monday morning. Now go home and have a rest and enjoy your weekend if you can.'

'I'll wait here, in case the police need me.' She had a feeling he wouldn't let her get away with it, but how could she just leave? She had to find out what had been happening, and why her presence had kicked off such a horrendous reaction in Rhian.

'No you won't. They're quite capable of handling it and it sounds like you being there might inflame things. Go home. I mean it, Kit. Don't get underfoot.'

'All right. Will you let me know what happens, though?'

'Sure.'

But she hung about halfway down the lane, listening intently for anymore sounds from the direction of the house. If that scream came again, she would go back, no matter what Dai had said. She couldn't wait for the police; if they were busy they wouldn't even prioritise the call. They could be hours getting there. But after thirty anxious minutes spent standing rigid in the shadows, barely daring to breathe in case she missed a noise or movement from the house, she chanced a quick walk down the lane to see if there was any sign of help coming and spotted a police car turning the corner into Sunnyside. She still didn't want to go but she knew Dai was right; her presence probably wasn't going to be of any help, in fact quite the opposite. She slipped down the street and got into her car just as the police pulled up behind her. She couldn't announce herself to them, not wanting Dai to find out that she'd ignored his advice and hung about, so she turned the car around at the top of the street and drove off before the two officers had even clambered out onto the pavement.

Dai rang her back at home a couple of hours later. 'I thought you might like to know – a couple of the boys called up. It all seems fine there.'

'Really?' It felt like the first proper breath she'd taken for hours.

'Yep. They saw the mother, she said everything was all right. Denied any disturbance there earlier. She seemed very sensible, the lads said.'

'It definitely wasn't all right, Dai. I know what I heard.' Her chest muscles tightened again. Had the police even got into the house? Rhian was easily capable of a couple of minutes of chat on the doorstep, coming across all polite-but-reserved. And Dylan would probably say whatever she told him to.

'Kit, go and have a drink and try to relax. You've done all you can, they are safe for now. Deal with it on Monday.'

'OK. Thanks, Dai.'

'No problem. Hang on a sec.' Martin could be heard in the background, issuing his instructions again. 'All right, give me a chance,' Dai told him. 'I expect you heard that, did you, Kit? Martin says he hasn't seen you in ages, do you want to come over to eat tomorrow night?'

'Can I let you know?' she hedged. 'It's just, things aren't great with my mother and I need to get her sorted. It could be complicated.' By this, Kit meant that she expected to spend Saturday night flat out on the sofa with a bottle of vodka to recover from the experience.

'Of course. Maybe next weekend instead?'

'Thanks, Dai, yes, if it's all sorted by then, that would be great.' Kit had worked hard at developing a group of friends for herself, and Dai and Martin had been a particularly successful addition. She found Martin hilarious and Dai's gentle kindness did her good. But right now, she had too much going on to be able to negotiate the social stuff, all the working out what you were supposed to say and do. It was like a new language for her, one she'd never learnt as a child. She hadn't taken school friends home, never knowing what state she might find Christine in. Later on, she'd found it hard to face inviting anyone to Huw and Menna's, hating that moment when she saw them comprehend that she was in foster care, and the way she'd immediately become an object of curiosity, or worse, of pity.

After finishing her call with Dai, she tried to settle and relax but found it impossible. Roaming irritably around her small flat, looking for something to do, her eyes fell on her rucksack and she remembered the journal John had given her the previous day. She pulled it out and unrolled it, taking it into the kitchen where she flicked through the pages while she waited for the kettle to boil. She saw at once that the journal was written in medical jargon. She didn't have the energy for it. She flicked through a few more sheets, intending to bin it as soon as she reached the end. But her attention was caught by a photo of a couple posing with cocktails in hand on a balcony. The man was tanned and muscular, dressed in black trousers and a plain white T-shirt, the simplicity of the look a perfect showcase for the complex tattoos covering both his arms. The woman had straight, glossy hair and neutral make-up. It was hard to tell whether the perfect curve and fullness to her lips was artificial. If so, it had been expertly done. She wore a beige wide-legged jumpsuit with a string tie at the waist and no jewellery apart from simple gold hoops in her ears. It was a typical Insta shot, designed to impress, captivating at first glance but then immediately forgettable amongst so many similar images. She stopped flicking the pages and searched out the text underneath, curious as to why a couple like this would turn up in a psychiatry journal.

Her eye caught on several words in quick succession, all of them seeming totally out of place. Delusions, psychosis, self-neglect. None of this seemed likely to relate to them at all. There was another phrase too. *Folie à deux*. The little French she could recollect told her that '*deux*' meant two, but she couldn't get anywhere with the rest. She went back to the start of the article and read with horrified fascination as it revealed how the couple had become obsessed with each other soon after meeting and had gradually alienated those around them, becoming isolated and seeming to want only to be together in a relationship that others disapproved of as unhealthily intense. Eventually they had disappeared from view altogether, giving up their jobs to live frugally on savings and rarely going out. When they disappeared off the social media radar, became uncontactable and stopped answering the door, the young woman's mother had insisted that something was wrong and raised hell until eventually someone listened. The police had gained access to the flat and found them both emaciated, eking out their dwindling food supplies and living in darkness. They were acutely psychotic, convinced that government agents had been listening in to their conversations and even their thoughts via their TV, phones, computers and the light switches and sockets. They'd turned the electricity supply off, destroyed all their devices and shut themselves away, afraid to risk going out in case they were seen by the government on CCTV. If they had been left much longer, they would have run out of food and money and it seemed they might have been prepared to starve to death.

Kit didn't stop reading as she pulled out a chair with one hand and sat, spreading the journal out on the kitchen table in front of her. She wanted to understand how it was possible that two people could have exactly the same bizarre beliefs and have them to such an extreme that they would be driven to these lengths. The material was hard to wade through, and full of other terms she didn't recognise, but eventually she pieced together what *folie à deux* meant. Madness of two, or shared madness. Not just that two people had the same psychiatric condition at the same time, but that one had actually transmitted the condition to the other.

By the time she reached the end of the journal she had the basics down. People in intense relationships of one kind or another, isolated from others, the stronger personality of the two developing a psychotic illness and the other eventually succumbing to that version of events and losing touch with reality themselves. No doubt that was the picture John meant to convey, and it did make some sense. The most common relationship to give rise to the condition was that of parent and child, so that fitted too.

There were other cases mentioned in the journal; a whole family who had absorbed the parents' belief that someone was bugging their home and set off on a chaotic road trip across America in an attempt to escape the surveillance. The three teenage daughters stared out at her from the page, in a photo taken before it all happened, normal-looking, healthy and happy. She saw with relief that they'd all been found safe and treated successfully in hospital. More worryingly, she saw that the condition could lead to violence; several horrific murders were described as having been committed by people in the agonising throes of shared delusions and even hallucinations. She flicked past those pages; Rhian could be volatile, but John knew the family well, and he was obviously a steady type. If he'd thought there was a risk of that kind, he would have raised the alarm long ago.

Finally, she put the journal down. She'd need to think about it and maybe get some help. It sounded feasible as an explanation but given how rare this condition was, she still wasn't sure that it could be the answer. And she couldn't figure out what to do about it either. If they did have this condition, if Rhian was unwell and was slowly dragging Dylan into her world, what could be done about it? They were both so guarded. And after what she'd heard in the shop, she didn't altogether blame them, either. If they thought people were watching what they were doing and talking about them, they weren't delusional, they were dead right. All that nonsense about Fflur disappearing, the implication that there was something suspicious about it. Just the usual village gossip and drama. All small places had it; Christine's estate had been the worst, and no doubt she'd discover that her own little block of flats was a hotbed too, if only she ever spoke to any of the neighbours to find out. A pang of loneliness hit her; she glanced at the now boiled kettle, poured a vodka instead, and called Tyler.

'Hey. What do you want?' He was panting heavily and 'Eye of the Tiger' was blasting in the background. 'I'm in the gym.'

'Yeah, I figured. I've been to Rock.'

'What? Hang on, can't hear a bloody thing.' After a few seconds the music level dropped. 'Right, I'm in the changing room. Did you say you'd been to Rock? What for?'

'It's a work thing.'

'What's it like up there now?'

'It's the same as it was. A bit scruffier, maybe.'

'So now you're all upset?'

'I am, yes.'

'Grandad wasn't a hero, you know, Krystal. He wasn't perfect.'

'He just didn't understand. You and Dan getting in trouble all the time, the drugs – he worried for you. He just meant to get you to stop and sort yourselves out.'

'He went the wrong way about that.'

'I know he did. He had a temper, so do you. He died before you could work out how to get on, that's all.'

'Whatever. Is that all you wanted?'

'Yeah. Well, no. Are you busy after the gym?'

His sigh carried a hefty weight of self-sacrifice. 'Well, I was, but I'll cancel.'

'Sorry. Don't screw it up for me.'

'Don't be daft. She's hardly going to pie me off, is she?'

'Can you get anymore full of yourself, d'you reckon?'

'I just know my strengths. I'll pick up a curry, be with you in an hour. No going on about Rock and Grandad and all that, though, I'm not interested.'

'Suits me.'

An evening of mindlessly watching Netflix with Tyler helped her to shift work out of her thoughts. But waking early the next morning, she found her anxieties had gone on the hunt in the night and had alighted upon the problem of her visit to Christine. She was tempted not to bother but then she remembered that she had promised Amber, so she'd have to face it sooner or later. Might as well get it done. She lay in bed staring at the ceiling, envisaging what kind of a reception she would get and trying to figure out how to deal with it. She wished Tyler would come with her but she'd given it another try the night before and he was still having none of it. After a few more seconds, she hit on a solution.

An hour later, Kit was ringing Jazz's doorbell. Jazz opened the door, face grumpy, still in her pyjamas and dressing gown.

'Bit early for a visit, isn't it?'

'Yeah, sorry. I need a word.'

'Sounds serious. Keep your voice down, then, Nath and the boys are still in bed.'

She stood to one side and let Kit into the hall, where they picked their way past bikes, skateboards and numerous pairs of grubby trainers to reach the kitchen. Kit sat at the table while

Jazz put the kettle on. She glanced around. Jazz, Nath and the boys lived in a constant state of chaos. Even the kitchen worktops were covered with cereal boxes, school textbooks and what appeared to be several parts of an engine. Jazz saw her looking at it.

'Nath's working on his motor bike,' she said, as if this offered sufficient explanation. Jazz clearly hadn't inherited Christine's OCD, but as she looked at the gritty brown stain around the rim of the mug that was handed to her, Kit started to wonder if she had.

'This wouldn't be about Christine by any chance, would it?' Jazz sat down opposite Kit, putting her own dripping mug down on top of someone's geography homework. Kit longed to move it but managed to restrain herself. She could see several mistakes in it too; she itched to correct them.

'You must be psychic.' Kit's tone was fake even to her own ears. She'd been busted and there was no pretending that this was going to be an easy conversation.

'Don't ask me to go over there with you, Krystal. I'm not getting involved.'

'Yeah, I'm hearing that a lot right now. Come on, Jasmine. She's ill, she's probably not going to last much longer. I can't deal with it on my own.'

'No one's asking you to deal with it at all. Leave her to it, like she left all of us.'

'I can't.'

'I don't see why not.'

'I don't know either. But she hasn't got anyone else, has she? And she wasn't all bad.'

Jazz adjusted her dressing-gown belt around her substantial stomach with a violent tug, giving Kit plenty of warning about what was brewing. 'About ninety-nine per cent, though. And I was the one had to pick up the pieces.'

'I know you did. And I'm grateful; we all are. I'm sorry it happened. But I can't change that now and someone's got to see to her. You know what she's like with me, and I don't know what to do about her anyway.'

'I'm pretty sure they must have taught you something all those years in uni.'

'Thanks, that's a fat lot of help.' It was always going to crop up, of course. Kit had landed a great foster placement, she'd done well at school and she'd got into uni. Jazz and Josie were incapable of seeing her without harping on about at least one of these resentments, and more usually all three. Even Tyler had his snarky moments. Only Danny had been outright proud of her. It amazed her how often she found new reasons to miss him.

Jazz was cradling her coffee, her elbows on the table and her eyes down. 'I'm sorry. I know what you're saying but I can't do it.'

Kit put her own brimming mug down, not having managed to brave the mucky rim. 'That's what Tyler said too. Looks like I'm on my own, then. I'd better get going.' Neither of them had even mentioned Josie; there was no point.

Kit stood and Jazz did the same. 'You should come over for tea. Joe and Connor have been asking about you.'

Kit bit back a petulant answer about being too busy to manage that, on top of everything else. But deep down, she knew where Jazz was coming from, just as she did with Tyler. 'Yes, I will. Say hi from me and tell them I'll be over soon.'

'All right, girl. Good to see you.' They trailed back through the obstacle course to the front door where Jazz leant against the wall, watching Kit as she zipped her hoody against the chill of the morning. Jazz was feeling guilty now, Kit knew. She hung on for a few seconds, fiddling unnecessarily with her gloves, giving her the chance to spit out an apology or a retraction.

'You could try Dad.'

'Sorry?' Kit looked at Jazz in astonishment. What the hell was she on about? Their parents couldn't be in the same room together for five minutes without a row breaking out. It was half the reason Jazz and Nath had never got married. Even at Danny's funeral, Christine and Gino had had to be steered apart at every turn.

Jazz nodded. 'I know, I know. I get you. But he owes us. He's trying to get back in our good books, maybe he could do something useful for once. He doesn't have to go over there, she'd kill him probably, but it sounds like you need someone to talk to, who can tell you what you need to do. Someone, you know – responsible.'

'A grown-up, you mean?'

'Yeah, I suppose so.'

'I'm not sure he's exactly that, Jazz.'

'We don't know, though, do we? We don't know what the truth is. Maybe it's time to give him a chance.'

'OK. I'll think about it.' She fully intended to dismiss the idea without further consideration, but after saying goodbye and getting into her car, she sat for a few minutes to think it over and it dawned on her that Jazz might be right – what was needed in this situation was an adult. It came as a surprise, because up until now she'd thought she was one.

Ten minutes later, Kit pulled up outside her mother's house. It was half past nine, so she reckoned Christine ought to be up. She'd never been a late sleeper anyway; her anxiety kicked in early every morning and drove her out of bed, whether she'd had a drink the night before or not. But when Kit got out of her car, she saw that the blinds were shut at all the windows. She pushed away thoughts of another house with closed curtains as she struggled to undo the rusty gate and walked up the short path, feeling in her inside pocket for her keys, including the one to Christine's house, which she had inexplicably kept on her key ring for all these years.

'Mam?' Kit pushed the front door open and listened. The floor creaked in the front bedroom and then came the sound of footsteps and hacking coughs. Christine appeared at the top of the stairs. Kit braced herself.

'Krystal? What are you here for?' Her voice was quieter than usual, wavering a little.

'I've just come to see if you're all right. Do you want me to go?' The new tremulous version of Christine was unnerving and she didn't quite trust it.

'Go in the kitchen. I'll be down now. Don't open the blinds, it's too bright for me.'

Kit did as she was told, her fingers going straight to the light switch just inside the kitchen door, a kind of muscle memory still operating even after all these years. She crossed to the kitchen counter where she boiled the kettle and made her mother a coffee. She listened to the sounds of Christine moving around upstairs: getting dressed, she assumed.

After ten minutes, Christine appeared. Kit was taken aback at the sight of her. She hadn't looked well the last time she'd seen her, but Kit saw now why Amber had been so worried. Her mother's skin had a dark tinge to it, beyond the yellow that she'd acquired from years of cigarette smoke. She was bone-thin, her joggers and T-shirt hanging off her hips and shoulders like sacks. She moved slowly, as if she were a generation older than her actual age. Christine was only fifty-two, about the same age as the robustly healthy John Ellis. She made her way across the room to the table where she lowered herself onto a chair with an exhalation of breath and then sat holding her stomach and looking away from Kit.

'Where's your fags? Do you want one of mine?' Kit started

to feel about in the pocket of her hoody, but Christine shook her head.

'No, not yet. I can't smoke first thing anymore. Makes me throw up. Can't speak either. Give me a minute, catch my breath.'

Her frailty was so disorientating that Kit couldn't speak either. They sat in silence, not looking at each other. After a while, Christine took a couple of shallow, wheezy breaths before launching into a sentence.

'I'm bad. Really bad.' A child, appealing for help.

'I can see that. Have you seen the doctor?'

'No point.'

'Yes, there's a bloody point. I'm going to call the out-of-hours now.'

'No, don't. It's the drinking, isn't it?'

Kit shrugged. 'I wouldn't know.'

'Well, I do. Googled it. I don't want to go into hospital. I'd rather be here.'

'For God's sake, let me call the doctor.'

'No. I mean it, Krystal: I want to stay here.'

'You need someone to look after you.'

'Can't you do it?' That child's voice again, setting Kit's teeth on edge.

'I've got a job, remember? Anyway, you need proper care – nursing care.'

'Well, don't expect to see me alive next time you decide to bother with me, because I'm not going into no hospital.'

Kit stood up, exasperated. 'Why the hell not?'

'I'm afraid.'

Looking down at Christine's bent head, Kit saw that she was trembling. For fuck's sake. She sat back down.

'Mam, look, I've got a job, but I'd be no good at looking after you anyway. I don't even think it's what you want, not really. You and I have never got on, have we?'

'I dunno why you'd say that.' Sulky now, a teenager.

'Because it's true. You weren't great with any of us, but you definitely didn't like me. I don't know why but it doesn't matter anymore. Huw and Menna are my mum and dad now and I don't care how you feel about me, I stopped caring years ago, so you don't need to pretend. But me looking after you, that is not going to happen. It wouldn't work.'

'What about Jasmine? Or Josette?'

'No chance. And don't suggest Tyler, he wouldn't even come here today.' She knew Christine wouldn't argue with that; she wasn't about to revisit why Tyler was angry with her.

'Looks like I'm on my own, then,' Christine snapped. She got up and started rooting through a kitchen drawer, eventually pulling out a cigarette packet and a lighter.

'You are choosing to be on your own, Mam. You should be in hospital, you won't go. I can't do anything about that, can I?'

'No. There we are then; you know where the door is.'

Kit stood and turned on her heel, heading for the door, speechless again but with irritation now. She had hold of the handle when Christine called out from the kitchen behind her.

'Why do you care what happens to me?'

Kit stopped and rested her head against the tobacco-stained UPVC of the door frame. 'Search me. Maybe I'm just a nice person.'

'Maybe you are, too. It wasn't that I didn't like you, you know. You've got that wrong. It was just – well, he doted on you, that's all.'

There was no need to ask who she was talking about. The nameless 'he' had only ever meant Gino in this house and the story that Kit had been her father's favourite and her mother had resented it was well known by them all. Kit regarded it as nothing but an excuse, and an unlikely one at that. She didn't bother with a response but pulled the door open and left without another word, slamming it behind her. She'd been in the house barely twenty minutes and they'd had a row. She was going to have to rethink how to manage Christine, that much was clear.

CHAPTER 8

Kit was in the office before anyone else on Monday morning. She'd spent Sunday sleeping off Saturday night's vodka and attempting to come up with a plan. She'd debated whether to ignore Christine and ring the doctor, but she knew there was no point. The doctor would phone Christine, she'd say she was fine and that would be that. Going back with a GP in person wasn't an option either; Christine would just shout abuse from behind her locked front door. Or worse, throw things at them through the window. On Sunday afternoon, Kit had texted her mother and established that she was still alive and that was as much as she could face for the time being. She didn't update her sisters or Tyler about events. They didn't want to know, so she didn't need to go to the trouble of telling them.

The police report from Friday night was waiting for her on the system. It said pretty much what Dai had told her; great play was made of Rhian's reasonable and calm presentation and the officers had obviously been disinclined to inquire any further than that. For a second time, they hadn't spoken to Dylan. It had been a waste of time and she hoped against hope that she hadn't blown her chances of working with Dylan by pointlessly sending them up there.

Georgia arrived just before eight thirty, looking just like an iron railing in her skinny black trousers and matching cropped jacket. As she stalked across the team room, her eyes fell upon Kit and her face took on an exaggerated expression of surprise.

'Oh hello! We don't seem to have coincided in quite a while.'

'No, we haven't, have we? I've been really busy.'

'Really? Got time for a catch-up now?'

'Sure.' Kit had set herself up for that one. She trailed into the office after Georgia, a feeling of doom closing in. Georgia would instruct her to try to close as many cases as she could, and there wasn't a single one ready to be closed. On the upside, if she kept Georgia busy with that old fight, she'd limit the chances of her stumbling upon the existence of the secret client.

'Right, let's bring up your caseload.' Georgia's long nails tapped on her keyboard for a few seconds, then she took a sharp breath and sat back in her chair, staring at the screen with a gurning expression which amounted to near horror. Kit felt a stab of pure panic. Had someone on her caseload died without her knowing about it?

'You're up to capacity,' Georgia said, finally.

'Oh, yes, I'm sure I am.'

'So, what can you get closed?'

'I really don't think any of them are . . .'

Georgia's palm went up in the air, a habitual gesture of

command which always made Kit perspire all over with irritation. 'I don't think you are understanding me. I have six cases waiting for allocation from last week and no doubt many more on the way this morning, plus four child protection enquiries outstanding. Everyone's got to make room, I'm afraid, and some of yours have been open for . . . let's see . . . three months. They all need to move over to the long-term team. What's this? Ella Evans – four months? And she's in a foster placement? Really?'

'I know. But the thing is, Ella's at high risk and she is starting to listen to me, a bit anyway. I think to move her to another social worker right now would be a mistake. She'd have to start again and it might destabilise things.'

A few moments of silence followed. During it, Georgia's face took on the strained expression of someone summoning up the considerable reserves of patience necessary to deal with a case of outright stupidity. Eventually, she leant forward in her chair, rested her elbows on the desk and fixed Kit with an earnest gaze.

'No offence, but have you ever thought you might be better off working in another team?'

'No. Why?'

'I just think the . . . er . . . *ethos* of a long-term team might suit you better.'

'In what way?'

'Well, "long-term". The clue's in the name, really.' She ended with a small laugh.

Kit longed to slap her. 'Sorry. Not with you.'

Georgia sighed. 'Look, as I've told you a number of times before, the point of this team is to screen for serious issues, get them closed off if we can and move them on to another team if we can't. Fast, targeted and effective, that's us. Ensuring there's no comeback on the department if something goes wrong with one of these kids later down the line. You seem to get very . . . *involved*. That's not our role. If you want to spend your time indulging teenagers who are running away from perfectly good foster placements, you need to be looking for a new job. As far as we are concerned, the likes of Ella Evans are nothing but backlog. And we cannot have backlog. The inspectors have been clear about that, and so far our statistics are shaping up very well in this inspection, especially as compared to the previous regime.'

It was the jibe at Vernon that did it. 'We're a social work team, Georgia. What the hell is the point of us if we don't do any social work? A trained monkey can screen cases against a tick-list. How do you think anything is going to get "closed off", as you call it, if we don't have time to get to know these kids? And by the way, Ella Evans is not backlog. She's a young girl who's been so badly treated she can't handle it when someone treats her well, so she keeps going back to what's familiar instead. It doesn't take a genius to see where she's headed if someone doesn't get her trust. That is what I trained to do and it's what I'm good at. Just let me do it, for fuck's sake.'

A fleeting expression of surprise had crossed Georgia's face during this speech. It was the first time Kit had completely lost her cool with her. Although deeply satisfying in the moment, it was not the best strategy. The shock departed from Georgia's face almost at once and was replaced with delight. She stood and moved out from behind her desk to face Kit.

'You are still not understanding me. I am the manager of this team, and you will do whatever I say. I could discipline you for the way you just spoke to me, but I will give you one last chance. I want three of your cases ready for closure on the system by the end of this week. I will email that instruction to you this morning, along with a record of our conversation. Defy me if you so choose, but you will take the consequences.'

A variety of retorts simmered in Kit's mind and she seethed at Georgia's headmistressy tone, but she had already crossed a line and it wasn't wise to do it again. She turned away and closed the door behind her, just about managing not to slam it. After signing out for the day, she grabbed her bag and left, trembling with rage.

Kit busied herself with visits all morning, this being the only way she could distract herself. To her delight, Ella had stayed put in her foster placement and had a good weekend. There would be many more slip-ups before Ella finally settled down but that would be someone else's problem now.

Around midday, she reckoned it was about time to set off for Rock. She would see if she could catch Dylan before he went to the shop. She still needed to confront Rhian but after what had happened the other night, it was best to speak to him first. The memory of his agitated face at the window made her shiver all over again. She was desperate to make sure he was all right.

She drove quickly up the Hir, barely noticing the scenery today, still preoccupied with Georgia and what she might do next. Arriving in Sunnyside, she parked a little way down the road from her usual spot. She wanted to concentrate on Dylan and not get drawn into a chat with John, cosy though that might be. She pulled her phone out of her pocket to while away the time while she waited for him to appear. She'd worked out that he probably left for the shop around about this time every day, and sure enough, a few minutes later he emerged out of the lane, head down against the rain. Kit started the car as she watched him cross over the road, then she did a three-point turn, drove a few yards and pulled up alongside him, winding the window down.

'Need a lift?'

He stopped and looked at her, unsmiling. 'I knew you'd turn up.'

'Wow, really? Are you psychic, then?'

'No. But you just keep coming where you're not wanted, don't you?'

She was unexpectedly hurt. She'd really thought she was making progress with Dylan. She was great with teenagers and she was going to turn his life around, that was the story she'd been telling herself. He'd cut her right down to size. Her immediate reaction was to defend herself, but that would just lead to a confrontation and he'd end up telling her where to go. She had no legal right to insist on seeing him, no evidence of any significant harm, no matter how dysfunctional this family seemed. It was entirely up to him whether he saw her again or not. His cooperation was necessary and she had hold of it by a thread. If she lost her grip now, that would be the end of it.

'Tell me about it, then, Dylan. Tell me what I did wrong and why you're annoyed.'

'You shouldn't have come to the house. And you didn't need to send the police, there was no need of that, none at all.' As his words tumbled out, something about them caught her ear. 'No need of that' – it was an old-fashioned turn of phrase; her grandparents would have said it, maybe even her parents at a push, but not a teenage boy. Was he passing on what Rhian had ordered him to? Or was it just that he was alone with his mum so much that he was picking up her way of speaking?

'OK, I'm sorry. I got it wrong. But I've been worried about you, Dylan. Really worried. What was going on the other day?'

He shrugged. 'Nothing. You frightened my mother, that's all, coming up, no warning, getting yourself in through that gap. It was sneaky. She didn't like it.'

'I'm sorry. I really wanted to speak to her. I just want to help.'

'Well, you shouldn't have done it. I've closed it up now so don't try it again, and I've put glass all along the top of the wall too, so you've got no chance of getting in. No one has.'

The rain was running down his face now, and the shoulders of his thin hoody were darkening.

'I really am sorry. We can talk about this some more but please will you just get in the car, you're drenched.'

He hesitated but gave in, his anger abating slightly now he'd said his piece. Once he was settled in the front seat, she turned to him.

'You had your dinner yet?'

He shook his head.

'Fancy a Big Mac?'

'I need to go to the shop. I have to be home by one thirty.'

'It's only fifteen minutes away. I can drive you to the shop after and then drop you home with your shopping. We can make it as long as we're quick.'

He was snookered. 'OK, then. I have to be back on time, though.'

He did up his seat belt and stared straight ahead, rigid in his seat, while she started the car, put some music on and drove through Rock and onto the main road, heading south towards the nearest McDonald's on the outer edge of Sandbeach. The fast-food chains hadn't made it up to Rock yet, but Dylan was bound to have tried a Big Mac when he was at school and she knew it was a sure bet for any hungry seventeen-year-old boy. She stayed quiet at first, recognising that getting into the car had been a big enough concession for him. He needed some time to sulk, so he wouldn't be seen to give in too easily.

As she drove, she noticed that his fingers were drumming slightly on his knees in time to the music. Taking this as a sign that he was ready to climb down, she searched about for a way to start the conversation.

'Do you like this?'

He wrinkled his nose. 'Not sure. What even is it?'

'Twenty One Pilots. "Stressed Out".'

He listened intently for a few lines. 'What's he saying about tree houses?'

'*Out of student loans and tree house homes / We all would take the latter.* It's about growing up.'

'So, like, he doesn't want to be an adult?'

'Yeah, I think. He means life's easier when you're little, you know?'

'Yeah.' He nodded then sank back into silence, staring out of the window. John had said that Rhian had managed quite well for a while. Maybe Dylan was thinking about the days when his mum had been better, and he'd been free to be a child.

'What do you think he means by that line, then, Dyl? *Wish we could turn back time to the good old days / When our momma sang us to sleep.*'

He turned to face her, eager to get the answer right. 'I guess he means he liked it when his mum looked after him, made everything all right, maybe?'

'Yeah, I think so too. It must have been like that when you were small, before your mum got ill?'

He nodded. 'Is that a message for me, then?'

'Sorry?'

'Did they put that in the song for me to hear, the bit about my mother?'

'Dylan, no, of course not. How could someone do that?' Anxiety flared hot in her chest and stomach as she strained to grasp his meaning.

'It's all right, I get what you mean now. You muddled me up, that's all, talking as if it was about my mother.'

'I'm sorry. I didn't mean anything like that at all. It's just a song.'

'Yeah, sorry, I don't know what I meant. It is right, though, it was different back then, when I was small. But that was only because we didn't know.'

'Can you tell me about that? What didn't you know?'

He rubbed his fingers across his forehead, eyes closed. 'It's hard to explain. We need to keep safe now, that's all. I can't say anymore.'

'Keep safe? From what?'

'Nothing. It doesn't matter.'

'It does matter. It's my job to understand and help if something's harming you. Just tell me what you mean and we can sort it out.'

'I said it doesn't matter. Now leave it.' He fidgeted in his seat and out of the corner of her eye she saw his fingers playing along the door and searching out the handle. Would he actually open it and jump out if she pushed him anymore? She'd had a kid do that to her once before, and although he'd rolled expertly over onto the pavement and run away unharmed, she wasn't about to chance it again.

'All right, sorry, I didn't mean to upset you. Tell you what, I'll see if I can find something you like on my playlist. What are you into?'

'Rap,' he answered at once.

'Great, so what, Kanye? Or Drake?'

'Yeah, and Eminem, Jay Z, Kendrick Lamar. But Drake's the best.'

'Of course. How did you get into it?'

'The boys used to play it – at school, in the break.'

'So you did have a few mates at school, then?'

'I used to.'

'Do you still see them?'

'Nope.'

It was on the tip of her tongue to ask him again what had changed but she could see she was on thin ice. She'd find a way to come back to it more obliquely later on. Flicking through her playlist, she found Hotline Bling and left him to enjoy it in peace until they arrived at the drive-through.

'What do you fancy? Big Mac?'

He didn't answer at once and when she turned to look at him, she could see his teeth worrying at his lip. 'I'm not all that hungry.'

'Have a double cheeseburger then, no fries and a Coke?'

'OK.'

After ordering and collecting their food she pulled out

of the car park and drove back up the main road for a few minutes until she reached a lay-by just past the entrance to the Hir. She pulled into it and handed Dylan his burger and drink. She'd hoped to be able to see right across to where the thick pine forest started on the other side of the valley, running all the way from there up to Rock. As kids, Kit and Tyler had loved racing around in the soft light under the canopies of the branches, hunting for fairies and elves. This distant view of the forest had always marked the start of the Hir in Kit's mind, bringing the joy of knowing that she would shortly see her grandad. But today it was obscured by the rain, which lashed down relentlessly, hammering in the otherwise silent, increasingly steamy car. She tried opening the window a crack to get a breath of fresh air but a wet blast on her face made her shut it again immediately. She was acutely conscious of the lapse in conversation, and of the confined, muggy space.

Glancing at Dylan, she noticed that he was fiddling with the straw she'd given him for his Coke, rubbing the paper wrapper back and forth between his fingers. His burger lay unopened in his lap. He looked sullen, but that was the default facial expression for any kid who felt acutely awkward. He was cross with her because the situation was uncomfortable, and she ought to know what to do about it. It occurred to her that she had tried all along to tread carefully with him; maybe that was where she was going wrong. Maybe he needed her to take control.

'Dylan, I'm going to speak to you now, a bit like I did that time before, when we were outside your gate. OK?'

He didn't say a word or make a movement.

'I'm going to take that as a yes. Now, I am not sure what is going on with you and your mum. She doesn't seem quite right to me; as far as I can see, she doesn't even go out and you are looking after her, doing everything. It's affecting your life and it's not fair. On top of that, people around here are bullying you and giving you a hard time, maybe because of your mum, I don't know. I want to do something about all that. But first of all, we have to help her, then I can help you. Proper help, Dylan. Your mum might need someone to assess her mental health. A psychiatrist or a community psychiatric nurse.'

At that, he turned to face her, his eyes clouding with fear. 'No. We don't want that.'

'Why not?'

He shrugged. It was becoming a familiar sight and Kit was starting to see that the gesture was born less of uncertainty and more of stubbornness. Once those shoulders went up, the conversation was over. Rather like Georgia's palm-in-the-air 'stop' sign and very nearly as infuriating. She was going to push past it this time.

'Dylan, I don't know what you've got against mental health services but let's put that to one side for a minute. I can see that you love your mum.'

A slight tremor around his mouth said she'd hit on something. 'I guess you are doing your best to protect her. I don't

133

know whether she's anxious or depressed or what, but you are a bright boy and you know she's not right. It's only going to get worse. All I want is to get into the house and have a proper talk to her. It must be such a worry, looking after her; you can't do it on your own and you don't need to.'

He was rubbing his palm back and forth over his mouth now, mulling it over.

'Come on, Dyl. If you don't take this chance, you might not get another one. I know I handled it badly the other day. But other than that, you've found me OK so far, so you're not going to get anyone better than me to help, are you?'

'No. What do I need to do?'

She could have hugged him. But she had to think quickly, before he changed his mind.

'Could you talk to your mum, get her to agree to us all having a chat? I've got a few ideas that might persuade her to get help.' Not strictly true but getting a foot in the door was the first thing.

'All right. Can we do it now?'

'I think that's a really good idea.'

'Come on, then.' Now his mind was made up, he was over-taken by an urgency that she hadn't expected.

'All right. Eat on the way, eh?'

He nodded and she started the car and pulled back onto the road, while he began to unwrap his burger. Out of the corner of her eye, she could see that he was handling it carefully, almost gingerly.

'Is it all right? Don't you like cheeseburgers?'

'I never have them.'

'Your mum not keen on junk food?' It hadn't occurred to her to question what his diet might be like. Although she couldn't imagine he got much fresh stuff from the corner shop.

'I just don't have burgers.'

She wondered if she shouldn't have bought it for him, if perhaps Rhian wouldn't like it. Then she remembered that he was seventeen. And it was only a cheeseburger, for God's sake. 'Give it a try. You might like it.'

He lifted it to his mouth and nibbled on the edge of the bun. 'Yeah, it's all right.'

Feeling pleased at having encouraged this little bit of teenage rebellion, Kit drove on up the valley. As she stopped outside John's house, he appeared at the window, but he must have spotted Dylan in the front seat because he immediately moved back discreetly into the room.

'Finished your food?' Dylan uncurled his powerful frame from the front seat and clambered out onto the pavement.

'Yep.'

When they arrived at the entrance to the lane, Dylan turned to her. 'You'd better wait here. I'll talk to my mother. Give me your number and I'll phone you when it's all right to come up.'

'You've got a phone?'

'John got it for me. In case there was an emergency or something. My mother doesn't know I've got it.' He drew out a cheap-looking pay-as-you-go phone with a flip-top lid and opened it up. She gave him her number and he tapped it in, then he made off into the lane, half running.

She stayed in the shadow of the bushes. The last thing she needed was for John to appear and get himself involved, overwhelming Rhian and upsetting the delicate balance of Dylan's negotiations. After half an hour, she was getting chilly and a bit concerned. Was Dylan going to come back? Had it just been a ploy to throw her off? She was considering going after him when her phone rang in her inside pocket. She answered it.

'Come now.' And he was gone.

CHAPTER 9

Kit started up the lane, her feet slipping on the uneven, leaf-covered surface. As she came around the corner into the clearing, Dylan was waiting for her behind the gate.

'Are you OK?' she called out. He had his phone clutched in one hand and started waving at her urgently with the other. It was similar to the gestures he had made from the window the other day. Had he changed his mind already? She was determined to ignore him this time. But as she gained a few more feet and pushed the gate open, he lifted his finger to his lips. He had not been telling her to leave, but to stop shouting.

'OK, but why?' she whispered.

'My mother's very upset. She won't listen to me. Will you try?'

'Can I come in to talk to her?'

'Yes. She's in the front room. Please be quiet, though.'

'I will, but why?'

He shrugged. 'Loud noises startle her.'

Dear God, the woman was like a nervous horse. Kit followed Dylan through the gate and up the path. When they got to the

137

doorstep, he stopped and switched his phone off and then put it away in the inside pocket of his thin jacket. The precise way in which he did it, patting to check that it was securely inside and doing up the tiny button on the top of the pocket, made Kit feel sad. It must be so precious to him, this cheap little phone; most teenagers she knew would treat a brand-new iPhone with less care. She put her own phone away in her pocket too, knocking the sound off first, in case it rang and caused Rhian to bolt or rear up or something.

The front door stood open, allowing them both into the dimly lit hallway. While Dylan locked up behind them, she glanced around. The wallpaper was heavily embossed with a pattern of leaves and painted over in a dark shiny green. The woodwork bore dingy brown varnish, peeling in places, an old-fashioned look that didn't correspond to Rhian's actual age. A strong smell caught at Kit's nose again, just as it had the first time she'd visited. Now that she was in the midst of it, she could recognise notes of damp, dust and stale cooking. It was nothing sinister, she told herself. Just the odour of a house in which doors and windows were never opened to allow the sun or the air to circulate. Or to allow anyone in or out. And this definitely wasn't the best time to start speculating about why that might be. She was feeling very claustrophobic as it was.

Dylan leant across her to push open a door that stood to their left and nodded to indicate that she should go in first. Passing closer to him than she'd ever been before, she registered with brief but acute pleasure that he smelt of warm skin and plain soap. She couldn't remember the last time she'd come across a young man who hadn't been doused in half a can of Lynx.

She entered to find a living room decorated in more dull brown and green tones. It was furnished simply, with a dark-green velvet three-piece suite, worn to a shine on the arms and the seats, and a couple of wooden occasional tables. A huge Welsh dresser stood against one wall, holding only a few pieces of blue-and-white china. There was no TV in the room, and Kit realised for the first time that the quietness of the house was in part due to the absence of technology of any kind. No TV, no computers, no texts pinging or vibrating, no Spotify, not even a radio. Nothing to disturb the thick, funereal silence. Her mind immediately threw up the picture from John's journal; the glamorous young couple who'd ended up cowering in their flat, cutting off all their devices in a desperate attempt to keep themselves safe.

Rhian stood in front of the big bay window, facing Kit as she entered the room. A bright shaft of winter sunlight had fallen onto the thin beige curtains behind her, creating a luminous honeyed backdrop, against which she stood out bony and stark in a charcoal outfit of blouse and straight-legged trousers, hanging loose at the neck and waist and drooping at the knee. Her hands were folded together tightly in front of her, as if she were anticipating a reprimand.

Kit looked at Dylan, thinking it best if he took the lead. But he shook his head. 'You explain to my mother,' he said. He moved to stand opposite Rhian, and she turned to face him so that the two of them were sideways on to Kit. They glanced at each other, their eyes locking for a moment, Rhian's dropping away first. So, they were both angry, Kit thought, but Dylan was winning. As she took in this fact, along with the sheer physical presence of him, taller and more substantial than his mother by far, she saw that she had miscalculated. Dylan wasn't just a timid boy, afraid of his mum. They were far more equal than she had realised. Fit for each other, her grandad would have said.

'Thanks for seeing me.' Both their faces swung towards her, as if startled by the realisation that she was still there.

'That's quite all right.' Rhian's nod of acknowledgement was as highly mannered as a curtsy.

'I wanted to speak to you both because I'm worried about you, Rhian. I feel you might need some help, and I want to find out how to get that to you.'

'Thank you, but we don't need help. We are fine as we are.' Rhian addressed Kit, but her eyes were already back on Dylan, and his on her. His fingers were curling and uncurling, his knuckles cracking quietly. After a few seconds, seeing that he wasn't going to help her out, Kit had to press on, but she kept a tiny part of her attention on him. More and more she was understanding that Dylan expressed himself physically, his feelings coming out that way far more vividly than they did through his words.

'I'm sorry, Rhian, but I think you do. I don't know what's

going on here, but it's not fair for Dylan to have to look after you. He's bright, he should be doing his A- levels. If you have anxiety or something that's making things difficult for you, we need to get you some help.'

Rhian flinched visibly. 'No,' she said loudly. 'I won't be locked away. We don't need any help, we are fine as we are.'

'You keep saying that.' Dylan's words echoed Kit's own irritation at hearing that phrase yet again. His voice came quietly but deliberately now, telling Kit that he was trying to steady himself. 'But we're not fine, are we? She wants to help us, Mam, and it's time someone did. We can't go on like this.'

Rhian's mouth twisted angrily. He was stepping out of line, defying her.

'What's the problem then, Dylan?' Kit kept her voice gentle. 'If you can tell me, we can talk about what to do.'

'I'm going to tell her, Mam.' He moved a step nearer to Rhian and took a hold of her shoulder, turning her to face him again. 'Let me tell her, and maybe she can tell us how to make them stop.'

'You know we can't do that. You know why. Please, Dylan.'

'Do you mean Aled and Joe?' Even as she said it, Kit knew those two idiots couldn't be the cause of all this. But her words were lost anyway; Rhian's breath had started to come from her mouth in jagged gasps, startling in the hushed room. Dylan reached out and took his mother's hand. His fingers curled into her palm first, kneading gently at the scant flesh, then he turned her hand over and ran them back and forth across her knuckles, caressing and soothing her. His eyes stayed on hers and his head moved up and down with the rise and fall of her chest, mimicking it at first, then slowing, leading her to follow his rhythm. After a few minutes, she exhaled audibly and he nodded at her. 'That's better,' he said, keeping hold of her hand and clasping it in both of his. 'That's better now, isn't it?'

Kit cleared her throat, uncomfortable for a reason she could not put a label on. 'Best if you leave.' His face was empty of hope now.

'I'm not in any rush.'

'I'll let you out.' He dropped his mother's hand.

'Thank you for coming.' Rhian spoke as if it had been a tea party. Dylan crossed the room and went into the hall, leaving Kit and Rhian to stand in silence.

'I'm a good mother.' She spoke without lifting her eyes from the floor. 'You think I'm not, but I look after him.'

'I don't think you're a bad mother at all. I know you're very strong, you must have been to bring Dylan up on your own. That must have been hard.'

Rhian looked her full in the face now, a smile wavering on her lips. 'Thank you for saying that. Yes, it was very hard, on my own.'

'And he's lovely, he really is. But you seem like you're . . . suffering.'

'We are. They're plaguing us. I wish you could help.'

'Then let me.'

'No one can. It's just not possible. But thank you for coming.'

She turned away to face the curtains, leaving Kit with no choice but to follow Dylan out into the hall.

When he had finished undoing the chain and turning the key in the front door, Dylan straightened up and she managed to catch his eye. He looked away, but not quickly enough to hide his red-rimmed eyes. Her heart filled with sadness for him.

'Will you meet me at the viewing point later this week? We can talk about this some more?' She ran through her schedule in her mind. Maybe it would be good to give him a few days' break from her. 'Friday, maybe?'

'I'm not sure.'

'Come on, Dylan. She doesn't even need to know and we can talk about a different way to do things. I'm not giving up, I told you that, so you needn't think I'm going away. I'm going to help you.'

'Whether we want you to help us or not, eh?'

'Well, that's about it, yes.' It was confusing, the way he could switch from coldly escorting her out of the house to teasing her in a matter of seconds. But she was flooded with relief. He couldn't bring himself to finally draw the line, in case she didn't come back. They were standing close together now, the scent of his fresh skin reaching her again. He made a small, self-conscious movement with his hand, brushing his hair out of his eyes and revealing his cheekbone just as she had before. There was no sign of the bruising now. But she felt sure that if she asked him in this quiet moment, as they stood so that they were almost touching, he would tell her the truth.

'Dylan, the first time I saw you, you had a bruise on your face. Did someone hit you?'

'No. Don't be stupid.' Tears welled and hovered on his lower lashes. He turned his face away from her before they could fall, pulling the door wide open, then stood with his chin up, staring out into the garden as if she wasn't there. She rested her fingertips lightly on his lower arm.

'Dylan, if someone hurt you, you can tell me. Was it your mum?'

His eyes were full of anguish when he turned to face her. His chest rose as he gathered himself to speak.

'You need to go now.' Rhian stood behind them, her face set and cold. Had she heard? Kit couldn't tell but she knew it was time to leave. She stepped out onto the path and turned to find that Rhian had pushed past Dylan and was standing framed in the doorway. But her attention wasn't on Kit. Following Rhian's eyes Kit saw something on the path glinting in the sunlight. It was a small handful of change, just four or five coppers.

'I guess someone dropped some money. Might have been me, actually.' Kit started to pat her side pocket, where she usually had a few coins. It was empty. Perhaps the money had fallen out when she'd put her phone away earlier. She leant forward to pick it up.

'Leave it.' Rhian's irritability was rising now. 'It wasn't dropped, look at the way it's lying. It's been placed.'

'Placed? What do you mean?'

'Just leave it.'

'All right, I will, I'm sorry. Dylan, will you meet me on Friday? Usual time?'

But he didn't answer or even look at her. He was looking over his mother's shoulder, pushing forward urgently to see what had caught her attention. She'd lost him. Making her way down the path, Kit swore under her breath. Every time she got near to him, he backed away. She turned at the gate, hoping to get another word in. He was on the doorstep now, his mother leaning into him, his arms encircling her upper body. They clung together, oblivious to Kit's presence, their eyes fixed on the coins, their faces taut with fear.

CHAPTER 10

For the next couple of days, Kit fretted almost continually about the Merediths. She kept a low profile in the office, managing to evade Georgia in person, although there was no escaping her terse emails of instruction, starting with the one ordering Kit to close three cases by the end of the week. Others followed, commenting upon her casework, picking holes, noting every tiny thing she hadn't done. Her expenses claim was returned with a note attached querying the exact locations of visits and length of journeys, right down to the last half-mile. Georgia was all over her, trawling through her work and boning up on every aspect of it. Reluctantly, Kit rang Ella's foster carers and told them she was moving Ella on to the long-term team. She recorded their angry comments and then filled out the case transfer, taking care to note that she was doing so on Georgia's instruction. When she sent it off to Georgia for authorisation, it snapped back immediately as if it were attached to a piece of elastic. Kit sent a silent apology to Ella and crossed her fingers for her.

Arriving at the office on Thursday morning with an

unsettling notion that she'd been told to be there on time but absolutely no idea as to why, she found her desk plastered with an array of shocking-pink Post-its. Peeling them off one by one, she read them, screwed them up and dropped them into the bin. They instructed her to amend her expenses claim, update her training planner, close two more cases TODAY WITHOUT FAIL!! and finally, to present herself in Conference Room J at 9.30 a.m. to meet the inspectors. So that was it; she vaguely remembered Nazia having mentioned this. She was surprised to find that Georgia hadn't put a stop to it. She wouldn't normally let Kit within ten feet of anyone influential.

Kit selected two more cases for closure, working on the basis of what would cause the least havoc. Again, she made a note on each one to the effect that this was her manager's instruction. She and Georgia were engaged in a game of chess now, and she wasn't about to surrender easily. After a quick coffee, she set off for the conference suite. Passing Ricky and Maisie on the stairs, she paused to explain where she was going.

Ricky was open-mouthed. 'And Georgia knows you're doing this?'

'Apparently. I don't get it either, but she told me to go so I'm going.'

'Please don't say anything you shouldn't. In fact, just don't speak at all if you can help it.' He leant precariously over the banister as she skipped down to the ground floor.

'Can't think what you mean.' But she planned to behave herself. No point in rocking the boat.

Arriving at the corridor that housed the conference suite, Kit could see Cole Jackson pacing up and down at the far end. He was glancing at his watch and adjusting then readjusting his vivid purple paisley tie. As she drew nearer to him, his aftershave floated out to meet her halfway. She inhaled carefully. He smelt like a half-baked muffin. Blueberry, that was definitely it. Was this a coincidence, or did he deliberately match his scent to his tie colour every day? It was an intriguing theory and she would share it with the rest of the team later. They could start cross-referencing daily, bringing a new dimension to their regular game of Describe Cole's Aftershave.

'Kit, glad you could make it. The inspectors will be ready for us any minute now.'

'I didn't realise you would be joining us, Cole.'

'Just pretend I'm not here. Say anything you want to, don't hold back. I'm keen to get your feedback. You know how I feel about transparency.'

She did indeed, and therefore also knew what a total waste of time this was going to be. But there was nothing to do except get through it, so she waited while Cole gave a servile little tap on the door, then slipped into the conference room. She followed, determined only to get back out again as soon as possible.

A man and a woman stood behind the long table. There were two chairs set out in front of it. Kit took one while Cole and the inspectors stayed standing to exchange pleasantries. The man was in his late thirties, sharp-suited, and wearing a striking lime-green tie. He had good skin and thick dark-blond hair, and he greeted Cole warmly. She had his number at once. He could have swapped places with Cole and it would be at least six months before anyone noticed. Even their dental implants looked like they'd emerged from the same mould.

The woman, though, was harder to fathom. She was in her early sixties and wore a neat black dress and a crimson jacket. She was tall and slim, with cropped ash-blonde hair accentuating her impressive cheekbones. She wore minimal jewellery and make-up, just enough to soften her businesslike look, but nothing too distracting. After Cole and the other man had stood chatting for several minutes, the woman drew out her chair and sat down. The two of them immediately followed her lead.

'Thanks, both, for coming along,' the man said. 'This is quite informal, so please relax. We want you to feel at home.' Kit knew it was a matter of time before he said the word 'transparency'. No doubt 'empowerment' would make an appearance too, which sounded all well and good until you realised that in the mouths of people like him, it amounted to leaving troubled families to get on with it.

'So, I'm Joshua Lomax. Call me Josh. And can we call you Kit, or would you prefer Ms Goddard?' He smiled, highly amused by himself.

'Ms Goddard, thanks.'

He shot her a look. 'OK. Er . . . OK, fine, then. And this is Maxine Cadwalladr.' He struggled slightly on the pronunciation of her surname. The woman's face was impassive, but that had to be irritating, especially if they had been working together for a few weeks. 'As you know,' Josh Lomax continued, 'we're from the inspectorate and our job here is to identify how Sandbeach Child Services is functioning against the quality standards and whether things are sufficiently improved to avoid special measures. Your team is right in the thick of it, and we are conscious that quality starts at the front door. We've been greatly assisted by Georgia already, of course. But we wanted to speak to staff, too, and you were suggested to us by your senior as a new member of the team who can bring extra value to those discussions.'

'Kit's happy to help, I'm sure.' Cole jumped in, probably fearing that Kit might be about to say she couldn't be arsed, which wasn't that far from the truth. 'What would you like her to tell you?'

'So, what would help us most, Kit,' Josh Lomax began, 'is to hear you speak freely about your first year or so in post. The challenges, what you've learnt, how you've been supported.' He opened the notepad in front of him and lifted his pen in readiness. Maxine Cadwalladr did the same.

Kit's working life so far had been divided into two distinct eras. Six months of working for Vernon, feeling excited and interested in what she was doing every single day and knowing for sure that he always had her back. And nine months of working for Georgia. Enough said. Except she couldn't say it, of course.

'I've really developed my skills. It's been such a challenge, a real stretch. I've become conscious of my own strengths and weaknesses,' she threw out randomly, feeling it safest to mirror Josh Lomax's meaningless wordy style. Perhaps she should have started all her sentences with 'So' for good measure.

Josh was nodding as he noted down her words. Kit noticed that Maxine Cadwalladr's pen remained suspended a few inches above her notepad. She wasn't surprised. She wouldn't have bothered writing this nonsense down either. Josh Lomax was scribbling away happily, though. After a few more rounds of the same pointless questions, in response to which she trotted out more of the same trite answers, he indicated that he was satisfied by capping his pen. She saw this was her cue and stood. Josh and Maxine did the same and after quickly shaking Kit's hand and thanking her in a tone that said he'd already lost any slight interest he might have had in what she had to say, Josh moved aside, indicating that Cole should follow him. They fell into animated conversation at once, leaving Kit and Maxine standing on opposite sides of the table.

'Thank you, Ms Goddard,' Maxine said. 'It sounds as if the culture of the team suits you very well.' Kit squirmed. There was no real reason for her to care what Maxine Cadwalladr thought of her, but somehow the idea of this cool, self-possessed woman believing that she bought into Cole and Georgia's management speak was excruciating. Glancing over, she could see that Cole was safely immersed in Josh and vice versa.

'Well, it's been quite a change in the culture really, with us having a new manager, you know? I feel like I've worked in two entirely different teams since I've been in the job.'

Maxine nodded absently, her attention diverted to smoothing out some near-invisible creases in the crisp skirt of her dress. 'Yes, I was sorry to hear from Cole that Vernon had left. I hope he's enjoying his retirement.'

'Oh, Vernon's not retired. He's on sick leave, that's all. He only had a minor heart attack.'

Maxine looked up at her sharply. 'Really?'

'Well, yes. Vernon's not really the retiring type.'

'No. He isn't, is he?'

Kit could hardly have caused Cole anymore trouble if she'd come into the meeting armed with a plan to get him sacked. But what the hell was he doing lying about Vernon's absence anyway?

'Well, Kit, thank you. It's been very helpful. No doubt you have things you need to get on with.' Cole had appeared at her elbow, blowing any chance she might have had of telling Maxine more. Had he heard? He was hovering as if he might be about to physically escort her out of the room. She pushed her chair further back and was about to do as he wanted when Maxine's voice stopped her in her tracks.

'Ms Goddard? I wonder if you would do something for me?'

'Of course.'

'I'd like to take a look at some of your cases.'

'We're due to do our file reviews tomorrow, Maxine.' Josh

was back in the conversation, sensing something slipping out of his control. Maxine gave him an icy look and continued as if he hadn't spoken.

'I'm after something rather different here. I'd like you to select some of your cases, Ms Goddard. Anything that can demonstrate the shift you've just described. Print the files out and give the copies to Cole's PA, by lunchtime if you can. She can bring them down to me this afternoon.'

Kit nodded and shook Maxine's firm, cool hand. Then she headed out into the corridor, relieved but guilty, leaving Cole to his fate. As she headed for the stairs, she heard a voice behind her.

'Ms Goddard?'

Turning, she found that Maxine had followed her out. 'Please call me Kit.'

'Thank you, Kit. I just wanted to say, it sounds like things may not have been going altogether smoothly for you in recent times.'

Kit hesitated, unsure how much she should say.

'Don't worry, I don't need the details, I'm sure I'll pick up anything I need from the files. But I appreciate that I've given you extra work to do, so if at any time you do have any concerns or there is anything I can help you with directly, please give me a call at the inspectorate. I owe you a favour. And thanks for your honesty about Vernon, too. He's well thought of in our department, and his absence has not gone unnoticed, but it seems we were somewhat misled as to the reason for it.' She gave Kit the tiniest of smiles as she turned to go back to the conference room, but her tone was clipped, suggesting that Cole would shortly have some explaining to do.

The team room was mercifully empty when Kit got back to it. She returned to her desk, even though she was longing for a fag, determined to get as many cases as she could printed off and delivered to Cole's PA before Georgia caught her at it. She started with Ella Evans. Then she ran down her allocation list and picked out another three that demonstrated Georgia's interference at its height. She was about to head for the printer room and was already feeling around in her rucksack for her ID badge to swipe in the machine when she realised that she didn't have it – bloody Aled Simms did. She'd been so preoccupied with the Merediths and with Georgia that she'd forgotten all about that particular incident. She'd have to do something about it pretty soon. But she needed her badge right now, to authorise the print job. She'd just have to see if anyone else was around to lend theirs.

The printer room was empty, as was the Youth Justice Team office next door, where she had a few mates who would have helped her out. She hesitated in the corridor, wondering what to do. The next office along was Leaving Care, which she couldn't risk entering for fear of running into her own support worker, the ever bouncy, high-fiving Andy, with his constant talk of taking responsibility and holding herself accountable. He'd been quite helpful with her uni fees and getting her set up in her flat, but she wasn't needy enough for him and the whole thing had got awkward, so she'd avoided him as much as she could ever since. She could ask Cole's secretary to print the files, of course, but then Cole might interfere. She didn't want any vital entries mysteriously going missing. As she pondered, she heard footsteps coming up the stairs and Tim Page appeared, a sheaf of papers in his hand, en route to the next floor.

'Tim!'

'Kit. Hi.' He looked wary, probably fearing that she was about to attempt to fob a referral off on him.

'Could I borrow your ID for a sec? I've left mine at home and I just need to swipe the printer.'

'Sure, no problem.' He took his badge from around his neck and held it out to her. She took hold of it but there was an awkward tussle. He was hanging onto the other end of the lanyard. What the hell was up with him?

'Actually, why don't I come along and swipe it for you?' he said.

'No, it's fine, I can do it. You get on – pick it up from me on your way back down.'

'Really, it's no problem. I'll come with. You can give it back to me straight away when you're done.'

It didn't look like she was going to shake him off. She let go of the badge and headed back into the team room, Tim trailing behind her. At her desk, he finally handed it over. She glanced at his photo, noticing that he'd been quite good-looking twenty years ago. She supposed he still was, or well-preserved at least; his dark-brown hair was turning grey but it suited his light-toned skin and steely eyes. His tall frame carried no extra bulk. His clothes were uninteresting but neat, and the pastel blue of his checked shirt was a good choice for his icy colouring. She still couldn't quite see the appeal of him; he seemed pleasant enough but totally bland to her. But then, she'd never been on the receiving end of his alleged charm in the way Maisie had.

After taking the personal ID code from Tim's badge and entering it against the print jobs queued up on her computer, she returned to the printer room, Tim still in tow. He stood watching in silence as she swiped his card in the machine and pressed the start button. Surely he'd sod off now. She wanted to have a quiet think about how she could get her own ID back. She tried handing the badge back and thanking him elaborately, but he still seemed to be welded to the spot. Kit glanced at the printer, which appeared to be running at about a tenth of its usual speed. Tim leant back against the wall now, settling in. She waited for him to give her a clue as to what he wanted.

'So, how are you, Kit? How are you getting on? I know you haven't been in the department long and you must miss Vernon. If you feel you need any help, my door is always open to you, of course.'

For a minute, she wasn't at all sure how to take his tone. The warmth and concern of it took her aback. He'd never so much as said good morning to her before. Dear God, was he flirting with her? But no, that was ridiculous; it seemed like he genuinely wanted to help and actually, it was nice to be asked. Maybe this was the perfect opportunity to get some advice from someone who knew about adult mental health.

'Well, actually, there is something. About the Merediths.'

'Ah, that one. Yes, that was a good piece of joint decision-making, wasn't it? I can take you through the rationale if you like. I was just going to ask you about it, funnily enough. I assume it's all closed down, as agreed?'

'Well, yes and no. I'm visiting the family now—'

'What are you talking about? Georgia and I specifically discussed closure.'

Oops. She didn't know what odds it made to him but he was riled. His back had straightened and he seemed to tower over her now in the small room. But there was no way out of it. 'Well, to be honest, Georgia doesn't know. Cole asked me to make a visit and find out what's going on. I'd appreciate it if—'

'My lips are sealed. Go ahead, tell me what's on your mind.' His tone had lightened; he altered his posture and leant back against the wall again. 'Honestly, you can confide in me. What's the situation?'

'Thanks.' His snappiness must have been a blip, probably not aimed at her at all, but just irritation at Georgia for not doing what had been agreed. 'The situation's very unusual, Tim. I'm not sure what to make of it.'

'Oh, really?'

'Yeah. I'd appreciate a chat about it, the mother's mental health is a serious concern—'

'You can't get involved with that. You don't have the skill set. It needs to be closed. That's what Georgia and I decided and I don't think she'd be very happy if she found out you were doing all this behind her back, would she?'

'No, possibly not.' The printer finally came to a standstill. Kit started gathering up the papers, dividing them into a pile for each case, trying to catch up with Tim's quick-fire changes of mood. He was edging towards the door now, keen to be on his way. She felt a spike of irritation; she didn't know why everyone was so reluctant to get involved with the Merediths. Why did she have to take all the responsibility?

'Tim, can I just check something with you, though, on the Meredith case. Are you one hundred per cent sure the mother hasn't got any psychiatric history? Rhian Meredith?'

'As I said right from the beginning, there's nothing against her name on the system. I'm quite capable of running a background check, you know.' His mouth had tensed, deep lines appearing along his jaw. She hadn't meant to insult him but it seemed pretty easy to do.

'OK. It's just – as I said, the situation's really odd there.'

'Odd? What on earth do you mean by that?'

'They are definitely being harassed in Rock, or the boy is, at least. But it feels like there's something more going on, you know?'

'Well, I mean – such as what?' There was that note of amusement again, just like he'd used with Georgia. It had seemed inoffensive enough at the time, but now she was on the receiving end of it, Kit found it surprisingly undermining.

'Mental illness can be inherited, right? So, could Dylan's gran have passed something on to her daughter? Schizophrenia or something? Isn't that how it works?'

'As I've also said right from the beginning, mental illness is a bit more complicated than that. The young man sounds like he's had a difficult time, he's reacting badly, that's normal. Don't pathologise it. That's a very uninformed perspective on your part, if you don't mind me saying so.'

'Right. But what about Fflur Meredith, though? I can't seem to get to the bottom of things with her. I mean, she was in hospital, so she was ill herself. That would be three generations, wouldn't it? And by the way, there's a bit of confusion over where she was towards the end of her life. Frankie thought she remembered seeing something on file about a care home. But you mentioned hospital.'

'Well, I don't know why Frankie's accessing her file at all. It's not relevant. It will simply be a muddle in the paperwork no doubt. Fflur Meredith died in Penlan some years ago. If I were you, I'd close it, pronto. It's an abuse of this family's human rights to have you poking about with no justification whatsoever. It could land you in a lot of trouble with the legal section, which would be a shame at this stage of your career. I'll need to mention it to Georgia if you persist. Now, I really do need to get on.' He pushed past her to the door and left without a goodbye.

Kit swore to herself as she finished sorting her piles of papers. What a condescending jerk he was. It certainly didn't bode well for the prospect of a happy pairing with the hopelessly tactless Maisie.

She glanced at her watch and saw that it was almost lunchtime. After making her way back to her office and sitting down at her desk, she put Tim Page firmly out of her mind and ran hurriedly through her copied documents, determined to finish before Georgia caught her. She clipped sections of each file together so that Maxine would be able to work through from referral to assessment and then on via the case recordings to closure. That done, she signed out, slung her rucksack onto her shoulder and ran upstairs, where she firmly instructed Cole's sniffy PA to make sure that the papers got to Maxine Cadwalladr personally, and at once.

Glancing through the window in the senior management suite, Kit could see that it was chucking it down outside. But she was desperate for a cigarette and some lunch. She ran back downstairs and out through the main doors into the hammering rain, reaching her car in seconds. Once in, she pulled out her fags and lit one before she'd even fully closed the door. She needed a moment to think; after putting some music on, she opened her window a touch to let the smoke out, then decided to go the whole hog and reclined her seat. Running over the cases she'd printed, replaying Georgia's caustic comments in her mind one by one, she relished the thought of Maxine Cadwalladr's reaction as she read them, that light frown appearing on her immaculate brow over and over again.

Kit was enjoying herself so much that she decided to light a second cigarette and linger a little more before going to pick up a sandwich. But as she pulled one out of the packet, her phone started buzzing. Reluctantly, she dug it out of her pocket. It was a missed call from Amber. The kids would text, message and Snapchat her, but they never rang her. She put her fag back into the packet and returned the call.

'Kit?' Amber managed before she burst into tears.

'Amb? What's wrong?'

'It's Nana . . .' Her words trailed off into more sobbing.

'OK, I'm coming straight away, where are you?'

'Mags's.' The shop on the estate. Dear God, had Christine started shoplifting again? No, that couldn't be it. Amber was a sensible girl; she didn't cry for nothing. If she'd seen her nan getting into trouble in public, she would have just walked away and pretended not to know her. It was a skill they'd all had to learn early on. No, it had to be worse than that. In the background of the call, voices rose in a shrill argument. Christine and Josie.

'What's happening now, Amber?'

'Mam wants to call an ambulance but Nana's saying no. She says she's going home. There's loads of people here and everyone's staring at her.'

'Tell her I said to stay there, I'll pick you all up.'

There was a bit more shouting and Kit could just make out Josie telling Christine she could drop dead in the street for all she cared. 'Nana's walked off now, Kit,' Amber said. 'I think you'd better meet us at her house.'

If Josie wanted to call an ambulance, things had to be bad. As she drove towards the estate, Kit's fears mounted along with her self-doubt. Should she have done something when she knew Christine was getting really ill? Insisted on the doctor, maybe? She drove past the parade of shops that housed Mags's, where she noticed a small crowd of people lingering outside and chatting. Christine's audience, presumably. Following the route her mother would have taken, she drove on down the hill. She spotted Josie and Amber almost at once, and then Christine, staggering along a few yards ahead, a combination of falling forwards on the incline and rebounding off garden walls somehow adding up to a slow progress towards her home. Kit pulled up next to Josie and Amber and they jumped into the car.

'What happened? Is she pissed?' She turned in her seat to face them. Amber was calmer now, but her face still bore traces of tears, along with a mutinous expression that was instantly familiar to Kit, being the one she would have adopted herself at the same age and in the same circumstances.

Josie shook her head. 'No, I reckon she's ill. I don't know what happened. We didn't even know she was there. We came out of the shop and there she was, on the pavement, sparko. Silly cow.'

'It was so embarrassing. Everyone was looking at us and then Mam and Nana started full-on screaming at each other.' Amber stared out of the car window, furious. She was just starting to wake up to how different her family was from everyone else's.

'That must have been horrible. It'll be OK now, though – let's catch up with her and I'll get this sorted out, eh?' She gave Amber a reassuring smile and hoped she would feel that an adult had arrived to take charge. From her own recollection, that was the one thing she'd wanted at the age of nine. And Amber was certainly unlikely to get any such thing from Josie, who was already looking like she had somewhere more important to be. It hadn't even entered Josie's head to reach out to Amber, to soothe or comfort her. She felt a throb of sadness; there had been a time when Josie had been capable of better. Like Jazz and Danny, she'd played with Kit and Tyler and helped to look after them, and she'd known how to give a cuddle back then, too. But over time, something had hardened in Josette; it was as if she'd decided that turning out like Christine was her fate and she might as well give in to it. Kit missed the old Josie, and for the first time, she wondered about it. Kit had come back to Sandbeach after foster care and uni to find Josie different. She'd accepted it without much thought, just as Josie herself seemed to have done. But what had caused that change in her? It was something else to think about, and sooner rather than later if Amber was to avoid repeating the cycle.

Turning back to the road, Kit saw that Christine had disappeared around the corner into her own street. Kit started the car and followed, passing her mother just as she was entering the last few yards before her gate. After grabbing her door keys from her rucksack, and telling Amber to stay put, Kit jumped out of the car and stood waiting on the pavement, taking the chance to get a look at what was coming towards her. Josie was right, Christine didn't look drunk; this was something else. Her mother was almost level with her now and Kit could see that she was deadly pale and was wincing with every lurching step.

'What the hell are you doing here?' Christine spat out. If it had been her last breath, Christine would probably have used it to have a go at Kit. She ignored her mother and headed up the path before her. After opening the front door, she stood back to allow Christine to struggle past and was about to follow when her mother turned, blocking her entrance.

'I didn't expect to see you again, not after all what was said last time you were here.'

'No, well, Amber phoned me. She was frightened.'

Christine's eyes closed for a moment. 'No need for being frightened. I was taken bad, that's all,' she muttered. Amber was the oldest grandchild, and when she'd been born, Christine had given the grandmother thing a real shot, to everyone's surprise. She'd doted on Amber for the first couple of years, buying her clothes and toys, cutting back on the booze. In the end, it had got the better of her again, once Amber reached the less cutesy, more demanding stage. But for all that, Kit didn't doubt that Christine loved Amber. Just not quite enough.

'Look, you were flat out on the pavement in front of everyone.'

'That's a lie. Who told you that?'

Kit sighed. It was just exhausting. 'It doesn't matter. Right, this time, you are having the doctor.'

'I'm not. I just took a bit dizzy.'

'I'm calling the doctor today.'

'Do what you like. No one's coming in here.'

And with that, she banged the door shut in Kit's face. Kit bent down and pushed the letter box open with her fingers. 'For God's sake, Mam. Open up!'

But silence met her. By the time Kit reached her car, she was already ringing her father's number.

CHAPTER 11

Kit was on her way to Dinas when her phone buzzed. She didn't bother to stop and check it. It was bound to be Gino calling her back. He might be saying it was convenient for her to visit right now or he might not. It made no odds. She'd warned him she was on her way and she intended to see him one way or the other.

She pulled up outside the High Street Tavern, knowing that her dad would most likely be doing the lunchtime shift. As she got out of the car, she glanced around with disdain. Dinas was a dormitory town for Cardiff. It was better off than Sandbeach, and well endowed in terms of out-of-town retail parks and cavernous warehouses offering soft play areas and trampolining. The town centre itself, where Gino's bar was located, had the usual line-up of major chains plus some higher-end boutiques and delis. Dinas was technically by the sea, in that it was only a ten-minute drive away from the high street. But Kit had noticed that there was a strange disconnect between the town and the coast here; Dinas people didn't seem to have the same passion for the beaches that Sandbeach residents had. The scenery wasn't anywhere near as gorgeous, of course; the coastline proper started with a flourish at Sandbeach and stretched west from there, and every cove and bay along its entire length was picture-postcard perfect. But the beach and cliffs near Dinas were pretty enough, in a more low-key way, so that couldn't be the whole explanation. Puzzling as it might be, it appeared that Dinas people simply preferred to spend their Saturday mornings trailing around the town centre, following it up with a two-for-one lunch of cheap sausages and bland mash in the Sleepy Slug or the Battered Badger or whatever the hell the ugly pub-restaurant in the precinct was called. In Sandbeach, you took your kids to the beach on a Saturday, with fishing nets and a football, and bought them chips and ice cream for lunch. If the weather wasn't good enough to do that, you stayed at home feeling miserable and fretting about whether you would be able to go next weekend instead.

Pushing open the heavy wooden doors of the bar, Kit blinked as her eyes adjusted to the lower light. She would have been quite disorientated had it not been for the female voice ringing out from behind the bar. She headed towards it, fixing her vision on the outline of elaborately curled blonde hair atop a petite frame, which eventually came into focus as her step-mother. Mal was pulling a pint and chatting to a customer in the overly loud, bantering tone she adopted for all such interactions.

'Well, hello, stranger.' Mal dropped her voice into the normal range in order to greet Kit.

'Hi, Mal.'

'I'll be with you now, girl.' Mal knocked the tap off and handed the brimming pint to the customer. 'There you go, love,' she bellowed at him. 'That's you set up for the day now, eh? Don't drink it too quick or your missus'll be after me.'

Close up, Kit could see that Mal had been on the Botox. Portions of her face were frozen solid; the bits in between were pretty much marooned, with limited room available to move in any direction. Mal was only in her early forties. She must be taking the ageing process quite hard already. Perhaps she worried that Gino might find a new Mal.

'Is my dad here?'

'Out the back. What's up?'

'Not much. Just need a word.' When it boiled down to it, Kit didn't mind Mal, not really. She hadn't been mother material, but that didn't seem like a good enough reason to hate her. The others thought differently, but Kit and Danny had always held to the view that the responsibility for the five of them had been all Gino's. Maybe Mal had refused to take them on, but they weren't her kids, they were his. He should have stood up to her. On the quiet, Kit didn't blame Mal for not being keen. She had been just twenty-three when she'd got together with Gino. By that time, Danny and Tyler had already been a right handful and Josie hadn't been a total delight either. Kit wouldn't have volunteered for the stepmother vacancy herself, especially as it would have come complete with the cast-iron guarantee of regular hassle from Christine.

'Take a drink with you, Kit?'

'Better not, I'm driving.'

'Coffee then? Sandwich? I've got some lovely ham and mustard made up, one of those do you?'

Kit realised she was starving, as well as parched. 'That would be great, yes. Thanks, Mal.'

'No problem. You go on, I'll bring it through.' It was totally a ploy to enable Mal to have a good nose into what Kit wanted with Gino, but it didn't matter. She was ready to have it out with the both of them, if need be.

Kit found Gino in his tiny windowless office, counting money ready to take to the bank. Piles of notes and coins lay all over the desk.

'Hello, love.' He looked up, his eyes crinkling at the corners in an expression of genuine pleasure.

'Hiya, Dad. You OK?' She sat down in the tatty armchair in front of his desk. Its faded pattern of birds and flowers against a pale-blue background was instantly familiar. It had been her gran's chair, salvaged when her grandad had died. The fact that it was there in the office said less about sentimentality on Gino's part, and more about his love of saving a few bob.

'I'm good. To what do I owe this honour, then?' Gino had adopted the tone he used to address punters in his bar. It was habit, Kit supposed, or maybe he was nervous about why she'd come. Either way, she suspected it would shortly be replaced by something less jovial.

'It's about Mam.'

'What about her?' Marilyn appeared at Kit's side, bearing a sandwich along with a cappuccino, which she must have extracted from the machine in record time in order to make sure that she didn't miss a thing. She placed the cup and plate on the desk in front of Kit, then stood with her arms crossed, all pretence gone, blatantly waiting for the details. Kit took a sip of coffee and a bite of her sandwich, playing for time while she tried to work out the best way to get what she wanted. Losing her temper was definitely not the way to go.

'She's not well.'

Gino snorted. 'Yeah, right. In the head, you mean? What's new about that?'

'No, it's different this time. She's really ill. I think it might be cirrhosis, I don't know. But she looks awful – she needs to be in hospital, but she won't have the doctor.'

'What's it got to do with me?' Gino's tone was top-grade dismissive. Kit felt a swell of desperation. She couldn't cope with Christine on her own, she really couldn't. She was the last person Christine would listen to, and what's more, she had more than enough on her plate with Amber and Tyler to worry about, not to mention work, what with the possibility that Georgia was going to sack her and the constant nagging worry about Dylan. And she missed Vernon, and Alex was miles away and God only knew when he'd be back.

'What is it, love?' Mal's hand was on her shoulder and she was bending down to Kit's level, her face kind in a way that Kit hadn't seen before. 'You look like you've got the weight of the world on you.' The unexpected concern, coming from Mal of all people, made Kit stop and think. Maybe it wasn't best to keep trying to be strategic. Maybe she should just say it how it was.

'Mam collapsed in the street. Amber was there and she saw it and she's terrified. No one cares about it, no one except me and Amber anyway. Jazz doesn't want to know, not really, and Josie's no help. Tyler's got his own problems. I don't want her to die on her own in that house. I know you probably think that's all she deserves and maybe you're right, but I can't let it happen. But I can't fix it either. She won't give me the time of day, she never has. You know that, Dad.'

He looked at her for a moment and there was a struggle written across his face. She imagined that he was weighing up his newly hatched wish to do the right thing by his children against the long-standing and adamant desire never to set eyes upon Christine again. 'And what do you think I can do? What makes you think she'll listen to me?' he hedged.

'I don't know if she will. But I can't do this on my own anymore. I've held the other three together for years now and it'll be Josie's children next. Tyler very nearly didn't make it. You didn't know that, did you?'

'What's up with the boy?'

'He can tell you about it if he wants to. The point is, he'd probably have gone the same way as Danny if it wasn't for me. I'm the youngest and I'm on my own with it all and I'm really good at it but it's not fair. I've got a job and I need to have a life of my own, I can't keep dropping everything whenever one of them fucks up. Thanks for the money at Christmas and everything, but it's not what we need. We need you to help.'

Gino's eyes had gone back down to his cash. Probably checking it was still there. 'And I want to help. I'll do anything else, Krystal, honest I will, but she's made her bed as far as I'm concerned. She's done nothing for you kids anyway, I can't see why you'd care.'

The cheek of it. If there was one person in the world who'd done less for them than their mother, it was their father. She moved forwards on the chair ready to stand. 'Fine then. Forget it. At least I know where I stand.'

'Now hang on a minute, you two.' Mal put her hand on Kit's arm and stopped her in her tracks. There were few things that annoyed Kit more than being interrupted in the process of a good old storming-out, but something in Mal's tone told her it might be worthwhile to take notice.

'You need to think twice by here, Gio. You can't expect Krystal to handle all this.'

'Don't you bloody start, Marilyn. What can I do? Last time I saw that bitch she chucked a vase at my head.'

'Not the point. You need to get over there and try.' She turned to Kit. 'And what's all this about Danny and Tyler?'

'It's a long story.'

Mal looked at her. 'I have heard something, I won't lie.'

Kit nodded reluctantly. She should have predicted this. Mal had grown up on the Coed too, and she still knew plenty of people. It had been a matter of time before news started to get around, especially as there were plenty more residents up there who had until recently made a secret of having been abused in the council-run youth centre that should have been their place of safety. Like Danny and Tyler, people had buried the secret deep. Now the perpetrators were in prison awaiting trial and the whole thing was about to become public.

'What the hell are you two on about now?' Gino asked.

Kit and Mal looked at each other. 'You'll have to speak to Tyler, he can tell you if he wants to,' Mal said. 'That doesn't matter right now anyway. First off, we've got to sort your ex-wife out.'

'Mal . . .'

'I don't want to hear it. Now, Krystal, what do you need him to do?'

'Someone has to get her to see the doctor. Or maybe if it's really bad, have an ambulance to the house.'

'Rightio. He'll go over there and sort it. That OK?'

Kit nodded. Gino wasn't giving up easily, though. 'Go over there and do what, woman? Get a glassing and land up in hospital having my face reconstructed? What help is that going to be?'

'Oh, shut up,' Mal said. 'It's not like your face is anything to write home about to start off with.' This was totally untrue. Gino had stayed annoyingly handsome, if a bit creased and puckered in places. It made Kit smile, though. A downmarket George Clooney he might be, but Mal still had the upper hand after all. 'You leave him to me, Kit,' she continued. 'I'll see he gets it done.'

Kit was only too glad to agree and end it there. She stood and gave her father a nod of goodbye, which he could barely bring himself to acknowledge, such was his unhappiness. The clink of coins being poured into a cash bag resumed behind her as he tried to comfort himself. Gulping her sandwich down, she headed into the bar.

Mal followed her out through the main doors and once they were on the pavement, lit a fag and handed it to Kit, then another for herself. 'Don't worry about him,' she said. 'He'll do as he's told.'

'Thanks.' Kit didn't know what else to say. She'd assumed that Gino's attempts at building bridges with his kids had taken place without Mal's knowledge; now she wasn't so sure. She had no idea what might have prompted Mal to take this new direction after so many years. She glanced sideways and found Mal doing the same.

Mal blew smoke out into the cold air in a long stream. 'I know we could have done more. Tell you the truth, I regret it now. We never had any of our own. Well, I never wanted any and I think your father . . .'

'He'd had enough?'

'Well, yeah. Sorry, but yeah, I think he had. No disrespect to any of you, mind, but your mother . . .'

'I know.'

'Anyway, what happened with Danny, it shocked us both. I

don't think your dad will ever get over it. And it's just me and him here getting older now, plenty of money and nothing to spend it on and I'm thinking we could have stood by you all more than we did. I wish we had. Maybe things would have been different with Dan.'

'I doubt that.'

Mal's face brimmed with gratitude. 'Well, you knew him best, love.'

Kit had let Mal off the hook, really. Of course it would have been different. The whole story would have played out some other way, and no doubt that way wouldn't have been great either. But if her dad had been around, the boys wouldn't have been left to run wild and Danny wouldn't have ended up killing himself, racked with guilt over not protecting Tyler from being abused, when it shouldn't have been his job to do it in the first place. Still, it was done now and making Mal suffer wasn't going to change it. She needed to get on with solving the problem to hand. Problems, more like.

'I'd better go.' She stubbed her fag out on the pavement before picking it up and chucking it into a bin.

'All right. I'll speak to your dad. See what we can sort out.'

It was a moment that called for a hug, but Kit couldn't push herself that far. 'See you, Mal,' she managed, before she got into her car and started back towards Sandbeach.

Glancing at the clock, Kit saw that it was already a quarter to four. She had to show her face in the office at some point, especially as she'd spent most of the afternoon dealing with her family. At the same time, she didn't want to be hanging about at work too long. Her presence just gave Georgia more of a broadside to aim at. She decided to take the longer way back, through the lanes and along the coast.

The rain stopped as she reached the coast road, and a few slender rays of sunlight emerged between the clouds. It was still light enough for the sea to be visible and although she didn't really have the time to stop, she couldn't resist it. She pulled in at the next lay-by and got out of her car, walking towards a stile which gave access over the fence and out onto the clifftops. As she reached it, she saw that daffodils were starting to appear in fresh green clumps across the grass beyond. A glimmer of yellow here and there amongst the green lifted her spirits. Soon they would be fully out, and summer would not be far behind. She longed to go closer to the sea but instead she leant her elbows on the stile and looked out, savouring the grassy air and picking up the distant sound of waves as they broke with a satisfying crunch on the pebbled beach. It soothed her at once; it was the first time she'd felt still in days. She was relieved, she realised. Not because she really thought that Gino could do anything about Christine, but because it was his turn to try. She'd passed the baton, and although it couldn't last long, he could damn well hang onto it for at least a few days while she took a break.

But she couldn't rest into the feeling of having nothing to worry about. There was still Dylan to sort out. She needed to take some time, sit back and try to put together a picture. She'd been bombarded with information and impressions from the start of the case and she'd completely lost her way. There was no time right now to think it through properly, but she pulled out her phone and went into Notes, ready to jot down a few pointers. Where to start? Maybe if she took it chronologically, from the first referral. And that was a question in itself. If Rhian and Dylan were so isolated, who in the world could have cared enough to make that call? The school wouldn't have had any reason to hide it and it definitely hadn't been John, because Frankie had said it was someone young. She'd said he'd been scared, too. But what of? She tapped herself a note and as she did so, the mention of the school reminded her once again that she needed to get her ID back from Aled. She started a to-do list with that as the first item.

The tricky bit came next; she needed to run through all the thoughts she'd had about what was going on in Ty Olaf, one by one, and try to get them in order. It was clear that Dylan was being harassed, and she had some idea about the reasons why he and Rhian were so isolated. Then there was the relationship between Rhian and Dylan. This bit was knottier. She'd thought at first that Rhian was unwell, and Dylan was a vulnerable and put-upon young carer, and she'd been determined to get the woman to seek help for herself. Kit had seen herself as a bit of a social work heroine, if she was honest, setting the boy free and gaining some kudos in the process. But her most recent visit had shown her that the dynamic between them was far more complex than that. She had no words to cover their relationship, couldn't get a purchase on the nature of the intimacy. Then there was Dylan's odd behaviour: the building of the wall, the thing with the pebble and the sudden, chilling comment about the message in the song. It was as if the two of them shared a world of their own, sitting parallel to the real one, with Rhian almost completely absorbed into the other world and Dylan stepping back and forth between the two. There was no denying that the whole thing seemed more and more like the cases she'd read about in John's journal, a shared illness, with Dylan being in the much earlier stages, more anchored and still trying to pull his mother back. It might mean that he was the one who could still be helped, if only Kit could catch hold of his hand before he slid over the edge. She didn't know what a psychiatrist would make of it, but she'd find someone to ask. It was going to be hard to explain, though, and she wasn't about to approach Tim Page with it after his snappy insistence that she should close the case. Besides, it would have sounded totally far-fetched to her if she hadn't seen it for herself.

And finally, there was Fflur, the fierce individualist who had never quite fitted in, even before the accident at the pit and her stand-offish attitude to the strikes. The domineering mother, still casting a shadow over her family. Had it all started with her? Was there an affliction running through this family, tumbling down from one generation to the next? Fflur's story had fascinated and moved her, but parts of it still evaded her too; the contradictions over where she'd lived out her last months and where she'd died. The wild rumours and gossip in Rock, and poor old Deri's conspiracy theories. Fflur obviously hadn't just disappeared in the way he had said, but had she come to some harm? And had the home covered it up somehow? It all added up to a fog, obscuring Fflur and swirling outwards to hide any part she might play in Dylan's story. It was driving her nuts, actually, and she was going to have to get to the bottom of it and draw a line. Fflur's death certificate would tell her something, but it would take time to get hold of that and it wouldn't give her the whole story. Snowdrop Court would have the records somewhere, but she'd already failed to prise any information out of them. She needed a go-between. She came out of Notes, googled the number of the inspectorate and called it.

'Maxine Cadwalladr, please.'

After giving her name to the telephonist there was a short pause before Maxine picked up. Kit wasn't sure that Maxine would even remember her.

'Kit, nice to hear from you.'

'Hi, Maxine. I'm sorry but I need a favour and you did say—'

'Indeed I did. What can I help you with?'

'It's about residential homes. The ones for people with mental illness.'

'EMI homes? Sure, fire away.'

'How do people get out of them?'

'Well, let's see – they walk through the door like everyone else, I suppose.'

'No, sorry, I meant . . . can people just leave?'

'Well, yes, they're not prisons, you know. People can check in and out of care homes as they wish.'

'What if someone didn't have mental capacity?'

'Ah, now I'm with you. That is rather different. There would need to be a process of assessment, involving the family and several professionals. It is possible to use certain legal safeguards to prevent someone from leaving, if it would pose a risk.'

'I see.' Maybe Deri had a bit more about him than she'd thought.

'It sounds like there's more to it than this. Is there something else you want to ask me?'

'To tell you the truth, I'm not sure. I'm working with a family and I'm after some information about the grandmother. I think she died in a residential home but I need to confirm whether she did, that she didn't manage to esc . . . leave. Under her own steam. Without anyone knowing. A missing person, is what I'm trying to say.'

'Why does it matter?'

'It's something that's probably completely irrelevant, but it's bugging me and I need to clear it up before I can see the rest of the picture clearly.'

'Ah yes. I noticed you have that tendency. I'm sure the children you work with are very glad you do. Look, if it's an issue about someone going missing, I can check the records here for you.'

'You have that information?'

'Yes, of course. All significant incidents in homes are noti-fied to the inspectorate, and someone going missing would definitely be that. We get notifications of all deaths in care homes too. When are we looking at?'

'February 2012.'

'And which home?'

'Snowdrop Court.'

There was a perceptible pause at Maxine's end. 'Snowdrop Court? In Hafod? Interesting.'

'Why do you say that?'

'There's been a change in regime at Snowdrop Court in recent years. I know my adult services colleagues were wor-ried about that home at one time. Lack of leadership, poor recording and so on. It's one of the few EMI-registered homes in the south so it was under pressure and it needed to per-form. There's a different owner now and it's much improved; I hear excellent things about the new officer in charge. Now, I think I'm right in saying that February 2012 would pre-date those improvements, so what you are saying is giving me some concern. Anyway, give me your number and I'll look into it for you. Is there anything else?'

'I just need to know as much about her as possible, her diagnosis and so on.'

'That may take a little longer, but it's definitely do-able. What's the client's name?'

After giving Maxine the information, Kit ended the call. She was desperate to linger, breathing in the scent of the sea, but she'd better get back to the office before it closed.

It was five to five when she pulled into the car park. She was up the stairs and into the team room within two minutes. Georgia's door was half shut but the click-click of her keyboard indicated her officious presence. Kit removed her hoody, draped it over the back of her chair and sat, debating what to do next. If Georgia hadn't yet looked in the signing-out book, there was still time to scribble in an invented location for her afternoon. But she couldn't risk it yet, just in case Georgia had already looked and seen the glaring gap in Kit's movements from lunchtime onwards. All things considered, it seemed best to hang around for a bit and gauge the temperature. As soon as she set eyes on Georgia's face, she'd know whether she was already in trouble.

Loitering at her desk, she rummaged in her rucksack, where she'd put the Meredith referral away before her first visit to Dylan and Rhian. She located it right at the bottom, with a couple of red wine gums stuck to it. When she scanned it yet again, nothing stood out as unusual. As she stared into space, she wondered whether it would be disgusting to eat the squashed wine gums.

'Where have you been all afternoon?' Georgia stood in the doorway of her office, raincoat tightly belted around her skinny waist, bulging briefcase in hand. Off to work through the night on her plans to get Kit sacked, no doubt.

'I'm sorry, I should have rung in. I had a few family problems. I needed to sort them out.'

'Family problems? So, you just disappeared, without so much as a by-your-leave?'

'Well, I . . .'

Georgia advanced into the room. 'So, what are you doing here now? Trying to cover your tracks? Because you may think you're clever, but I've cross-referenced the signing-out book, your case recordings and your expenses claims for the past couple of weeks, and I don't mind telling you there are some discrepancies. I've drawn up a spreadsheet setting it all out. There are gaps last Thursday and Friday. Where were you?'

Kit didn't need a spreadsheet to tell her she'd been in Rock both times. She became acutely aware that she had Dylan's referral out on her desk and sat helpless as Georgia advanced, leant over her and also took in this fact.

'Dylan Meredith? That's the case I closed, isn't it? That mad family, the inadequate boy? What are you doing poking about in that?'

Kit's temper flared in a trice. 'Jesus Christ, Georgia, where the hell do you get off talking about people like that? They've had a horrible time, things have happened to them that you can't even imagine.'

Georgia's eyes glinted. 'And how would you know? What's been going on here?'

But Kit was past caring. 'Cole allocated the Meredith case to me. Take it up with him.'

'Oh, believe me, I will. So, this explains some of your unau-thorised absences. Apart from the one you decided to take to deal with your personal problems, of course.'

'If you say so.'

'I think I get the picture. Get the case closed right now. I've nothing more to say to you today.'

She stalked off, leaving Kit to make a quick calculation as to whether she could get sacked for something the head of service had told her to do. Clearly not. But that wasn't the problem anyway; she'd handed the excuse to Georgia on a plate by going AWOL. If she'd just rung in that afternoon, said she had an emergency and was taking some of her overtime back, she'd have been covered. Instead, she'd set herself up for trouble and on top of that, Georgia would make sure she really did have to close the Meredith case now. Cole wouldn't put up a fight, not when it came down to it. As she turned back to her desk, Kit wondered whether she'd finally blown it. She gathered up her belongings and, after locking the Meredith referral in her drawer, left for home.

The light on her answer machine was blinking as she opened the front door. It would be Menna, of course. No one else used the landline. It was at least two weeks since Kit had called her. She felt guilty, and it would be good to hear Men's voice right now, too. She dropped her bag and coat, made a coffee and settled on the sofa to ring her back.

Menna answered, yelling a greeting over the sound of Jess

barking wildly. 'Hang on a minute, Kitty, she's a flipping nuisance with this phone, I'll just shut the door.' Kit waited, smiling at the thought of Menna's long-standing struggle to manage Jess, which ran hand in hand with her ruination of any training by means of a constant and undeserved supply of cheese. It was such a familiar image that Kit felt suddenly and painfully homesick for her little room in that warm, messy house, for her walks with Jess on the wild Cliffside coast and most of all, for Huw and Menna. She hadn't seen them since Christmas. Maybe she should take a few days off soon, go for a visit. It wouldn't hurt to be in the area either, just in case Alex did turn up at the start of March.

'Right, how are you, then?'

'Not great, Men, to be honest.'

'What's up, love? Work again? I thought that was all sorted months ago?'

Kit had had a very similar conversation with Menna the last time she'd been struggling with work. She couldn't keep doing this, running to her foster carers whenever things got tough.

'No, it's something different, but it's nothing. Don't worry, I'll handle it. What's your news?'

She half listened to Menna chatting away about Huw and their new puppy, updating her on Jess's latest bad behaviour and throwing in a few titbits of gossip from the village. It was an easy and comforting rhythm, and she started to dread it coming to an end.

'On your own this evening, then?' Menna had sussed her.

'Yeah. It's fine, honestly. Don't worry.'

'Where's your brother?'

It was an idea, she supposed. 'Maybe I'll text him.'

'Do that. You know you're not good alone when you're worrying about something.'

After Menna had gone off to cook the dinner, Kit texted Tyler then deleted it. She was still furious that he had refused to help her sort out Christine. She hadn't felt this let down by him in a long time. Maybe not ever. She wandered into the kitchen where she put some beer in the fridge, then sat down at her small table. Looking around at the pristine white cabinets and the shiny cooker, she was reminded of the determination she'd had when she'd moved into this flat to do some proper cooking. Have people round maybe. She had an idea how to do it; Menna was a brilliant cook and had shown her. But once she'd started living on her own, she'd lacked the motivation and had quickly joined Tyler in his love of takeaways, something that hadn't been easily accessible in Cliffside, and had been frowned upon by Menna in any case. Now she wondered if she was failing at this bit of her life and ought to pay it more attention. Maybe when things were a bit easier at work, she should ask Dai and Martin over to hers for once. She could even ask Ricky and Meg. But that would be five people, and it might feel awkward. She'd have to cultivate a new friend just to fill the gap. Were things this hard for everyone her age? Life seemed to flow along for other people without much effort or forethought. She was having to build hers, slotting together the parts as deliberately as Amber making houses and families out of Lego. Maybe it was because she'd been in care. Or maybe it was just her.

CHAPTER 12

The buzz of her phone woke Kit early. Her temples throbbed slightly, the result of too much beer and too little food the night before. She'd settled on cheese on toast and it hadn't been substantial enough to soak up the alcohol. Grabbing her phone, she could see it was only six thirty. Who could be texting her at this hour? Her heart executed a startling jump as the penny dropped. It had to be something to do with Christine.

She sat up in bed and took a long drink from the glass of water on her bedside table, steeling herself. But when she read and then reread the text, she couldn't immediately make sense of it.

dont come up today we r going away

As she tried to decipher it, her phone pinged again.

dont ever come back to the house

Dylan. She'd been due to see him later on. She checked the number against the one on her phone list from the other day. It was him. What the hell was this about? It didn't seem very likely that Dylan and Rhian would be planning a nice weekend away, so where could they possibly be going?

She rolled out of bed and onto her feet in one motion. Her head swam. But after swallowing two paracetamols with her morning coffee, and then another tall glass of cold water, she felt more human. She showered and dressed in black jeans and T-shirt, gave her hair a blast with the hairdryer and a quick straighten, and then pulled up her bedroom blind to ascertain what outdoor clothes she needed. It was wet and blustery outside yet again. Her burst of energy disappeared, her mood dropping back down to its recent low levels. How much longer could this weather go on? She pictured what it would be like up in Rock and selected a pair of flat-heeled ankle boots and her grey Nike fleece. She added her hooded Superdry coat over the top, threw her fags and water bottle into her bag, and hurried out to the car park. As she opened the car door, she was assailed by the smell of stale fried onions and had to stop and lean her forehead against the roof for a moment until a wave of nausea subsided. How could the McDonald's smell still be lingering after four days? That was the last time she'd be eating junk food in her car. After a few breaths of fresh air, she felt a bit better and got in, winding her window down as far as the rain would allow before starting the engine.

She was already on the road to Rock before it occurred to her that she was about to replicate yesterday's big mistake. She hadn't signed out in the office or phoned her location in, and the last thing she needed right now was to give Georgia more ammunition. She pulled over and called Ricky.

'Kit? Are you all right?'

'Yes, fine. Sorry. Did I wake you?'

'No, I'm up.'

'OK, good, would you do me a favour?'

'What now?'

She briefly considered telling him to forget it. But she pulled herself back; there was too much at stake.

'No, it's nothing dodgy. It's just, my car's not starting and I'm waiting for the AA. They said it'll be a couple of hours. Can you put something in the signing-out book? Just to cover me in case Georgia's sniffing around?'

'I can come and pick you up on my way in if you like?'

'No, don't worry. I'll need it sorted for my visits today anyway.'

'Kit, what are you up to? Georgia was going through the signing-out book yesterday. Is that something to do with you?'

'Me? No, I don't think so. Thanks, Ricky.' She ended the call before he could argue further and resumed her journey. She was taking a big risk, but something was going on with Dylan, and once she was back in the office, she'd have Georgia standing over her until the case was closed. It was her last chance to get to the bottom of it.

As she pulled up outside John's house, she saw that his living-room curtains were open already, and his lights were on. She might have known he'd be up. He appeared on the doorstep as she got out of the car.

'You're an early bird. Everything all right?'

There didn't seem to be much point in covering it up. And

after today, it was unlikely she'd set eyes on John again anyway. She took a few steps up the garden path so that he would hear her whispered response. The neighbours would be stirring by now and if she wasn't careful, they'd hear every word.

'I'm just going up to check on them. I had a text, saying they were going away.'

John's brow creased. 'Going away?'

'Yeah. I mean, where would they go?'

'Well, that's it, isn't it? As far as I know, they've got no one but each other. There's nowhere for them to go. And why would they want to?'

'Right, well, I'm going to go and see what's happening.'

'All right then. You popping in, after?'

'Not today, John. Sorry.' It was surprisingly hard to know that she was saying goodbye to him. His memories of her grandparents had made her feel connected to them and to Rock for the first time in quite a while. She'd realised that she didn't spend enough time up here. Maybe she could pop back and see John, after a decent gap. Surely no one could complain about that? It wasn't as if he was a client himself. Then again, if she was about to get sacked, it would hardly matter anyway.

After a wave in John's direction, she started the trudge up to Ty Olaf. The light was rising now over the distant sea, but the lane was still dark. As she went, she tried to figure out what could be going on. Her stomach churned, but she couldn't say exactly what she was frightened of.

Kit found the house all closed up and the curtains shut,

as usual. She headed for the gap at the end of the wall, only remembering as she reached it that Dylan had said he'd blocked it off. He'd tried to do a really good job this time; several more layers of chicken wire had been pushed into the gap. But he hadn't fixed them to the wall or to the rock on the other side. Maybe he didn't know how, or perhaps he didn't have a drill. She got her gloves out of her coat pocket and, after putting them on, worked at the chicken wire patiently, pulling each layer aside and bending it back as far as she could so it wouldn't catch her if she had to make another hasty exit.

Once past the wire, she headed straight for the front door and used the knocker to bang on it as loudly as she could. As the sound of it fell away, the silence that followed struck her at once. No barking; Dylan must have already gone out with the dogs. But then she remembered that it was only eight o' clock. He went out in the afternoon every day and he was pretty rigid in his routines. She knocked again, waiting for Rhian's tentative footsteps to sound in the hall. Still nothing. But she must be in there somewhere. Of course, they might be in bed, although the nervous energy the two of them carried didn't make them likely candidates for long lie-ins. She hammered hard on the door a third time, not caring if she did wake them. The racket rang through the silent house. There was no way they could have missed it, but looking up at the bedroom windows, there was not a flicker of life. She turned away from the door and followed the path around the side of the house. Maybe there was a back door she could try.

Reaching the rear of the house, she emerged onto a small, crumbling concrete terrace. A flight of steps led down to a tiny lawn, bounded by a tatty wooden fence. Beyond that, the whole of Rock stretched out in front of her, coming to life in fits and starts as the light rose overhead. The view stopped her in her tracks; she stood mesmerised, absorbing it. There was no doubt that, at its best, this house would have been one of the more desirable ones in the area. It was not much larger than John's, but it was detached, and slightly superior to the terraces where the colliers would have lived. She remembered John saying that Rhian's father had been the deputy in the pit. Like him, the house and its location were a cut above.

Turning her attention back to the house itself, Kit saw a peeling wooden back door with a pane of glass set in it. There was a small porch, which she entered, shining her torch around. A pile of logs a few feet high sat to the side of the porch, an axe balanced carefully on the top. She peered through the glass pane, and found she was looking at the kitchen. The room was large but bare, empty apart from an old-fashioned cooking range against the opposite wall, a butler's sink set in a wooden worktop and a big pine table. The floor was made up of worn red tiles. Three glasses stood on the table and a kitchen chair lay overturned on the floor. Kit rapped on the door a few times, but without any real hope. If they were going to answer, they would have by now. For God's sake, where the hell were they?

She moved on to the next window along on the terrace,

but the heavy curtains were tightly shut. The same at the one on the side of the house. Returning to the front door, she accepted that she had no choice but to give up. It bothered her, but maybe Rhian had finally decided to venture out and they had gone away, just as Dylan had said. The chair lying on the kitchen floor seemed strange, but there was no reason to think it meant that anything was wrong.

But it was not good. It just didn't feel right. Rhian's terrified face was burnt into her memory. Even opening the front door scared the wits out of the woman. And besides that, where would they have gone? As John had said, they had no family, and they were hardly likely to get a room in a nice B & B with three berserk collies in tow. She leant her back against the door, trying to figure out what to do next, staring up at the Oer, as it started to loom out of the semi-darkness. It was the first time she'd realised how much it overbore the house, as if Ty Olaf had been forced out onto the edge of its narrow perch. From this perspective, the position of the house seemed less superior and more precarious. Her mind wandered, returning once again to the strangeness of the three generations of Merediths, the way they had mostly lived in their own world, set apart from everyone else. And it had started with Fflur, who had spent such a long time in a psychiatric hospital.

Kit's heart leapt as a muffled bark emanated from behind the door. Then there was the sound of movement, something being dragged sharply across the floor, followed by a high-pitched yelp. If the dogs were inside the house, then Rhian and Dylan must be too. But Kit would know that sound anywhere. It was one of pain. Dylan would never hurt one of the dogs or allow anyone else to. Something was very wrong. She hammered on the door over and over but not another sound emerged from inside. It was clear that they weren't going to open up. She could call the police, but they'd been to the house twice now and Rhian had fended them off both times. She was going to have to get some help.

Kit was back at the office in less than twenty-five minutes. As she hurried across reception, she spotted Georgia disappearing into the lift, no doubt on her way up to a 'performance meeting' with Cole. As the doors closed on her, Georgia spotted Kit too, and her face emitted a glare so exceptionally hostile it took Kit by surprise, and sent her anxiety soaring. She was determined to put it to one side. She had other things on her mind. Hoping there would be someone around for her to unload her worries onto, she headed for the stairs but was stopped by someone behind her angrily shouting her name. Turning, Kit found that Georgia had emerged from the lift and caught up with her. She was carrying a huge cardboard box and her face was as grim as Kit had ever seen it.

'I don't know what you had to do with this. But I will find out. Social work is a very small world, you know, and reputation is everything. You'd better hope you don't ever want a change of job.'

Kit stared at her. 'I have no idea what you are talking about. But you don't get to speak to me like that, whatever it is.'

Georgia shot her a look of angry disbelief and stalked off in the direction of the lift. Kit exchanged glances with the woman at the reception desk, who had sat openly staring, taking in every word. Then she took the stairs as quickly as she could and burst through the door into the team room, where she found most of her colleagues at their desks, heads up, openly chatting on work time and clearly enjoying themselves. Now she was looking more closely, they looked ridiculously happy. What was up with them, the bunch of bloody idiots?

'What's wrong with you?' Nazia had caught sight of her face.

Kit didn't even stop to sit down. 'Something's going on with Georgia, but I don't know what the hell it is. She just had a massive go at me downstairs. But never mind that for a minute. You know that boy from Rock, the one I got Cole to allocate to me, Dylan Meredith? I thought he was all right, well, he is, sort of, but his mum's not and I think maybe she's ill and so he's not all right and neither is she and I need to do something but Georgia said I have to close it. And I'm worried about him, Naz. I've been there and I think she's got him locked in the house and I know they're in there because I heard the dog cry and he would never hurt the dog so it must be her. I think she's lost it. I'm really worried about both of them. They're so scared.' She stopped, noticing that everyone was laughing.

'Well, stop bumping your gums and get the police up there sharpish.'

Kit swung round with a jolt. Vernon was leaning against the door frame of his office, faking nonchalance. She'd run across the room and hugged him before she even knew she was doing it. 'Bloody hell, get a grip,' he mumbled, shaking her off, but she could see he was chuffed. 'Do as you're told for once and get onto the control room.'

'Already on it. What's the address, Kit?' Nazia had the phone tucked under her chin.

'There's no point, Naz. They've been before and the mother can present really well; they didn't even speak to Dylan.'

'You leave that to me.' After a few minutes of gentle but firm negotiation, she put the receiver down. 'All sorted, they'll send a couple of officers up now and let us know what's going on in a bit.'

Kit turned to Vernon again. 'Are you back to stay?'

'Thought I was past it, did you?'

'No, of course not. But what about Georgia?'

'Not a clue, but that's Cole's problem. I had a call from the chief exec herself out of the blue last night, begging me to come back. Search me as to why, I can only assume the union had something to do with it. It's my substantive post after all and I've been declared fit for work. Anyway, Nell says I'm driving her up the wall at home, so now you've got the benefit of my superior management abilities for the foreseeable. Right, let's have a word, shall we, see if we can get this boy of yours sorted? I've already had Tim Page on the phone about this case.'

'Have you? Why?'

'He wanted us to close it, for some reason. He was expecting

197

to find himself speaking to Georgia, of course. We had a frank exchange of views. He's threatened to go to Gail Wilson about it.'

'So am I closing it?'

'What do you reckon?'

He stood back to let her past him into his office and, after a few minutes spent allocating duty cases to the team with the rapidity of gunfire and a fair bit of swearing, followed her in. On the way past his desk, he picked up the wastepaper basket in one hand and used the other arm to sweep all of Georgia's Post-it notes, highlighters, air fresheners and low-carb snacks into it in one fell swoop. His eyes scanned the desk and fell on the department's brand-new procedural manual next. He flipped through a few pages, guffawed loudly and dropped that into the bin too. Finally, he got a paper bag out of his briefcase, selected a sausage roll from it, and sank down into his chair. She had already noticed that he didn't appear to have lost any weight. The reason for this was now obvious.

'Shoot,' he said, indistinctly.

Kit had never been so happy to be sprayed with a mouthful of soggy pastry. As Vernon worked his way through the rest of his food, she brought him up-to-date with the Meredith case. The sheer joy of being able to talk without having to second-guess what she might get criticised for next was dizzying. She didn't imagine Vernon would be able to help her that much, not really. It was more and more obvious that John's journal had been the big clue she had needed. Rhian was the source of the problem and if her mental health got sorted, Dylan's would too. Vernon wouldn't know about *folie à deux* anymore than she had herself, but at least he would back her up. They could go and see the two heads of service together, and Vernon would deal with Gail Wilson, and get Rhian allocated to the CMHT, where she should have been all along. Then Kit could finally get on with her own job.

'There's a six-million-dollar question staring me right in the face by here,' Vernon said, once she had finally come to a halt.

Was he annoyed with her? 'You mean, why's this not in the Mental Health Team? I know, Vern. I kind of agree. But like I said, Tim didn't want it. Well, you've heard for yourself, he doesn't think anyone should have it. I wasn't happy, no one had spoken to the boy. So I persuaded Cole to let me visit. Without Georgia knowing.'

'Did Nazia know about this? Well? Lost the power of speech, have we? I'll ask her myself. Naz! Get in here a minute!' he yelled in the general direction of the door.

'Back five minutes and you're shouting at me already. Problem?' Nazia absorbed all Vernon's unreasonable behaviours with this combination of indulgent humour and mild exasperation, as if he were a toddler who was bound to grow out of it eventually.

'You knew about Kit taking this case behind Georgia's back, did you? Decided to ignore it, eh?'

'Yes, I did. What of it?'

He sat back in his chair looking from one to the other and back again. Kit began to get a familiar quiver in her stomach.

'Nah, I'm not pissed off, I'm messing with you. Your face was a picture, though, Kit. Nice work, you two. I mean, really, really excellent. Sounds like this kid's in a desperate state and no one else wanted to know. God knows why Tim's so set on closing it. Sod whose responsibility it is or isn't, somebody needs to act. Looks like I've taught you something after all.'

Of course, Vernon would think like that. It was just that she'd had a feed of Georgia over the past ten months and it had left its mark.

'Right, sod off now then, Naz, I'm trying to speak to Kit.'

'It was you told me to come in here, mind.'

'I know that, now I'm telling you to go back out again.'

'Oh all right, keep your hair on, don't have another heart attack.'

He threw a screwed-up pasty bag at the door as it closed behind her. 'Right, Kit, time to get on with this one, eh? If the mother does turn out to have some issues, we'll insist on getting Tim's team involved. He should be helping you with this. Have you spoken to him?'

'Yes. He was an arse.'

'Was he now?'

'He certainly was. I don't know what's up with him.' Tim's behaviour was starting to trouble her. Why was he so intent on getting the case closed, even willing to have a ruck with Vernon about it? She recalled what Maxine had said about

Snowdrop Court having problems, the inspectors being worried about the place. Had something gone wrong there? Was it
possible that the home hadn't looked after Fflur properly, and
Tim's team had failed to pick up on it? Maybe he was worried
that if she started work with the Merediths, she'd trip over
some information about Fflur that hadn't been picked up on
at the time and that Tim would rather was left to lie.

Vernon shrugged. 'Perhaps he's under pressure. He was
quite difficult with me on the phone earlier too, it's not like
him at all. He runs a tight ship over there and that is not easy,
let me tell you. It's quite a tough gig, mental health. I mean,
not as hard as it is for us here, not by a long chalk,' he added,
hurriedly. 'But demanding enough.'

'How do you know that then?'

'I was in that team myself for a bit.'

'Were you? When?' Vernon had always been a Child Services
man through and through, as far as she'd known.

'A way back. Early on in my career, before I saw the light.
Anyway, I expect Tim's preoccupied with the inspection,
although Mental Health Services always get a gold star or a
balloon or whatever it is these people hand out. Anyway, it
seems you're stuck with my expertise, but luckily for you, that
is not inconsiderable. Now, what I'm saying is, when it comes
to mental health, I wouldn't go too far down the medical line
of things if I were you.'

'No? Why?' She saw that Vernon was pulling out a notebook
and a pen. 'Is there a Venn diagram involved in this?'

'No. It's more of a spectrum. No, scrub that. It's a pair of scales.'

'Go on.'

'Well, you seem to be very focussed on whether something's inherited and so on, chucking about terms like mental illness. Like it's a disease.'

'Isn't it?'

'Try dropping the labels.'

'Pardon?'

'I know you think I'm not politically correct, but I do know one thing. You'd never speak about a child like you do about people with mental health problems. You're starting to sound like Georgia. Try to think of it more in terms of vulnerability on one side and stress factors on the other. So, look, here's your scales.' He drew a pair of old-fashioned scales on his notepad. 'We've all got a certain weight here.' He drew a small bowl onto one side of the scales and added a pile of something indeterminate to it.

'What's that?'

'That's . . . well, I don't know, flour or something, it's irrelevant. The point is it represents our ability to deal with stress. It might be made up of lots of things – personality traits, good childhood experiences, etc. But then there's also the negatives, the bad experiences, abuse or not being loved. We all have a few of those. Plus, some people might have a susceptibility to certain conditions, maybe that's inherited or maybe it's the effect of being brought up around an adult who has those conditions, or a bit of both. That kind of thing takes a bit away, makes our side lighter. It all adds up to create our individual weight, if you like. Our strength. But we all have a tipping point then, don't we? The point where what's loaded on the other side outweighs what we've got on our side of the scale. Some of us are heavier, more solid, we can take more, some of us can take less.'

'OK.'

'So, when the weight adds up enough on the other side, we will tip.' He started drawing a stack of discs on the other side of the scale. 'Stress, illness, bereavement, loneliness. There's a certain unique combination that will do it for each one of us. Some people may have a predisposition for all we know, but their life events don't stack up against them, so they never tip. Others don't have any particular predisposition but their life events pile up so high that they do.'

'Makes sense.'

'Of course it does. I'm not putting it up for debate, I'm giving you solid information here. But what I'm saying is, don't other people with mental health problems, Kit. Think beyond that, you're clever enough to do better. We can all get there. And it's all very well to go on about mental illness and disease and whatnot, and medication might have a part to play, but we can't ignore what's on the scales. We need to alleviate this end.' He tapped the pile of weights. 'Or bolster this end.' He tapped the bowl. 'Or ideally, both. Then we can get the scales to balance up again.'

'I see what you mean. And you are right about the Merediths, they have been through a lot. So yes, I can see all that. But something's definitely not right with Dylan's mum, Vern, whatever you call it, and the gran had mental health problems of some kind. What do I do next?'

Vernon lobbed a second greasy paper bag across the room, missing the bin by a wide margin. 'It's still not adding up to me. Someone cared enough to refer it in the first place, so maybe these two have got more support than we know about. Are you sure it's not the neighbour, this John guy? Sounds like he's a bit besotted with the woman to me.'

'I think he is too, but no, it wasn't him. Frankie said it was someone young, very nervous, didn't know what they were doing.'

'Well, all right, let's accept that for a minute. The gran is clearly on your mind, so start there. Find out what happened with her, maybe something on her records will give you a clue about the daughter. See where that takes you first.'

'I've already started looking into that. There's a problem with opening her file on our system and the home wouldn't tell me anything, so I've spoken to Maxine Cadwalladr in the inspectorate. She's going to chase it up for me.'

A broad grin overtook his face. 'Maxine? Is she still around? I thought she'd retired. Well, well.'

'She's on our inspection. You know her?'

'Oh yes, me and Maxine, we . . .'

'Don't tell me, you go way back.'

'We do. What a woman.' He flipped onto a new page in his notebook and started doodling, a faraway expression over-taking his face. Kit vacated the room before an inappropriate image of Maxine could appear on the page. Outside, Nazia had heard the exchange and was rolling her eyes. She looked more like herself than she had for ages. Kit wondered if this was how it felt when your parents got back together.

Maisie was busying herself in the kitchen area. Upon Kit's arrival, she reboiled the kettle and handed over a mug of coffee then followed Kit over to her desk where she hung around, picking up photos of Kit's nieces and nephews and staring at each one without any sign whatsoever of genuine interest.

'Any news, Maze?'

Maisie put a photo down so fast she nearly dropped it. She hoisted herself onto the edge of Kit's desk. 'Yes, as a matter of fact there is. Tim's finally asked me out. I'm going for a drink with him tomorrow night.'

'Good.' Kit hesitated, unsure whether she could be both-ered to get involved. Maisie was an adult, after all, and rather thick-skinned to boot. But something about Tim's changeable behaviour the other day in the print room was still bothering her. Maisie had been attacked by an irate client the previous summer, and although she would never talk about it, that had to have got to her on some level. She definitely didn't need anymore hassle right now. Kit cleared her throat and braced herself for the inevitable rebuke.

'Maze?'

'Mmm?'

'How do you find Tim? As a person?'

'Oh, he's so easy to be around. Very warm. Ambitious, but caring, I'd say. Principled. It turns out we share a lot of interests.'

'That's great. You don't find he can be a little . . .'

'A little what?'

But Kit didn't know. Domineering, condescending, stroppy. They all came to mind but none of them quite fitted the bill. And Maisie was right, he could be warm too, she'd seen that for herself. 'Never mind. As long as you're happy.'

'I am.'

'OK, good.' She'd leave it for now. She turned to her computer and started it up, waiting for Maisie to get the hint. Once she'd ambled off, Kit sat staring at her screen and sipping her coffee. She'd intended to think again about the Meredith referral, try to figure out who had made it. But after a few minutes, she was still totally stuck with that. What could she usefully do next? Vernon's words had reminded her that she hadn't heard back from Maxine about Fflur yet. Maybe she'd have one more go at Fflur's file.

But after she clicked on it again the same message covered her screen: *Incorrect permissions*. She glanced behind her. Nazia had disappeared and Vernon's door was still shut. She and Maisie were completely alone. Well, she'd give it a go. After all, Maisie had been in the team for five years; presumably she'd picked up something along the way.

'Maze, can I ask you . . . ?'

'Don't call me that, Kit. It sounds ridiculous. I don't know why you Welsh have to shorten everyone's name.' Maisie was English, something which no one apart from Maisie herself ever made an issue of. Apart from Vernon, of course.

'It's our way of being friendly.'

'Well, it's really annoying.'

'OK, I won't do it again, I promise. But can I ask you a question about something?'

Maisie brightened. She crossed to Kit's desk, hauling herself up onto the one next to it this time, her short legs dangling and her patterned combat trousers riding up to reveal her purple DMs. 'Is it about your love life? Because I can't help noticing you're still single, which is unusual at your age, isn't it? Should I ask Tim if he has a friend?'

'God, no, you definitely shouldn't.'

'Oh, all right, no need to get offended.'

'Maisie, it's not that. It's about work. The Mental Health Team – their old case files have been loaded onto the database, I should be able to get access to all of it, yes?'

'Oh yes, I know all about it. I'm surprised you don't. Mental Health went electronic before we did. So we had a special project, a few years ago, to link their records into our system, so we'd be alerted if a child had a parent or relative with a mental health problem and vice versa. Joined up working and all that.'

'So, what does this mean? I've had it come up twice now.' Kit clicked on the folder again and showed Maisie the message.

Maisie leant across her to read it several times over, unwilling to admit that she didn't know.

'Must be a problem with the system. They loaded thousands of records onto it, after all. I expect there were some blips. Why, what do you need?'

'I just want to have a look. I'm not even sure what I'm looking for, to be honest.'

'Bit of a fishing expedition? Well, you could arrange to go over to the CMHT to view the file on their system, they'll probably get it open since it's theirs. Would you like me to ask Tim to sort it for you?'

'No, don't worry.' She couldn't be faffing about with Tim. Anyway, he'd already shown his disinclination to help her. She'd go over there herself and speak to whoever was on reception, get into the file immediately. She'd need her ID badge first, though.

'Right, I've got to run.' She stood, prompting Maisie to dislodge herself.

'Suit yourself. You'd be better off asking Tim, though, he's on the ball.'

'It's fine, Maze, thanks. I really do have to go.'

As she was signing out, Nazia arrived back in the room. 'Kit, before you go, the police have been out already. They spoke to the mother, actually managed to get into the house and got eyes on the boy, nothing of concern. The officer rang through himself, he was a bit tetchy actually. Seems to feel we're wasting their time.'

'Did they speak to Dylan on his own?'

'Apparently not. He refused to cooperate with that.'

'Great.'

'Well, at least you know they're both in one piece.'

'I suppose so. Thanks, Naz.' It was some comfort, but not much. Something was wrong there, she knew it. She'd been so sure she could get through to Dylan but now he'd lied to her about them going away and obviously didn't want her involved at all. His mother's influence over him must be growing by the minute. But the wall of silence and collusion around this family was as unyielding as the physical one that Dylan had built to shield Ty Olaf. No matter which way she tried, she couldn't find a crack in it. For now, she'd just have to plod on, pushing at the spots that seemed vulnerable until one of them crumbled away.

She finished signing out, giving her location as the CMHT and Sandbeach High School, and then headed to her car. As she opened the driver's door, her nostrils were hit by the oniony smell again. She got in, knelt on the front seat, and started sniffing the air, checking around her seat first and then leaning over to the back. No, the smell must be coming from the passenger side. But she couldn't see anything on the seat or in the door pocket. Leaning across, she tracked the smell downwards and after two more sniffs, pushed her hand under the front seat where her fingers made contact with something soft and crinkly. She pulled it out; Dylan's double cheeseburger, wrapped up in its grease-soaked paper. She pulled it open, fighting back her queasiness; apart from a tiny bit missing from the outside edge of the bun, it was untouched. He had pretended to eat it then hidden it. What the hell was wrong with him?

CHAPTER 13

After running through the rain to chuck the burger into the dumper bin at the back of the building and getting dripping wet in the process, Kit threw herself back into the car and set off for the CMHT. Her mind kept returning to the trip to McDonald's. Dylan had been reluctant to eat at all, she remembered, and once she'd handed him his burger, he'd behaved like it might blow up in his face. Or like it might poison him. Was that it? Had Rhian given him weird ideas about food? She knew now from reading about the couple in John's journal that people were prepared to starve to death if a delusion dictated it.

Kit found the tiny car park at the Mental Health Team offices almost empty. It wasn't quite lunchtime so most of the staff would still be out on calls, but the reception was bound to be staffed. She'd have to find a way round not having her ID, but that wouldn't be insurmountable. She spotted the door to reception and headed into a cramped lobby, which carried a thick smell of damp and dust. There were a few tatty leaflets and posters stuck haphazardly on the walls, advertising mental health groups and workshops the dates of which had long since passed. What would it feel like to come into this place feeling low, maybe even suicidal? Perhaps it wouldn't be a big deal, in the scheme of things, or perhaps the air of neglect would seep into you, surreptitiously confirming how bad you felt about yourself.

There was a desk to the right of the lobby. Behind its glass screen, a young man sat with his slim legs outstretched and his feet up on the desk, head down to his phone, scrolling through Twitter. She waited a few seconds, fidgeting with irritation, but he didn't notice her so she banged her knuckles quite hard on the glass.

'Jesus Christ!'

'Sorry. Couldn't seem to get your attention.'

'That's OK. What can I do for you?' He set his feet down on the floor and slid a portion of the screen back. He had white-blond hair pulled up into a topknot, and wide-set hazel eyes behind light-framed glasses. He also had trouble written all over his freckled face. But he was smiling at her now and she was already smiling back.

'I need to view a file, if that's OK? I'm Kit Goddard, from Child Services.'

'Nice to meet you, Kit Goddard. Child Services, eh? Who is it you're interested in over here, then?'

'A client called Fflur Meredith. She's dead now but I need to take a look and I can't seem to access her file from our system.

I think something must have gone wrong when they copied it across to the Child Services database.'

'The name's not ringing a bell. Tell you what, I'll buzz you in, we can take a look on here.' He tapped the top of the computer that sat on his desk.

By the time she got into the office he had already pulled another chair over and placed it very close to his own. 'Have a seat. I'm Ben, by the way. So, what's the story on this one, then?'

She wasn't sure she ought to be telling all of the Merediths' business to the team's receptionist. She wondered if she should insist on viewing the file alone, as she had originally planned. But now she found she didn't really want to.

'It's a family I'm working with, and this woman was related to them. I just want to check whether there's anything else I need, anything significant in her history.'

'All right then, what did you say the name was?'

She gave him Fflur's details and watched as he turned to the computer and typed them into the search fields. She liked the way he'd done his hair and she was busy registering an intricate Celtic tattoo on the inside of his pale-skinned left wrist when he spoke.

'That's weird. The file's there but I can't open it.'

She peered at the screen. 'That's the same message I got. Are you not authorised to get into it, maybe?'

'Well, no, it wouldn't be that. Even a junior doctor gets full access.'

'Sorry, I . . . er . . .'

'You thought I was the receptionist? No, he's off sick, we're all taking it in turns to cover for a couple of hours. My fault, I didn't introduce myself properly. I'm Ben James, I'm Dr Del's specialty registrar.'

'Dr Del?'

'We all call her that. Just not in her hearing. Delilah Carver, consultant psychiatrist. But yes, I am an actual doctor and I ought to have access to everything. Looks like the bug's at our end, in the original file.'

'So how do we get into it?'

'I'll get on to IT now. We won't get an answer for a while, though, they're short-staffed. Do you want to give me your number, I can drop you a text once I sort it?'

'Sure. That would be great.' She gave it to him and stood up. But it seemed a shame to leave so soon. She loitered about, waiting for him to finish his call to IT.

'Could I tell you a bit about the case? I could do with some advice.'

'Well, since you're a social worker, protocol would say I hand you over to Tim Page for a consult.'

'Please don't. I've tried that, he didn't seem too interested. He wanted the case closed from the start.'

'Well, that's Tim for you.'

'Meaning?'

Ben shrugged. 'Tim treats cases and clients according to how

214

much use they are to him. I guess your guys here didn't seem like they'd be particularly career-enhancing.'

'I've heard that elsewhere actually.'

'Yeah? Well it's dead right. Recently he's seeming a bit anxious, though, which is not like him. His mood's all over the place, we'll be having him in Outpatients himself at this rate.'

She heard herself laughing even though it wasn't all that funny. 'Well, it's not his love life that's the problem, I happen to know that much.'

'Ah yes, well, nothing puts Tim off that. He's quite a player, apparently.'

'Seriously?'

'Apparently. I don't get it either. Maybe it's an age thing.'

'Maybe.' His words were making her uneasy but she couldn't deal with it right now, on top of everything else. She could always text Maisie in a couple of days' time, see how her date had gone.

Ben was standing now too, picking up his phone from the desk and slipping it into his back pocket. 'Look, no worries, I'll run over the case with you, if you like. Do you fancy getting out of here, though? I could knock off, it's nearly lunchtime. Buy you a glass of Coke in the Red Lion?'

Kit hesitated. She was worrying herself sick about what was happening in Rock. But then again, there was nothing to be gained by going back just to bang on the door some more. She'd hadn't even eaten yet today and she desperately needed to get a better understanding of Dylan and Rhian if she was going to be any use to them whatsoever. 'Chuck in a pasty and a bag of crisps and you're on.'

'Deal. Wait for me here, then, I'll just find someone to take over.'

Watching as he left the room, she took in that he was of medium height, perhaps a few inches taller than she was, and had a slender, neat build. He reappeared five minutes later, pulling on a fitted denim jacket in an unusual sage green and carefully tucking a few loose strands of hair back up into his topknot. He could not have looked any less like her idea of a psychiatrist.

'Ready then?' He pushed the front door open and held it back for her to escape into the fresh air. She was so grateful to be away from the stale smell. If that had been her office, she'd have sorted out the posters and whipped round with a can of Pledge, so that her clients didn't have to feel insulted on top of everything else.

They walked round the corner to the pub, hurrying in the driving rain and wind, not bothering to attempt speech. Once they were installed at a table with drinks and food, Ben rested his elbows on the table and his chin on one hand and fixed her with a disconcertingly attentive stare. 'Go on, tell me about your Fflur Meredith.'

'It's less about her really. It's about her daughter and grandson. It seems like since Fflur died a few years ago, the daughter, Rhian, hasn't coped very well. Fflur was in Penlan for a long time before that so I'm not sure why it affected her so badly when her mother died.'

'How long was she in there for?'

'About fourteen years, I think.'

'Are you sure? I mean, that would have been quite unusual, to be honest. The care-in-the-community policy was well bedded in by then. Anyone who came into hospital at that point would usually have gone straight back home after treatment, or they might have had a spell on the rehab ward first, but that would be about it. She'd have to have been severely ill to have stayed in Penlan that long.'

'There is a suggestion she was discharged to a care home eventually, but it's all a bit confusing. The social worker who took the referral on the grandson thought she saw some paperwork about it on her file.'

'Well, have you checked with Tim?'

'He said it's just an admin error, reckons she definitely died in Penlan. Very insistent actually.'

'Well, it seems odd to me but I guess if that's what he said that's probably right then, isn't it?'

'I don't know. Maybe. I just want to be sure I've understood it all. And as I said, Tim's been weird about it from the start.' And Ben was the second person to mention Tim's determination to make his team look good. She wondered again whether he was trying to cover something up. 'Ben, is it possible that someone in your team made a mistake of some kind with

Fflur's case? Maybe Tim's trying to hide it. In case it gets him into trouble, affects his career or something.'

'What makes you think that? What kind of a mistake?'

'I don't know. Like I said, he wanted it closed and he's insisted all along she died in hospital when our intake worker says she saw on the file that she was in a home.' She wouldn't mention Deri right now. It might not add to the credibility of the story. 'Maybe the team chose the wrong community place-ment for her. Or maybe there was negligence at the home and the team didn't spot it.'

'I wouldn't put it past him. And yes, as I said, she had to have been pretty unwell to be in Penlan for that long. So it's feasible the home found they couldn't cope with her, perhaps they'd bitten off more than they could chew. Did you speak to anyone there?'

'Yeah, but they wouldn't tell me a thing. And as you've seen, I can't even get into her file. I've chased it with the inspectorate and now you've spoken to IT, I guess I'll get the information one way or the other. I'm just not good at waiting for anything.'

'How did she get into the file?'

'Who now?'

'The other social worker. The one who took the referral. You said she saw something on Fflur's file. You couldn't get into it and neither could I – so how come she did?'

Kit hadn't even questioned that point. He was doing a pretty good job of pointing out all the holes in her story. She probably wasn't impressing him much. 'Oh, I don't know. Maybe the bug only kicked in after she'd accessed it.' But as she said it, her mind was pulling back to Tim Page again. She'd need to find out more about why the file wasn't opening and whether he might have had anything to do with that.

'Mm, maybe. Anyway, we'll see what IT have to say about it. What about the daughter and grandson? Rhian and . . . ?'

'Dylan. They're very isolated and they only relate to each other – they don't let anyone else into the house as far as I can see. They're kind of . . . unnaturally close.'

'Sexually, you mean?'

To her annoyance, she felt a burn rising upwards from her neck. 'No, obviously, I didn't mean that. Well, not exactly.'

'So where does granny's mental health fit into all this?'

'I don't know if it does. I don't even know what mental illness she had. I suppose I thought if I could find that out, I'd get some idea whether she'd passed it on to Rhian and whether Dylan might be at risk of inheriting it too. But it's been a dead end so far.'

'What makes you think either of them might be mentally ill in the first place? I know you said they're a bit strange but so are lots of people.'

'There's been a couple of odd things.' She wondered whether to wade right in with the *folie à deux* but now that she was talking to someone who knew their stuff, she felt suddenly shy about it, in case she'd got it wrong. She decided to build up to it, starting with the Merediths' reaction to the coins on the path. As she told him, Ben chewed on his pasty, nodding his head.

'OK, that is unusual. It's hard to say based just on that but I suppose it's feasible that there's something delusional going on.'

'Meaning?'

'Delusions are basically false beliefs. Sounds like maybe this woman's mildly paranoid; she sees coins lying on the path, and whereas you or I would think nothing of it, she thinks someone's put them there deliberately, it means something. A message, a threat. She believes they're under attack.'

'In some ways they are. The family's got a long history with the locals, some of it not good, and they've had a bad time of it all round. So, she's not completely wrong.'

'There you are, you see. Interesting, isn't it? What came first? Did the hassle with the neighbours trigger something off, or was it there all along? Is she paranoid, or do people genuinely hate her guts? Or a bit of both, maybe. They're not mutually exclusive. This is the type of thing we deal with all the time in psychiatry.'

It didn't sound far away from Vernon's scales theory, but it didn't help her much. She still felt a pull to put a label on what was going on, in spite of herself.

'All right, but if Rhian does have something . . . clinical, what would we be talking about?'

'Oh, it could be a few things. Delusional disorder, a psychotic disorder, schizophrenia.'

She seized on the name she vaguely recognised. 'And isn't schizophrenia inherited?'

'I wish it were that easy. Working out where mental illness comes from is a lot more difficult than that.'

'Trust me, I know it. I'd ask you to explain, but I'm noticing that you mental health guys just can't give a straight answer to that one.'

'Ah well, there's a very good reason for that. It's because we don't know, but we don't want to admit it.'

'Great.'

'All right, I'll tell you this much. If you have a first-degree relative with schizophrenia, a parent or a sibling, that is, you are slightly more likely to get it yourself. Whether that means it's inherited as such, or the predisposition is, we don't really know. There's loads of research about the genetics of it and all the possible causes, inflammation and loss of synapses in the brain and the impact of stress and trauma and God knows what all else. Cortical thinning is a pretty interesting area just now, I could go through that with you if you want?'

'You're all right. Just give me the headlines.'

'Well, what it boils down to is that she might be at higher risk of schizophrenia if that's what her mother had, and stress can play a part in someone developing that too, just like it can in any mental health problem. But to be honest, we're assuming a lot based on how you interpreted her reaction to seeing money on the floor. You might have misunderstood.'

'There's been a few other things, especially some things Dylan has done.'

'OK, let's have another Coke, shall we, and do the second instalment? I'm not in any rush.'

'Go on then.' She could happily have stayed put too. It was an old men's pub, converted from one of the terraced houses that crowded into the not-yet-gentrified streets in this part of town, close to where the docks used to be. The two downstairs rooms had been knocked through and still only just gave enough space for the bar and a tiny lounge area. It had a heavily patterned red-and-brown carpet, scuffed wooden chairs and tables and no particularly appealing features, but it was warm and quiet. The rain was still beating against the windows and Kit slipped away into a fantasy about leaving her car in the CMHT car park and changing her order to another pasty and a double vodka.

'Here you go. So, what's this other thing that's happened, then?' He handed her a glass of Coke and used his free hand to do another tidy of his hair as he sat down.

'They've got some weird ideas about food. They only go to the local shop, and that's because they know the woman there. Dylan said something about only trusting her. Then I bought him a burger a couple of days ago and he kind of pretended to be eating it, but he was looking at it like it might not be safe. He's never had a McDonald's, as far as I could make out. And he's seventeen.'

'Whoa, now that is crazy.'

'Yeah, I know. Then I found it in my car afterwards. The burger, I mean. He'd hidden it.'

Ben sipped his Coke. 'Maybe he just didn't like it and he was too shy to say.'

'Well, maybe.' She wasn't getting it across to him at all. The strangeness of it all, the way Dylan and Rhian had been when she saw them together. Time to come out with it. 'Can I ask you something? It's going to sound a bit weird.'

'Sure.'

'Do you think they could have this *folie à deux* thingy?'

'Is that the technical term?'

'Don't laugh at me. I know it's very rare but it seems to me they've got the same delusions, as if their whole understanding of the world is completely skewed. But Dylan's got more of a foot in reality than she has, he's not sure whether he completely believes it or not. So sometimes he tries to talk his mother round to getting some help. Then he goes back over to her side again. Are you getting me?'

'I'm not sure I am. If by chance you're right and she's ill and he is too . . . well, that's it, really. There they are, side by side, both untreated and getting more and more ill.'

'But that's it exactly. That's what I'm trying to tell you – they aren't side by side, both with their own delusions, some of them similar, some of them not. It's the same, the whole thing. Their understanding of what's happening to them, and why, it's exactly the same. Dylan's got some doubts but he half believes it as well, like he's starting to fall in with her more and more.'

'They share a delusional network but Dylan's still got partial insight so he's ambivalent, is that what you mean?'

'I was hoping you'd tell me. With you being a psychiatrist and so on.'

'No need to be sarky. Yes, it is what you mean.'

'And it's possible?'

'As you said yourself, it's rare. But yes, all right, it's not unheard of. I'm a bit rusty, let me read up on it and get back to you.'

'That would be great. It really would.' She'd dropped another iron into the fire. Now she had Maxine working on Fflur and Ben working on this, she felt less alone. If she kept throwing rocks at the wall, something was bound to shift.

'Are we having another one?'

'Sorry, I'm going to have to go. I need to make a visit to a school.'

'That's a shame. When are you going back to see these two? I'm thinking I should come along. It doesn't sound totally safe for you to be going up there on your own, to be honest.'

'No, I don't think that would be a good idea. For them, I mean. Obviously, it would be a good idea for me. What I mean by that is, professionally, it would be good. Because you know a lot of things. You're quite clever.' She could feel her cheeks starting to flush. Could she be any less cool?

He was lolling back in his chair now, hands clasped behind his neck, openly laughing at her. 'Ring me if you have any problems, then? I'll send you my number now. I can be quite clever over the phone too.'

'Yes, I bet. I mean, I will. Thank you.' She headed across to the swing doors and bundled through them, before she could embarrass herself any further.

CHAPTER 14

As she pulled into the school car park, Kit swallowed down the familiar swell of apprehension. Her time in this school had been short but bitterly unhappy. Everyone in the place had known her family's story, so expectations of the Goddard kids had been pretty low to start with. But Tyler and Danny had managed to push them right down to the ground. No one had known what to make of Kit and her attempts to be different from her siblings; perhaps they hadn't quite trusted it, they'd thought that blood would out in the end or something. She'd been a puzzle, so teachers and pupils alike had opted to ignore her. That had suited her in some ways, but she still remembered arriving in the school at the age of eleven and wondering whether she had suddenly become invisible and inaudible. It didn't take much insight to picture what Dylan's experiences would have been like here.

After locking her car, Kit headed into main reception where she signed the visitors' book and then leant on the counter, waiting for the receptionist to finish her call.

'Kit, nice to see you, what can we do for you? Nothing wrong, is there?' June had only been in the job for five years, so Kit had a clean slate with her, and she'd been careful to make a friend of her too, knowing that she was bound to need a favour some day.

'No, no problems, June. I just need a word with one of your pupils, if that's OK? Aled Simms? I think he's in sixth form?'

June's eye roll was magnificent to behold. 'Oh yes, we still have the pleasure of Mr Simms. Retaking his GCSEs; his parents insisted, apparently. Rowena Simms can be quite . . . er . . . *vocal*. Do you know her?'

Rowena. Well, well. There couldn't be many of those around in Rock. 'I think I may have run into her.'

'You'll know what I mean, then. I'll send for him now, Kit. Got your ID for me?'

'No, I haven't, to be honest. Left it at home. Come on, June, you know who I am. I'm here every five minutes.'

June wanted to say no, but Kit's carefully planned charm offensive had rendered her unable to do it. 'Oh, go on then. You can use the counselling room. I'll send him in.'

'Thanks, June. While I'm waiting, could you check something for me?'

'You may be pushing your luck now, but go on.'

'Dylan Meredith. He was a pupil here until recently.'

June's plump face brightened. 'Yes, he was, very nice young man, very clever too. We were sorry to lose him.'

'Did anyone in the school make a referral in to us after he'd left? Raising a concern about him?'

June turned to her computer. 'I don't think so. I mean, we were all worried about him but no one mentioned that. At the end of the day, he was old enough to decide to give up school, wasn't he? And I don't think his mother encouraged him much, she hadn't been to a parents' evening since about Year 9.'

Kit recalled the school having told Frankie that Rhian had never been seen at all. But that hadn't been quite right and there it was again, that odd cut-off point, with Dylan and Rhian functioning almost normally before Fflur died and going to pieces afterwards. It was incredible what grief could do. But then she thought about Danny, and it didn't seem incredible at all.

'No, no one from here referred him, Kit.' June turned back from her computer. 'Sorry I can't be more help.'

'No problem. I'd better go and wait for Aled.' It was what she had thought and it seemed she'd been right. Then again, if a teacher had decided to make the referral anonymously, perhaps going against the opinion of the head, they wouldn't have put it on school records anyway. None of it made sense and it had been more than a long shot, given Frankie's description of the referrer, but she'd ended up giving it a try because she still couldn't see who else would have made the call.

She crossed the reception to the side room, where she settled down to wait. Fifteen minutes later the door swung open and Aled entered, his face a picture of amusement.

'Ooh, Dylan Meredith's social worker's here to see me.

What's this all about, then, Miss?' He let the door go behind him with a slam.

'Sit down, Aled.'

'All right then, I will.' He flopped onto the chair opposite hers, letting out a satisfied sigh and stretching his arms above his head with a loud yawn. She waited patiently for the display to end.

'Am I in trouble, Miss?'

'Not yet.'

'Uh-oh, scary. What have I done?'

'You took my ID badge. I want it back.'

He shrugged. 'Can't help you, sorry.'

'Come on, Aled, what's the point? It's no use to you, is it?'

'Sorry. I binned it.'

She'd been worried about this. Dammit, she should have just bitten the bullet and gone to HR for a new one straight away. It would have been a hassle but this was an even bigger waste of her time. In truth, though, she wasn't just there for the ID badge.

'OK, let's talk about something else, then.'

'Go on. I could do with a break, to be honest.'

'What's your problem with Dylan?'

He shrugged. 'He's a weirdo. His whole family are.'

'Not good enough. He's not bothering you, even if he is weird, so why have you been bothering him?'

He was grinning at her, still full of himself and totally

unwilling to cooperate. The radiator was on full, too, the heat causing Aled's unpleasant personal scent to seep out into the room. Sweat and cannabis, just like last time.

'So, does your mother know you smoke weed, Aled?'

'What d'you mean?' He was a trier, she'd grant him that much, but there was no hiding the look on his face.

'Does your mother know about the weed? No, I didn't think so. She's got the shop up in Rock, hasn't she?'

His sudden inability to speak was as good as an answer.

'Right. Two things, then. Number one, have you really chucked my ID badge away? Because I'm willing to give you one last chance to come up with it before I pop into the shop and have a word with her. And number two, I want to know what your issue is with Dylan.'

He looked like he might be about to beg her not to tell; he might even be trying not to cry. Rowena Simms must be bloody terrifying when she had one on her.

'It's just . . . Dylan used to be my mate. Mine and Joe's.'

'Did he? When?'

'In primary. He was all right for a bit after we moved up here but then he didn't bother with us no more.'

'That's not really a reason to be bullying him, is it?'

He shrugged. 'Dunno. I just hated him after that. We all did, me and the boys.' She could see now that Dylan had become their target, something they could rally around, the outsider they needed so that each of them could feel sure they were on the inside. Aled was the ringleader but hidden deep down at the root of it all was his hurt over losing a friend and not being able to understand why.

'Well, do me a favour and leave him alone. He's having a rough time. I can't say anymore, but him backing off has got nothing to do with you. He's got his own stuff going on.'

'I know.'

'Do you?'

'Yeah. He told me a secret once, before he got weird. Told me what was happening up his house.'

'Fancy telling me at all?'

But he had stopped dead. 'Nah, it's nothing. All right, I'll call the boys off. Are you going to tell my mam?'

'Well, see, I don't know. What about my ID badge?'

He stood up and fished in his back pocket, pulling it out by the lanyard and holding it out to her, looking hopeful.

'Thanks.' She wondered whether there was anything else she needed from him, while she had the advantage. 'One more thing?'

'What?'

'What do you know about Dylan's nan?'

'What do you mean?'

'Don't piss about. When I saw you up in Rock that day, you and Joe were shouting at Dylan about his nan. Why?'

'She was mad too, wasn't she? Like I said, the lot of them are.'

'Your mother told you that, did she? Or your aunty Cath?'

'That's right, yeah.' He'd seized on it too quickly.

'Well, don't believe everything you're told, eh? And just leave Dylan alone, then I'll have no need to speak to your mum. You can go now.'

'OK. Thanks, Miss.'

'You can call me Kit.'

'Thanks, Kit. And by the way, you're not fat.' He was halfway out of the door now.

'Sorry?'

'Joe said you were a fat cow. You're not. You're quite fit, as a matter of fact.'

'Leave it there, Aled.'

'OK, Kit.'

Aled knew more than he was letting on. She hesitated, wondering whether to call him back and push him further, but the worry about what was going on with Rhian and Dylan was still shadowing her mind. She'd leave it for now; she could catch up with Aled another time.

Her phone rang as she was on her way to the car. Maxine Cadwalladr.

'Kit, I have some information for you.'

'Thanks, that's great.'

'I've checked the records for Snowdrop Court and no residents went missing in February 2012. Or for three months either side of that. I took a look, just to be thorough.'

Poor old Deri, he obviously wasn't as well as he thought he was. Fflur had died, that was all.

'What's more, no one called Fflur Meredith died there during that period either.'

'Are you sure?'

'Certain.'

So Tim had been right all along and Frankie had been wrong. Fflur had died in Penlan, after all. It was the same story that John had given, now she came to think about it, and he seemed to know the family pretty well. It was the first time she'd known Frankie to get something wrong, though. 'And there definitely isn't any way the records could have an error in them? You said things weren't good back then.'

'Up to a point. But they'd have been in serious trouble if they'd failed to report a missing or dead resident. It would have been picked up on their next inspection without a doubt. They were very sloppy about processes, but they weren't outright negligent.'

'Right. I see.'

'So, what I'm saying is, Fflur Meredith didn't die in Snowdrop Court in February 2012. Either the date or the location is wrong.'

'I'm one hundred per cent on the date – it's on our system and that was transferred across to us from the CMHT.'

'Then it must be the location. Could it be a mistake over which home – perhaps she was placed somewhere else all along?'

'Maybe.' She'd taken a guess at it being Snowdrop Court, based on Frankie's vague reference to spring flowers. Not very clever of her. But then again, how could Deri have known so much about Fflur? 'Actually, no, Maxine, I'm pretty sure she was in Snowdrop Court at some point.'

'Well, if you're quite sure and you feel it's significant, I'll ask the home to chase up her file and see what her story is. As I said before, it will take a bit of time for them to get it out of the archives.'

'Thanks, Maxine.'

'By the way, how's Vernon? – is he enjoying being back at work?'

'About as much as he enjoys anything. Wait, did that have something to do with you?'

'Let's just say I had a quiet word and leave it at that. I'll call you as soon as I have anything for you.'

As Kit ended the call, her phone was buzzing again, the screen showing the caller to be Ben Hot Doc.

'I've looked into what you were saying and I've got some info for you. Where are you now?'

'Sandbeach High.'

'Can you call into the office?'

'No. I've got to get back up to Rock and see what's happening with them. Can't you tell me now?'

'Easier in person. And more pleasurable.'

'I really can't.'

'All right, can I meet you somewhere after I get off work?'

'McDonald's car park, then.'

'Wow, romantic.'

'It's on my way.'

'OK then. See you about five thirty.'

She was there five minutes early and spotted him straight away as he pulled into the car park in his sporty white Audi, twenty minutes late. She flashed her headlights as he passed, determined to stay on her own territory, and caught the lift of his body and the flash of his courtesy light as he checked his appearance in the rear-view mirror before getting out of the car.

'Stinks of onions in here.' He wrinkled his nose, settling into the passenger seat and flapping the door back and forth several times.

'I've explained that already. Right, I haven't got long, so what've you found out?'

'I think you might be right. It could well be a *folie à deux*.'

'Really? Can you tell me more about it? I mean, I got the gist but I'm still not one hundred per cent I understand how it can happen.'

'OK, well, as you know, you have two people. Can be more than two, but that's even more unusual. So in the case of these peeps of yours, we're talking a parent and child, but occasionally it's a couple or siblings. Socially isolated, no contact with the outside world. It's what we call an enmeshed relationship. And one is transmitting symptoms to the other one.'

'That's the bit I don't quite get. Transmitting? How?'

'It's not that hard to understand when you think about it. It's to do with power, really. One of them, the dominant one in the relationship, is ill. That's the primary, or inducer. They pass on their delusions to the other one, that's the secondary or the receiver. Have you ever spent a lot of time alone with someone you really wanted to please? Like a boyfriend, or would it be a girlfriend, maybe?'

'I suppose.' She cracked the window open, to allow the build-up of steam to escape.

'Pretty non-committal, but OK, let's say you have. So, you start to go along with things they say even if you don't agree. Let things go for the sake of keeping it peaceful. They get upset if you don't see things exactly the same way, so you pretend you do. Now imagine being with that person 24/7, with no break, and no one and nothing from the outside world to give you a reality check, to remind you that what they are saying isn't right. Maybe that goes on for years, day in, day out. Gradually, you end up taking it on board, half believing it at first until in the end you lose track of whether it's true altogether. And paranoia's self-reinforcing, isn't it? As I said, you think people are against you, you find some coins on the path – it proves they are. How else did they get there? It's got to be a message.'

The whole thing hit every single nail on the head with a resounding smack. She couldn't believe she'd got it so right. 'And this is definitely a recognised condition, textbook and all that?'

'What, you think I got it off Wikipedia? I'm a psychiatrist, it's all legit.'

'Very sorry.'

'I should think so. I've spent the afternoon on it, fascinating stuff. As I said, we are all susceptible to it to some extent – falling in with the people we want to please, taking on their reality. If one person happens to be psychotic, then it might get noticed. But as for the rest of us – well, maybe all close relationships have an element of *folie à deux*.'

She remembered the glamorous couple in John's psychiatry journal. How normal they'd looked and how frightened they must have been to fall into that state of neglect rather than risk going out. Then there were the other cases, the mention of murder. 'Can it be dangerous?'

'Not to anyone else, not usually anyway. Almost all people with mental health problems are less risk to others than you or I would be. The same goes for these people, they tend to live quietly and avoid interaction. They're unseen, they stay off the radar, and it can go on like that for years. All the time they're getting more and more deluded and distressed, though, so it's them we have to be concerned about. But obviously it does depend on the nature of the delusions. Occasionally it has led to something criminal happening. And if the primary's got hallucinations – well, that can be a worry.'

'Why?'

'You know when you did your training – did you skip a lot of lectures?'

'Spot on. So come on, enlighten me.'

'Well, voices can torment people. And they might tell you to do something. Fine if they're telling you to . . . I don't know . . . keep the window open. But not if they're telling you to jump out of it. Or to throw someone else out of it, come to that.'

'And you get those with schizophrenia?'

'You can do, yes.'

'How would you know if someone's getting voices, though? If they don't want to tell you, I mean?'

'That happens quite often. Sometimes people don't accept there's anything wrong, but they know we will think there is, so they hide it, become guarded. But we're all over that kind of behaviour – we look out for clues. Responding to what we call unseen stimuli is a big one – laughing for no reason, maybe, or looking around suddenly as if someone's speaking when they're not. But remember, this is all speculation, really.'

It was a bit late for him to back off now. He'd planted the worries in her mind and they were growing tall. 'So how do you deal with it?'

'You separate them, and you wait to see which one gets better.'

'What, really?'

'Well, yes. You admit them to two separate facilities, making sure they can't bump into each other or communicate. Sometimes the secondary will need a bit of help, just some gentle talking-through, so ideally you get psychology to see them both, but their delusions will run out of steam pretty quickly once they haven't got the primary there fuelling them. The other one will stay deluded and need treatment. That's how you find out who's really ill.'

'It's obvious in this case. Who's ill, I mean. It would have to be Rhian.'

'How long have they been like this for?'

'About four years, I think.'

'So the boy would only have been about – what? Thirteen, at the start? It would be very rare to get a psychosis at that age – not impossible, but rare. Plus, she's the mum, she's likely to be the dominant one. So overall, I agree with your assessment, Ms Goddard. Nice work.'

'Thanks.' But an image came to her mind of Dylan and Rhian, standing in the front room at Ty Olaf, his hand sliding over her knuckles, the way he'd calmed her, and she'd submitted to it. 'I'm not one hundred per cent she is the dominant one, though, to be honest. Sometimes it seems that way and sometimes it doesn't. It's not a normal mother–son relationship.'

He shrugged. 'Like I said they're enmeshed, so normal rules don't apply. That's why I asked about the sexual intimacy – these are relationships where all the boundaries between two people break down, so sometimes that's a feature. But really, you are only ever going to know for sure by separating them.'

'How do I go about it?'

'Oh, you're a long way off that yet. It's a theory but it's all too vague. You need more information. Maybe if you go back and observe them, try to work out what might be going on and let me know. I can guide you through the next bit. Over a proper drink if you like.'

She parked that. Her head was too full. 'I don't know – they wouldn't even let me in earlier.' She shouldn't have let his words unsettle her, but it had been easily done. Her triumphant mood was ebbing away fast. The whole thing was still a mess, with loose ends everywhere and nothing certain. 'Right, thanks for that, I'm going to need to run now.'

'You're not seriously going there now, are you? It's a bit late.'

'Maybe you're right. Maybe Monday would be better. I don't know if I ought to leave them that long, though.'

'Come on. What can happen over the weekend? This is clearly a long-term situation, it needs careful handling. You're not going to solve anything by running up there right now. They probably won't even let you in.'

'No, maybe not.'

'Cool, what about that drink, then?'

'I'm knackered. I'm going home.'

'One drink.'

'Get out of my car, Ben.'

'Oh all right. I'll call you, yeah?'

'Sure.' She didn't miss how quick he was to get onto his phone as he strode off across the car park. She wondered who he was texting and felt a stab of regret. She should have agreed to have a drink with him. But she was missing Alex, so was it just the attention that she was enjoying? Ben was obviously a world-class expert in that department, and it was flattering.

But then again, if she really had screwed things up with Alex, if he had got fed up with waiting for her to say what she wanted to happen, then maybe it wouldn't hurt to think about moving on. She'd get off home and then she'd text Ben and they could go to the pub near her flat. Work could wait until Monday.

She almost made it home before she changed her mind. She could actually see the blurry outline of her building a few hundred yards to her left as she sat at the junction. Staring at the red light in front of her, she weighed things up. She'd fought against traffic all the way across town. She'd been soaked through several times today, she was starving again, and she had a gnawing pain in her back and ribs from holding herself rigid ever since Dylan's text had arrived that morning. Ben was probably right: nothing dramatic was likely to happen over the weekend, and besides, she didn't stand much chance of getting into the house now. Definitely best to take a break and regroup. All she'd heard was a dog yelping, after all. The light changed to amber; as she turned left, she replayed that sound, and remembered the claws scraping the floor as the same dog was dragged sharply by its collar. She pushed her indicator down, turned into a cul-de-sac, executed a tight three-point turn and headed back the way she'd come.

CHAPTER 15

It was six forty-five by the time she turned onto the valley road. There was no break in the rain all the way up the Hir and she had to slow down after the first couple of miles, the sleek surface of the road threatening to send her over the open edge and plunging down towards the valley floor.

Rock itself was deserted as she drove through it, everyone obviously having tucked themselves away at home. All she could think about was whether Dylan might be in danger. She ramped up her agony by listing all the times she'd failed him. The anonymous referral that said he'd been injured, right at the start. That bruise on his cheekbone the first time she'd met him. The moment in the doorway when he'd been about to tell her who had hurt him and the way Rhian had cut him off before he could do it. Why hadn't she pushed harder to get an explanation? She'd let the simple fact of that injury disappear below a pile of irrelevancies, fretting about who his father was and what had happened with his grandmother, instead of focussing on what mattered. Had Rhian done it to him? It still seemed impossible, that was the bald fact of it; he was huge compared to her. But Dylan wasn't the type to retaliate, even when he was easily capable of it; she'd seen that much in his encounter with Joe and Aled. It had puzzled her at the time, but maybe it was learnt behaviour. Maybe he knew better.

She pulled her car over well before reaching John's house, and after jumping out, hurried past before he could appear on the doorstep for a conveniently timed vape. Seeing his living-room window glowing cosily against the rain, she was drawn back to the question of whether John had been the referrer. She had been sure he wasn't, but now she wondered again; she really could not see who else would have known that Rhian had injured Dylan. She checked herself: *might have*. It was becoming a fact in her head but, really, she had no idea whether it was true. As Ben had said, it was all speculation, the whole thing, including this *folie à deux* business. But still, it was almost irresistible; the word Ben had used was *enmeshed*, and that was the word she'd been grasping for all along to describe Dylan's relationship with his mother.

Arriving at Ty Olaf, Kit saw that there were no lights on at the front of the house. She kept her torch on for now, sweeping the beam across the garden to see if anything looked different, then walked down to the end of the wall where she found the chicken wire still bent back exactly as she had left it. She slipped through the gap and out onto the lawn.

A few seconds with her ear pressed up against the front door told her nothing. She made her way round to the back, where gloom lay behind the glass of the kitchen door. Moving up close to it, she took a deep breath before shining the beam through the glass. The kitchen looked exactly as it had earlier, except that someone had picked up the chair from the floor and set it at the head of the pine table. She exhaled, leaning her head on the glass for a moment, then stood and at the same time tried to turn in the narrow space of the porch. She misjudged the space and her boot caught hard against something at floor level; she pulled it away sharply and all at once, the porch filled with an explosion of noise like gunfire as one solid weight after another came pounding towards her, battering her lower stomach and legs and almost knocking her off her feet. She threw herself backwards as the last of the rain of logs fell, the sound of steel ringing then echoing in her ears for several seconds as the head of the axe just missed her foot and smashed on to the tiled floor.

She leant her back against the porch wall for support, shaking all over, her knees weakening underneath her and her legs throbbing. It was a few minutes before she could stop crying and get a deep breath, cursing her own clumsiness that had brought the logs crashing down from where they'd been stacked. But as soon as her mind cleared a little, she realised that there had been no movement, and no bark or whimper from the house when the logs fell. There could be no doubt about it now, no one was in there. Where could they have gone, when their world had shrunk so much? Where else did they have? There was, she saw now, only one other place that was theirs.

She managed to ring Ben's number as she started up the mountain path, labouring in the heavy rain and the biting wind, but he didn't pick up. She was halfway to the viewing point by the time her phone buzzed with his return call.

'You OK? You need me to be clever?'

'I think maybe I do.' She told him quickly about the empty house and where she was heading.

'I knew I should have come with you. It's not safe for you to be up there on your own, especially not at the viewing point.'

'I don't need an escort. Just tell me what to do if it gets difficult when I get there.'

'Oh all right, just showing concern. It depends what sort of difficult you mean. The police have powers to convey to a place of safety if they think one or the other of them appears to be mentally disordered. You just need to quote Section 136 of the Mental Health Act to the control room and insist they get someone out.'

'All right, will do.'

'But Kit?'

'What?'

'How do you even know that's where they are?'

As he spoke, she picked up the sound of frantic barking coming from above her.

'They're up the mountain. What I don't know is why.' She ended the call, and stepped up her speed.

It was hard going. The freezing rain drove into her mouth and eyes, half-blinding her even with her phone torch for light, and her feet kept going out from under her on the sodden path. She was filled with a throbbing panic, desperate to get to them but terrified at what she might find, not understanding why they had gone there but knowing full well the risks they were taking in the furious storm and the stony darkness.

Finally reaching the threshold at the eastern end of the viewing point, she hung back to gauge what was going on. She found Griff and Tomos first, a lone sliver of moonlight picking out the white flashes in their coats. Moving forward, she tried to take in what else was in front of her as quickly as she could, willing her eyes to make out the pieces of the picture and her brain to interpret them. Both the old dogs were on high alert, ears back, eyes wild. Following the direction they were facing she located two figures at the western end of the ledge. She saw at once by their differing sizes that this was Rhian and Dylan. They stood tight together on the crest of the ledge, highlighted against the lights of Rock to the south. They were holding hands and looking out towards the blur of Sandbeach further south still, its streetlights glittering yellow in the far distance; oblivious to her presence, absorbed in the sight.

After a few seconds more, Kit spotted Bella; she was to the back of Dylan and Rhian, growling, her body lowered to the ground. There was no mistaking that posture. All the dogs were agitated, but Bella must be overwrought to the point of confusion, because her attention was not on Dylan and Rhian at all but on the bushes to the side of her, where the viewing point came to its western end. Something must have moved there, a bird or an animal, and she had homed in on it furiously. In that muddled state, she could easily turn if she was startled.

Kit edged along, keeping well back in the shadow of the mountain. The wind and rain were battering Rhian's tiny frame, throwing her back and forth, Dylan's outstretched hand her only anchor. The two of them shifted their attention in unison, away from Sandbeach to the drop below them, then to each other, then back down again. Communicating, urging each other on. She was behind them now, ten feet or so back and still in shadow but close enough to see that a decision was being made. In a few seconds, it would be too late. But if she got this wrong, there wouldn't be another chance.

'Dylan.' She tried to call it loud enough for him to hear but not enough to frighten them. Bella's haunches lifted, the aggression dropping away a little at the sound of a familiar voice, but she stayed where she was, unsure. Dylan and Rhian stood unhearing, pulling closer together now, looking out over Rock. She recognised that this had somehow been agreed, that it was the final drinking in of their home, their lives. She called again, louder, and Dylan's head came up as if he had heard. But he wasn't following the direction of her voice coming from behind him. Instead, he was looking towards the spot to his left, the one that had caught Bella's attention.

'I'm back here, Dylan. Please come away from there.' They swung round in surprise, dropping each other's hands, the motion unbalancing Rhian. She stumbled, slipping on the mud, falling onto all fours; scrabbling, she tried to catch hold of the top of the ridge to stop herself going over but she was losing her footing, sliding down the other side. Kit launched herself forward, knowing that she couldn't get there in time, flinching as Rhian screamed, not wanting to see but unable to look away.

In the next moment, Dylan had bent to his mother and snatched her up by her arms, lifting her easily to stand next to him again, his arms going around her waist. They both faced Kit now, their backs to the drop. One step backwards and they would both be gone over the edge, seriously injured or worse. She moved forward a few more paces.

'Dylan, I don't know what's happening but you have to get down from there so we can talk. Your mother's in danger, you know that.' She kept walking, her movements slow, not taking her eyes off them. Dylan was blinking repeatedly, disorientated. She searched for something to say, frantically running back through her conversation with Ben, then trying to imagine what it must have been like for Dylan to live with Rhian all these years, and how he might be feeling now. There had to be something she could use to reach him, to get hold of his hand.

'Listen to me, Dylan. Keep hold of your mother and just listen for a minute. Will you do that one thing for me?'

He ducked his head in agreement for a fraction of a second, then his eyes were back on her.

'I think it must have been so hard for you to understand what was happening the past few years. You didn't know what was real and what wasn't anymore. That must be so bloody frightening. I know you trust your mother more than anyone in the world and if she tells you things, you believe them, even if your own mind tells you they're not right. But look where she's led you – something's wrong, Dylan. It's not her fault and she'd never hurt you on purpose but she needs help. You and I, we need to help her, and put everything back how it was, before all this started. Like in that song I played you. *Turn back time to the good old days.* Remember? It made you think about how things used to be. Maybe we can get that back, get your mum back, like she used to be?'

Still he stood rigid, Rhian pressed tight against him, her face turned into the side of his body now, blocking everything else out. Kit was begging silently, the closest she had ever come to prayer in her life, *please, please, please, just make him move, make him move.* She held herself ready, nothing left to say; she'd taken her shot and it had either landed or it hadn't. She could only wait.

He glanced towards the same spot in the bushes again. Her eyes followed as she tried to pick up what it was that scurried there, but the wind and rain made it impossible. His next movement was so sudden that, at first, she couldn't comprehend which way he had chosen to go. Then she understood that he had swung his arms forward, Rhian still circled within them, trying to propel her away from the edge and from the drop behind them. But she was fighting back with animal force, her hands slapping against his chest. They clung to each other, silhouetted against the lights of Rock, swaying in one direction then the other, until Dylan finally seized hold of his mother's arms with both hands. 'No,' he screamed. 'No more.' And he lifted her and flung her away from him with such violence that she half stumbled and half flew forwards onto the ledge, landing on the stony ground close to Kit's feet with a sickening smack.

Rhian lay curled up on her side, not moving. Dylan was at her side in seconds, dropping to the ground, his hand out to touch her shoulder then moving up to stroke her hair away from her face. She didn't move and he started to cry then, an awful low whimper that quickly gathered force, rising into a frenzied, desperate wail. Kit was immobilised, her entire body ringing with shock, as if she had run full tilt into an invisible sheet of glass, the sound Rhian's body made when it hit the ground reverberating over and over in her ears. Dylan slumped over his mother now, his head going down onto her chest. All three dogs were milling around them, and as Dylan's cries reached an excruciating pitch, Bella began to bark frantically. The sound brought Kit back to herself. She reached into her pocket for her phone, her teeth chattering, not knowing how she was going to manage to speak, and whether an ambulance was needed or whether it was too late. As she tried to punch the number in with useless fingers, Dylan's head stayed on Rhian's chest and he stretched out, fumbling to locate her hand on the wet ground, missing it each time, until her arm lifted from the ground and her hand rose to meet his. Kit moved back into the shadow of the mountain, rested her head on the freezing rock and threw up three times into the water-logged gorse.

As she straightened, wiping her mouth with her sleeve, Bella let out another ringing bark behind her and shot off in the direction of the mountain path. Seconds later, Kit heard voices and was dazzled by torchlight as two uniformed police officers emerged onto the viewing point, two other figures that she couldn't yet identify bringing up the rear. Kit ran after Bella, managing to catch hold of her collar before she could go for anyone. Then she sank to the ground to soothe the dog, putting her arms around her neck and burying her face in her soaking fur.

'Thought you might need a hand, so I brought the police with me.' Ben James stood looking down at her as she sat, mud soaking through her leggings, shivering uncontrollably. She managed to pull gently on Bella's ears and whisper to her, feeling the dog start to calm and trying to tap into it for herself. The rain had died down and the wind was dropping but she felt like she'd never be warm again.

'I had it under control.'

'Looks like it too. Is she hurt?' He nodded towards Rhian, who was being helped to sit up by two police officers and the other person. It was Dai Davies, she realised.

'She had quite a bad ... well, it was kind of a fall, really. I was about to call an ambulance. You could check her over, couldn't you?'

'God, no. I'm a psychiatrist, me, nothing from the neck down. I'll get DS Davies and you can tell us the story.'

He made a beckoning motion towards Dai, who ambled over in his own time. 'You all right down there?'

'Yes, I'm fine. How come you're here?' She was so relieved to see him. Nothing much fazed Dai. Even now, he was looking around, slowly absorbing the sight of Rhian on the ground and Dylan pacing furiously back and forth, as if he encountered this kind of thing up a mountain in the dark every day.

'Seems my name's on the system after that visit I organised to the family. I got alerted when the call came in. I think the uniform boys were a bit worried about handling it. I was at home having my tea.'

'Sorry, Dai.'

'Not a problem, Martin will put it in the microwave for me later. No need to look so worried, Kit, we'll get this sorted now. What happened?'

She told them as quickly as she could then returned her attention to Bella while Ben went away to speak to Dylan. Dai approached Rhian, crouching down to the ground where she sat hugging her knees. She started to uncurl slightly after just a few minutes of listening to him. Then he went over to join Ben with Dylan, where the three of them stayed talking for a long time. That done, Ben came back and sat down beside Kit, the mud squelching under him as he lowered himself to the ground.

'OK, it's impossible to get any sense out of either of them, so I've explained to the officers what happened and they're going to take them in on a 136. I don't think the mother's hurt, just winded and very scared. But we can get her checked out.'

'Where will they take them?'

'The psych assessment unit. I'll call Dr Del now, she can meet us there.'

The relief left Kit light-headed. At last, someone else could take responsibility for all this, someone who knew what they were doing and knew about hallucinations and *folie à deux* and all the rest of it.

'What will happen to them?'

'You don't need to say it like that. It's a hospital, not a torture chamber.'

'And you don't need to say it like that, I'm not an idiot.'

'Are you always this spiky?' he snapped.

'Pretty much.' She pulled herself to her feet. 'I'm going to speak to Dylan, I need to explain what's happening.' She left him sitting and called Bella to come along with her.

She found Dylan and Rhian standing with one of the police officers, who was talking to them quietly. She would hang close, waiting until she was needed. They were bound to refuse to go, and she wasn't sure what would happen then. Would the police physically drag them in? Were they allowed to do that?

Dylan noticed her immediately. 'They want us to go to hospital.'

She moved alongside him and took his arm, guiding him to turn away from his mother so she could speak without Rhian hearing. She remembered what Ben had said. If Rhian was the one in control, the one who was ill, it was best to keep reasoning with Dylan; he would surely be easier to reach?

'I think it would be a good idea, Dyl, don't you? We talked about you getting help, and this is a chance for you to do it. You two could have been hurt up here; if you'd gone over the edge you might even have died.'

He nodded, head dropped, embarrassed.

'Was that what you were going to do? Were you and your mum going to jump? Why?'

His mouth moved slightly but he'd lost his words. She waited, her hand tightening on his arm, encouraging him. His other hand came up and covered hers, grasping at her fingers.

'Right, time to make a move.' Ben appeared at her elbow, all ready to chivvy them along.

'For fuck's sake, wait a minute.'

'All right, all right, keep your hair on, what's happening, then?'

'Just go away, I'm speaking to Dylan.'

He moved off without argument, but when she turned back, she could see that the moment had been lost. Dylan still held her hand but his attention was on his mother as he saw that she was being led away by a police officer.

'What were you going to say, Dylan?'

'Nothing. I wasn't going to say anything.' He snatched his hand away and turned to follow after Rhian.

Ben appeared at her elbow. 'Meet us down there, Kit? Dr

Carver wants to speak to you.' He held his arm out to usher Dylan away and the police officer did the same to Rhian. Kit watched the two of them walking off, perfectly compliant now. Then she saw Dylan turn.

'Kit – the dogs – what's going to happen to the dogs?'

Dammit, she hadn't even thought of that. 'I'll sort them out.'

As everyone trooped off onto the path, she hung back, looking around for the dogs. She found all three of them sniffing about in the undergrowth. She called them over to her and then started to lead them away, trying to figure out as she went what she was going to do with them. The two older dogs came along obediently enough but Bella was still upset, running around erratically and refusing to keep close. Kit took off her belt and looped it around the dog's collar. She should have asked for a door key, she realised, then she could have just dropped the dogs at the house. But then again, if Dylan and Rhian were going to be in hospital for a while, that would be no good at all. Who would feed them or walk them? She couldn't take them to her flat, she didn't have the room and besides, her contract didn't allow pets. She had reached the bottom of the mountain now and was standing at the mouth of the lane to Ty Olaf. She could ring Vernon, but he might suggest putting them in kennels. She couldn't do that; Dylan would never forgive her.

John opened his front door in his pyjamas, a glass of whisky in his hand, his wary face breaking into a grin as soon as he saw it was her. 'What are you doing here at this time of night, love?' His gaze fell upon the dogs. 'Everything all right up there, is it?'

'It's fine, John. I can't tell you the details but there's nothing to worry about. Dylan and Rhian are going to be away for a while. I'm not sure how long for. You couldn't possibly look after the dogs, could you? I don't know what else to do with them.'

He stood back from the door. 'Of course, I'd be glad to help. Come on, you look like you could do with a coffee and a Welsh cake.' Warmth and the scent of baking poured out of his house.

'I wish I could but I need to get Dylan and Rhian sorted. Thanks, John. What about dog food for tonight? I can't get into the house to get whatever they usually have.'

'Now, I have got a key, Fflur gave it to my mother for safe-keeping years ago, see, I don't think Rhian even knows about it, to be honest, but I've hung onto it just in case I ever needed to get in there. In an emergency. So, I could pop up. But no, tell you what, I've got some chicken in my freezer, they can have a bit of a treat. I love dogs, they'll be spoilt here with me.'

He really was a lovely man. She drew her belt out of Bella's collar and chivvied the dogs into the house, watching them trail wet mud all over his immaculate cream carpet as they went. 'Dylan and Rhian are safe now, John. Please don't fret about them, I'm sure it will all be OK.'

'Never no doubt about it, love. I hope that bit of info I gave you helped.'

'It did, yes.'

'Good, I'm glad I was of use,' he said.

'You were. Thanks so much.'

John was still hanging around. She raised her brows at him, wondering what he was fussing about now.

'Mind, as soon as I found out you were Ceri and Martina's granddaughter, I thought, She's a sharp one, then. She'll sort it.' He winked at her as he closed the door.

Kit chain-smoked all the way back down the valley and right across town until she reached Sandbeach General Hospital, which was located in the middle of an industrial estate on the west side of the bay. As her nicotine levels rose, she started to feel a bit more with it and it was only then that she comprehended how wet she was, her clothes sticking to her skin, her hair plastered to her scalp and her socks squelching in her boots at each press of the pedals. She couldn't stop shivering, even with the heater turned up to its highest. She wanted to go home and get a warm shower and clean clothes, but Ben had said the psychiatrist wanted to speak to her, and besides, she needed to make sure that Dylan was all right. Maybe she could get some time alone with him, then she could find out what he'd been about to say before Ben had interrupted.

She parked easily in the near-empty hospital car park, checked her appearance in the rear-view mirror with a stab of despair, and then got out to look around for a clue as to the whereabouts of the psychiatric unit. It turned out to be located right at the back of the hospital, at the very end of the main corridor. When she got there, she found the swing doors locked, but there was an entry phone on the wall and after using it to give her name and a brief explanation, it wasn't long before she heard hurried footsteps on the other side and the door swung open to reveal Ben James. He looked almost as bedraggled as she did, but he definitely wore it better.

'Just in time. Del's with the mother now, she's already seen the boy and she'll want a word. I've told her everything you told me. Come on in, I'll show you down to the unit.' He looked closely at her as she passed him. 'Get you a coffee, maybe?'

'That would be great.'

Ben indicated a door on either side of the lobby and then a third on the far side. 'These are the two acute wards. And the assessment unit is the one over there. Take a seat, I'll be right back.' She sat on one of the hard plastic chairs that were attached to the floor in a row outside the unit. It was warm in this lobby, and it didn't smell weird, but no one had taken down the out-of-date posters here either. Were these mental health types lazy or did they just not care? She leant the back of her head against the wall for a moment, closing her eyes and trying to process everything that had happened. All she could see was Dylan and Rhian teetering on the precipice above Rock, and what would have happened if she hadn't got there in time.

'You OK?' He handed her a thin plastic cup brimming with boiling-hot coffee.

'Yeah. I'm fine.' She took the scalding cup and sipped a tiny bit. It was foul, but she couldn't stop, it was so comforting.

'Let me just warn you about Dr Del. Don't let her intimidate you . . . something funny?'

'I'll cope, don't worry.'

'It's just . . . I did fill her in quickly before she spoke to them, about our theory, you know, the *folie à deux* thing, and she was a bit doubtful. It is very rare, and the fact that you're only a social worker and a children's one at that . . . well, I don't think she was impressed. Think I've talked her round but she might push you a bit on it.'

Kit wasn't sure whether that *only* had emanated from Dr Del or from him, but either way, it pissed her off. 'Thanks for the warning. But it's not necessary.'

The door to the assessment unit opened, cutting off any retort or apology he might have been about to offer. Ben jumped to his feet so quickly he nearly knocked Kit's coffee all over her.

'Dr Carver, this is Kit Goddard – the social worker I told you about.'

Delilah Carver was a diminutive woman in her mid-sixties. Her steel-grey hair was cut very short, and she had tanned, sun-damaged skin. She wore straight-legged trousers with knee-high leather boots and a plain shirt, all in black. She stood in front of Kit and Ben, looking from one to the other for several seconds before she settled her gaze on Kit and spoke.

'It was you discovered these two?'

It was an odd way of putting it, but accurate too. She remembered what Ben had said about cases of *folie à deux*. How they usually managed to remain unseen. 'I suppose so.'

'You did well, then. Very interesting.'

'What's going to happen to them?'

'The boy's agreed to be admitted, the mother isn't having any of it. They are extremely guarded but they do have some odd ideas. I'm going to call the out-of-hours team now, see if I can get a section organised for her. We'll put them on separate units, the boy here; the mother can go over to the ward in Dinas. I'll ask the psychologist to visit them both, try to tease out what's happening and then we can see what's what.' She turned her attention to Ben now, and Kit would swear she felt him shrink against her slightly. 'You went about it in totally the wrong way, Dr James, and we will be having words about that in due course. You don't give out informal advice in the pub in future, you direct people through the correct channels. But we are where we are. We don't see a lot of *folie à deux* but it's feasible in this case. Dr James, you will liaise with Child Services in respect of Dylan from here on in. Try to keep within procedures, if that's not too much of an imposition on your love life, that is.'

Kit watched her leave, walking very fast down the corridor, pulling out her phone as she went and barking orders as soon as it reached her mouth. 'Well, she seems lovely to me.' It was mean, but she still wasn't sure about that *only*.

Ben sighed. 'I think it's just me she hates. By the way, what did you do with the dogs?'

'I took them to the neighbour.'

'Well done. Look, Dylan and Rhian are going to need some stuff. We keep a few toiletries but they'll need clothes and so on.'

'I can't see her agreeing to anyone going in the house. I'll have a word with the neighbour, maybe he wouldn't mind calling in a shop for them. Can I have a chat with Dylan?'

'Sure. He's in there.' He indicated one of the side rooms off the lobby. 'I'll wait here.'

She found Dylan slumped across a radiator, his head down on his outstretched arm as if he were about to fall asleep.

'You OK, Dyl?'

'I'm so cold.'

'Yeah, and me.' She placed herself opposite him, trying to get a look at his face. 'You a bit scared too, maybe?'

'Bit.'

'They will look after you here, you're safe.'

'I don't know. I think maybe we shouldn't have come.'

'What's changed your mind?'

He sat up a bit, using his fingers to wipe muddy splashes from his face then wiping them on the pink upholstery of the chair. 'We don't need to be here. There's nothing wrong with us.'

'They just need to check, don't they? If that's right, they'll send you home.'

'Will they? They won't make me stay here? I don't want to live here.'

'Dylan, you won't live here. It's a hospital, not a home. But we need to get you both looked at, especially your mum.'

'I don't know, Kit. I trusted you but I shouldn't have.'

Leaning forward, she took hold of his mucky hands. 'It is the best place for you to be. They won't keep you here any longer than they have to. Once you're well, you'll go home.'

'What about my mother?'

'That may take a little longer. But yes, once they can see she's well, they will let her go too.'

'As long as we're well, we can go?'

'Dylan, honestly, I promise you. What is it that's worrying you about this?'

'I just want to be at home, and my mother to be there too.' He pulled his hands away and slumped back down onto the radiator, closing his eyes.

'All right, I think that's enough for now, don't you? I'm going to ask John to call at a shop and get you some clothes and toiletries. Is that OK?'

He shrugged and turned his face to the wall.

Ben looked up from his phone as she emerged from the side room. 'Don't look so worried, we'll take care of him. I'll look in myself tomorrow morning if you like, make sure he's OK. There's nothing for you to do here now, so why don't I go get this sorted and then I can come over to you for a drink later? Where do you live? I'll pick up a bottle of wine on the way.'

'Sorry, but no. Not tonight. I've got to go home, I'm dropping. And I'd better call my manager and tell him what's happened.'

'Not tonight? So, a different night might be OK, then?'

'Yes, maybe. Probably.' She could have said yes to tonight. She'd have plenty of time to warm up and sort herself out before he got there. But now that the responsibility was lifted, she was starting to feel weak and trembly and she needed to be alone. And that wasn't all of it. Something about what had happened on the mountain wasn't sitting right. She couldn't shape it yet and she sure as hell wasn't going to share it and risk disrupting things. Dylan and Rhian were safe and that was what mattered right now. The best thing for her to do was to keep quiet, go home, and let the scene on the Oer run through her mind over and over again until she found the snagging point.

CHAPTER 16

As soon as she got back to her flat, Kit went into the bathroom, stripped off her wet clothes, threw them into the laundry basket and got into a hot shower. She stood under the water for ages, turning the heat up and up, waiting for the shaking to pass, knowing that it was delayed shock and fear. Finally it steadied, and she got out and wrapped herself in her thickest dressing gown, luxuriating in the fluffy warmth as she went into the kitchen to make herself a hot drink. She took her tea and a large vodka through to the living room, where she put the fire on and ordered a pizza, then settled down on the sofa with her phone.

'It's 1 a.m., you know.'

'Sorry, Vern, I didn't realise the time.'

'I've had a heart attack, mind, I need my sleep.'

'It's OK, I'll tell you Monday.'

'No, go on, I'm wide awake now anyway, thanks to you. What's up?' Vernon couldn't bear to not be in the know.

She filled him in on the events of the day, relieved to be able to do it quickly, no tedious explanations necessary, knowing that even at 1 a.m. Vernon would absorb and understand it all at once.

'Sounds like you did well. Though I'm not happy with you for going up there on your own, and you didn't let anyone in the team know either. If you'd been splattered all over the Oer, we wouldn't have had a clue. That was bloody stupid.'

'Sorry, yes, you're right.'

'Still, it was a good call otherwise. So what's bothering you about it? Because I'm assuming you're not ringing me at this hour for no reason. Unless you've got a death wish.'

'I haven't quite worked that bit out.' She stopped and screwed up her eyes, pulling the scene back into her mind, searching for the hitch. 'Something about the dogs. One of them, anyway.'

'What the bloody hell are you on about? What dogs? Are you drunk?'

'No, I'm not. I don't know. Ignore me. But also, Dylan was going to say something and I think it was important. We got interrupted.'

'You're tired and shocked and you're overthinking it. Try to put it out of your mind until Monday. It's all sorted for now. I'm glad about that too, because I've had Gail Wilson ordering me about today, telling me to close it. I've told her where to get off, of course. Now I can tell her we were right.'

'Yeah.' So Tim had gone to Gail over it, just as he'd threatened. He really was relentless. The question of why that might be was looming up once again. But for the moment, maybe it was more important to keep him out of her way than to spend her time trying to figure out what he was up to.

'Vern, do something for me? It's a bit unusual.'

'I am not liking the sound of this.'

'If Gail asks about closing it again, just try to sound like you agree with her.'

'That goes against all my natural instincts. What the hell for?'

'Tim's been hassling me all the way through. It's a complex case and I don't want him barging in and upsetting the Merediths. I need a bit of elbow room.'

'I'll tell him to back off, then. I'm happy to have the row.'

'I know you are. But I think it would make my life easier, only for a week or two. Please? I'm not asking you to outright lie, just be a bit . . . evasive.'

'It's fine, l'll outright lie. Now, are we done?'

'Yes.'

'Good. And by the way, Nell says don't ever call at this time again.'

'I won't. Good night.' She ended the call and sat sipping vodka until her pizza arrived. She ate it quickly, turned the fire up and lay down, intending to think through what had happened. She fell asleep at once.

She woke after nine with a shock, perspiring inside her dressing gown, her mouth dry. She was off the sofa and on her way to the shower before she realised it was Saturday. She felt a twinge of disappointment, followed swiftly by another of self-pity. Had she really turned into a person who had no private life, who'd rather be in work? When had this happened? She'd need to take herself in hand. She'd start by trying to get her focus away from what had happened last night. Vernon was right, there was time enough to think about it on work hours.

She had her shower and dressed, and then made herself a proper breakfast. As she sat eating at the kitchen table, she thought through her options for the weekend. There was Tyler, of course. She hadn't checked in with him for a while, but that was because of the Christine problem, which still lay between them, creating an unusual distance. And she certainly wasn't up to dealing with that whole thing today. Huw and Menna would be thrilled to see her; the thought of Menna's cooking, a cliff walk with Jess, and a night in the cosy bedroom they still kept for her was definitely appealing. But it was a long drive out to Cliffside, and besides, she'd already decided that she ought to start developing some friendships here in Sandbeach. She was doing pretty well with her logic, leading herself exactly where she'd intended to go all along, but then her phone buzzed. Gino. She knew before she even picked it up that something was going to be demanded of her, and that Ben James was going to have to wait.

'Hiya, Dad, what's up?' As if she didn't know. She started walking around the flat, trying to work out where she'd dropped her boots when she came in the night before.

'I went up there first thing, like you asked. You were dead

right; your mother was really bad. Well, she must have been, like, because she didn't chuck me out or throw anything at me. She didn't even give me a mouthful. I thought she was dead for a minute. Then she started talking rubbish.'

'So, what happened?'

'I called an ambulance. They've took her into A & E. I'm going over there now. I've called the other three, seems no one's interested in coming with me.'

Of course they weren't. 'It's OK, Dad, I'm on my way.'

'Thanks, love. You'd better be quick, I reckon. If you want to see her, you know.'

She pulled on her boots, grabbed a coat and her bag, and set off. As she crossed the car park, she called Tyler. He picked up on the second ring.

'Before you start, I'm not going.'

'And before you start, yes, you are.'

'You know why . . .'

'Yes, I do, I know all of it.'

'So what are you going on about, then?'

'You're not getting it, are you? It's not about her. I know you don't understand why I bother and I don't either. But I've stuck with you through everything that's happened and now I need you to do something for me. Just to be there. Because my life is too hard right now, and none of you ever bother asking me about that, do you? It's always my job to look after you lot.'

She was in her car now, pulling on her seat belt, and realised she was shouting, that she had been shouting all the way across the car park. 'I've had it, Ty, I have just had it. I need a favour. You're my twin, for fuck's sake, and you are either going to do it or you're not, and if you don't, I'm not sure where that leaves us, to be honest. I'll see you there.' She ended the call before he could answer and took a few deep breaths to calm herself before she started driving. Then she lit a fag, started the engine and set off for Sandbeach General once again.

As she pulled into the hospital car park Kit remembered that Ben had said he would call in to see Dylan that morning. It was unlikely that she would bump into him, but still, she wished she'd stopped to straighten her hair. After parking as close as she could get to A & E, she followed the signs to reception where she gave her own name and Christine's at the desk. She was directed to a packed waiting area where she eventually located Gino sitting in a corner right at the back. He was huddled over, his head down, a cup of the nasty hospital coffee cradled in his hands. He glanced up as she approached and she saw with surprise that he was upset.

'You OK?'

'Not really. It's given me a shock, it has really. Thanks for coming.'

'It's fine. Tyler'll be along in a bit.'

'I doubt it.'

'He will. I told him to.'

'You always were in charge of him.'

'Yeah, I know. How is she, then?'

'There's no news yet. But I don't think she's got long.'

He was trembling, the coffee tipping over the edge of the cup and dripping onto the floor. She reached out and took it from him gently. 'I'll hold that for a minute.'

'Sorry. I don't know why I'm so upset.'

'Me neither. You two haven't had a good word to say about each other for the last twenty years.'

'I know. It's just – well, it wasn't always like that. You wouldn't remember, only Jasmine would, and Josie, maybe. It wasn't bad right from the start. She could be a great girl, your mother, when she was in the mood, you know?'

'Really?'

'I don't suppose you saw that side of her much, did you?'

'I only saw one side of Christine. Ever.' It was more complicated than that, though. The confusing thing about her mother was that she had been capable of better. In a good mood, on a good day, with a new man in her life and money in her purse, she could suddenly become the other Christine. Funny, happy, treating everyone in sight with ridiculous generosity. Christine could do the ups better than anyone; she just wasn't any good at the downs. She shattered into a thousand fragments as soon as anything went the tiniest bit wrong.

'Yeah, I know what you mean. Always drama with her, wasn't it? I loved all that at first, it's exciting when you're young, you think that's how it ought to feel. But I grew out of it pretty quick and I just wanted to know where I was, what I was coming home to every night.'

'The rest of us wouldn't have minded a bit of that.'

'I know, I'm sorry. You were just kids and you had it worse. I was weak, I see that now. My mam and dad used to tell me to fight for you and maybe I should have. But Christine wanted a fight, that was the thing, just to keep something going between me and her. She'd have dogged me for the rest of my days. So when she said I couldn't see you, I just accepted it. I let her win, but it wasn't a win for me or for you kids. Nor for her, really.'

Kit didn't know that she could be bothered. It seemed late in the day to be asked to reframe her entire childhood. And while it was plausible, and she definitely recognised Christine in there, it wasn't quite enough to excuse him. He'd missed something out, the crux, the bit that should have been the turning point of the story. 'But you knew about us being in care, Dad. You could have got us out, you could have stopped it, and you didn't. Why?'

'Well, they treated you all right in there, didn't they?'

It was all she could do not to get up and walk away from him right now. She'd hoped he'd have a plot twist up his sleeve, something she hadn't seen coming that would let him off the hook so that she could love him again, or maybe just like him. But all he had was spin, a desperate attempt to make himself look better in his own eyes. 'It was better, a lot better, in care than out,' she snapped. 'That ought to give you an idea how bad the out was.'

'What do you mean by that? Are you talking about this

business with Tyler? Mal's heard something, I know she has, but I can't get it out of her.'

Well, good for Mal. 'Yes, that's some of it. Something happened when me and the boys were still living with Christine. They should have taken us in sooner. I wish they had. But I can't tell you anymore. You can ask Tyler if you like.'

'I doubt he'll want to tell me.'

'I doubt it too.' She stood and felt in her pockets for change. 'I'm going for a proper coffee. Text me if anything happens.' She left before he could speak, stopping at reception on the way to ask for directions.

She retraced her steps back to the main entrance, where she spotted the small coffee shop over to one side of the doors. The queue was long, but her need for caffeine and a break from her father was desperate. She waited in the queue, staring out into the car park. She hadn't registered until now that it was sunny outside and the sky was icy blue. If she looked at it for long enough, it was bound to lift her mood. She watched the passers-by outside the hospital windows, thinking that everyone seemed smiley and less hassled now the weather had changed. Visiting time must be about due on the maternity unit; numerous bouquets and bunches of balloons were passing through the main doors. Pink, pink, blue, pink, blue. Green. Green denim. Ben James. Walking alongside a very pretty, petite, dark-haired young woman in a red knitted dress and white Converse. Smiling down at her. She had a stethoscope around her neck. Well, she was a doctor, then. A colleague. Nothing unusual about that whatsoever.

'What can I get you?'

'Two flat whites, please. Actually, three.' Tyler was coming through the doors, his face set in a mega-sulk. He upped the intensity when he spotted her, but she didn't care. He was there, he didn't need to like it.

'She dead yet?'

Kit handed him a coffee and picked up the other two herself. 'Not yet, but Gino reckons she's on her way.'

'He's still here, is he?'

'Yeah. I know, I was surprised he didn't leave me to it. Come on, it's this way.' As they walked towards A & E, she thought back to her conversation with Gino. 'I'd better warn you, Mal knows something.'

'How the hell . . . ?'

'Gossip. It's going round the whole estate. She hasn't told Gino any details but he knows something's up too. It's going to come out sooner or later, Ty. Might be better to get it over with. I've told him he needs to ask you.'

'Well, ta very much. He can ask away.'

'All right, up to you.'

'Yes, it is.' He wasn't relenting on her yet, but he would. They reached the waiting area, where Kit handed a coffee over to her father. Tyler and Gino nodded at each other and then the three of them sat in a row, sipping their drinks. Finally, the doors swung open and a nurse emerged and called Gino's name.

Gino got up reluctantly. 'What's he want me for? I'm not the next of kin.'

But who was? She supposed it must be Jasmine, as the eldest. 'You brought Christine in, though. I guess they've decided on you.'

'What've they done that for?'

'Oh, for God's sake, I don't know, just go and see what he wants.'

'Not got much choice, have I?' He stomped off, disappearing through the swing doors with the nurse. Kit settled down for a long wait but within minutes he was back.

'They're moving her.'

'She's gonna be all right, then? I might have known.' Tyler glared at Kit.

'No. That's not it. She's in a coma, acute liver damage, they said. They're taking her to ITU. They don't think she's going to wake up.'

It was unbelievable how cheated Kit felt. If anyone had asked her whether she was hoping for a deathbed scene, for her mother to finally explain everything, she would have laughed. But it turned out that it was the case. That, in fact, she'd been waiting for just that, and for years now. Instead, Christine was going to bugger off, leaving them all in the dark.

It was another three hours before the nurse came back to tell them they could come up to ITU. Jazz and Josie had been summoned in the meantime. They trooped into the room in turn,

Jazz and Josie first then Kit and Tyler together. As she looked down at her mother, it was clear to Kit that she had already decided to check out. The yellowed, puffy body connected to the ventilator and the lines was an empty shell. There was no real point in all of them being there. It was just admin.

They hung around anyway. No one spoke much. Kit fretted about what would happen if they were asked about switching the ventilator off. Would they all agree, or would someone opt to be awkward just for the sake of it? Meaning Josie, most probably. But at 4 p.m., a different nurse came back, took them all into the relatives' room, and told them with unnecessary gentleness that Christine was brain-dead and there was no point in continuing treatment. No one argued, when it came to it.

'Would you come with me, Mr Goddard? We need to complete some forms, I'm afraid.'

Gino stood and Kit was on her feet along with him. 'No, it's all right,' he told her. 'I'll take care of it.'

All four of them stared at his retreating back as he followed the nurse out of the room, oblivious to their surprise. Jazz and Josie went off for a smoke outside, leaving Kit and Tyler alone in the bland, overheated little room. It was an exact replica of the one downstairs where the two of them had sat clinging together in shock and disbelief after hearing that Danny had killed himself.

'Well, that's that, then. Are you OK?' He was feeling guilty for being mean to her.

'Yeah. I'm just sad that I don't feel that sad.'

'You know that thing about you can't miss what you never had?'

'Yeah?'

'That's bollocks, then.'

'Seems it must be. You miss the hope of having it one day, I guess.'

'That's deep, that is. You could get that put on a tattoo.'

'Shut up.'

'You'd better not be on your own, judging by the absolute state of you. Greasy takeaway, shed-load of booze and an evening in with your annoying brother?'

'Perfect.'

'Let's get this out of the way, then – do you really think I should tell Gino about what happened with me and Danny, and about the court case and all that?'

She nodded. 'I do. I mean, he is trying now, isn't he? In his own way. But I was talking to him earlier and he just doesn't get it. I think he needs to face up to things, understand what he abandoned us all to. Perhaps if he could do that, we could find a way to get along with him.'

'You want to use what happened to me to punish him, you mean?'

'Is that what your therapist reckons?'

'Yeah.'

'She's right. I do.'

'Fair play. I'll think it over, then. Come on, let's go for a fag. I can't sit in here, it's reminding me too much.'

By the time they got back to the relatives' room after two fags each, Gino had reappeared. 'There's a few more bits to do here. There's no point in you lot hanging around, you get going. I'll sort it. I'll call you all tomorrow about the funeral.'

'Funeral?' Tyler muttered, as they all took the opportunity to pile out of the room. 'I wasn't banking on that. Can't we just chuck her in a hole? I'll dig it.'

'That's so disrespectful.'

They all stopped dead and looked at Jazz.

'Quite right.' Josie's tone was serious. 'I think we should have a meaningful ceremony to celebrate the value of Christine's life.' She broke into a grin and all four of them doubled up, blocking the corridor, helpless with laughter.

Once they'd managed to compose themselves, they walked towards the exit, Jazz and Josie leading the way. It was only Tyler's arm going around Kit's shoulder that told her he'd seen when her tears of laughter had turned into something else.

CHAPTER 17

Kit took just over a week off on bereavement leave. She didn't know why, except that Vernon and Nazia seemed to expect her to so she figured that if she didn't, she'd look like a monster. There was nothing to do at home anyway; Gino was dealing with the funeral, and Tyler had gone back to his own flat, perhaps having realised that sleeping on his sister's sofa might cramp his style, Tinder-wise. In the end, she'd packed a bag and gone to Huw and Menna's for a few days. It didn't take her long to find out that the Bayside café was still closed up. Maybe it was time to think about that dinner party, now she had a way to even up the numbers. Whether Ben could ever be anymore than just a way to even up the numbers, she didn't know. But she was lonely, her own procrastination had probably lost her Alex, and Ben seemed like an appealing enough distraction for the time being.

Arriving back at work on Wednesday morning, she felt better at once. News of her work on the Meredith case had spread and she found herself fielding queries from curious colleagues as soon as she arrived. She felt like quite the expert on *folie à deux* by the end of it. It was manically busy, too, the way she loved it, and she happily took a pile of urgent referrals from Vernon and buried herself in them for most of the day. When she finally had them all under control, she took five minutes to run through her messages. She'd dropped Ben a text to let him know she was going to be off work and when she was planning to be back. He'd sent a standard 'sorry for your loss' one in reply and that was that. She'd half expected an update on Dylan to be waiting for her. But there was nothing. She'd give him a call in the morning and see what was happening. And she'd need to pop up and see John, too. She hoped he was doing OK with the dogs.

She was finishing her last bit of recording with thoughts of an early finish when her desk phone rang.

'Kit Goddard, please?' Kit didn't recognise the clipped female voice.

'Speaking.'

'It's the charge nurse on the psychiatric unit here. We've got a discharge referral for you. Name of Meredith.'

'Oh, that's great. When are you thinking of?' Dylan had got better even more quickly than she'd expected. She wondered why Ben hadn't called her himself.

'She's ready to go today, to be honest, but Dr Carver asked us to check with you in case you need to organise anything.'

'Sorry, which unit are you calling from?'

'Ward 2b. Dinas General.'

'Sorry again, but what's the patient's name?'

'It's Rhian Meredith.'

'And she's ready to go? Are you sure?'

'Dr Carver's seen her this afternoon. As I think I did just say, she's fit and well for discharge. So can you get it organised? Say, tomorrow morning?'

'Tomorrow afternoon would be better.' There was nothing to organise but this woman didn't know that and at least it would give her some time to figure out what was going on. First stop, Ben James.

He didn't pick up, of course. She left him a voicemail and set off for home, leaving the volume turned up on her phone. She was back in the flat and busy cooking herself some pasta when it finally rang.

'Hi Kit, are you back at work, then?'

'Yes, I am. Why didn't you let me know about Rhian?'

'Missed you too. Let you know what?'

'I just had a call from a rather snippy nurse. They're discharging her.'

'Are they, now?'

'You didn't know?'

'I'm not in work. I've had a few days off too. Study leave.'

'Really?' Thumping music and numerous voices in the background made this seem an unlikely tale.

'Yeah. Interesting, though. Maybe we were looking at the Merediths the wrong way round all along.'

'Dylan's the one who's ill, you mean? Is that possible? I

mean, he's seventeen, and the story is that this has been going on for a few years. Surely he'd have been too young?'

'As I told you before, it's possible to be psychotic at thirteen or fourteen. It's unusual but it can happen.'

'Right.' She wasn't going to accept it yet. She didn't want it to be true.

'By the way, before I went off, I did a bit more research. I couldn't get hold of anyone in IT to sort the community file. So I pulled Fflur's hospital records out of the archive instead.'

'And?'

'You don't sound very interested. I've chased all this up for you.'

'Well, things have moved on a bit. We know what's wrong with them now, don't we? Or we did until five minutes ago. But go on.'

'She was discharged from Penlan and admitted to a home in November 2011. That'll be why there's placement plans on the community file. Don't know why we couldn't open them, but mystery solved.'

'Does it say which home?'

'Snowdrop Court, as you said.'

'Right. And does it tell us what her mental illness was?'

'Of course. She had schizophrenia. She was very unwell, treatment resistant, hence the long hospital admission. Very paranoid, auditory hallucinations, believed the hospital food was poisoned, etc., etc. Some really intractable beliefs about someone powerful putting her away in the hospital. In the end a new consultant came along and twiddled with the meds and got lucky. The illness might have burnt itself out to an extent by then too, that can happen with schizophrenia. So she stabilised, not enough to go home but enough to be discharged to a place where they'd make sure she took her tablets. The hospital file ends there but from what you said, she died in the home quite soon after. That's not all that unusual, sometimes people don't cope that well with the change of being out of hospital after a long time. It's a shame.'

'Yeah, it is. So, where are you? And when are you back?'

'Not sure. Lots of work to do. I'll give you a call when I am.'

'OK.' The location was definitely right so she was now turning over once again how it could be that Fflur had died in Snowdrop Court when the inspectorate had no record of it.

She called in at the shop on her way home to pick up pancetta, eggs and parmesan for a carbonara, putting it all on to cook as soon as she got into the flat. Once the pasta was boiling, she took out her phone. Four forty-five. She might catch Maxine before she went home.

'Maxine, hi. Sorry to bother you, I was just wondering if you got any further with that case we were talking about. Fflur Meredith.'

'It's proving to be a little more difficult to get to the bottom of than I thought. I can tell you that your information was not quite correct.'

'What? I'm pretty sure now I did have the right home.'

'You did. Fflur Meredith was a resident in Snowdrop Court. But she didn't die there on 14th February 2012.'

'Someone must have entered the wrong date of death on our system, then.'

'No, that's not what I mean. She may well have died on 14th February, but not in Snowdrop Court. She discharged herself from there that day. So if she died, she died after she'd gone home.'

'She can't have. She wasn't safe to go. She had this thing about Mynydd Oer.'

'Where did you get that information from, Kit?'

'I . . . I can't quite recall. But I'm sure it's reliable. It makes sense, based on what I know about the family and their history.'

'I ask because I understand the home did express some reservations, and they were broadly of that nature. But they were overruled. Perhaps they shouldn't have allowed themselves to be.'

'Overruled by who?'

'I haven't got that far, I'm afraid. It was assessed to be a capacitated decision and Jane is looking into it further for me. The archives are a mess there, if I'm honest with you. I can chase her for an update tomorrow?'

'Thanks, Maxine.'

She concentrated on assembling her meal. It looked pretty good. Maybe she could make this when she had people over. She ate it standing up at the cooker, trying to figure out where to go next with the Merediths. It had all been neatly tied up and now it had bloody well unravelled. If it was true that Dylan was psychotic, Rhian had already shown herself to be of no use to him. In fact, she was the opposite. But she was all he had. Where was his father? And what the hell had happened to Fflur? They were all valid questions, but as she poked around in her mind, she knew she was about to dislodge something that had sat on a ledge for ten days, just out of sight. The feeling that she'd read something wrong on that dark, rainy night on Mynydd Oer. She'd pushed her doubts away, because she wanted to believe it was all sorted. It was time to pull them back into view.

After a restless night, she overslept and arrived at work late morning. Only Vernon and Nazia were there, sitting side by side at his desk, getting the allocations done.

'Ah, good. I've got another three for you.' Vernon had emerged from his office and was trying to push a pile of referrals into her hand before she'd even got her coat off.

'Can they wait? Just until tomorrow?'

Nazia glanced at Kit's face. 'I'm sure they could, couldn't they Vern?'

'No, they bloody well can't. I'm short of hands here as it is.'

'Can't Maisie take them?' Kit knew this was unlikely to be successful, but she really didn't need any new work right now. It was worth a shot.

'Says she's got personal problems and I'm overloading her. Blathering on about grievance procedures again.'

'Really? Is she OK?'

'Why do you ask?'

'Remember the last time Maisie was struggling and none of us took much notice?'

'Not likely to forget in a hurry, am I? Irate father finally loses his temper and comes looking for her and I leap in to save the day and land up in cardiac care.'

'Precisely.'

'She didn't say it was work, she said it's personal, therefore I'm not interested. Now, take these off me, will you?' He shoved the papers at her again.

'I can't.'

'For the love of God, not you as well. What's your excuse?'

'It's the Meredith case. It's gone a bit . . . pear.'

'Thought you had that one sewn up? Very good work.'

'Yes and no. It's still definitely a mental health issue but the mother's the one who's got better. Seems like it's Dylan who might be unwell – you know what I was telling you, about one of them being the primary, the one who's really ill?'

Nazia shrugged. 'Well, that's sad to hear but does it make that much difference? He's in the right place. They can treat him, then you can work with him, help him get back on his feet.'

'I guess. It's just I've got a few things I need to follow up on.'

Vernon was about to object but Nazia gave him one of her stern-parent looks. 'That would be fine, Vern, wouldn't it?'

'Depends what you're going to do. No treading on the

delicate little toes of the Mental Health Team, all right? I don't need Gail Wilson down here shouting the odds.'

Nazia tutted. 'Ignore that. He loves a fight with Gail; she's nearly as bloody awkward as he is. Look, there's something about this that's worrying you, Kit, so go and look into it. Trust your own judgement.'

'I will.'

'By the way, Cole's PA brought some papers down for you. I popped them on your desk in case you needed them.'

'Thanks, Nazia. I don't, I'll chuck them now.' It was the print-outs she'd done for Maxine. She picked up the sheaves of paper, crossed to the shredding bin and dropped them in. It reminded her about Fflur's file and her suspicions that it contained something that Tim didn't want to become general knowledge. 'Naz, can I ask you something? If I try to open a file and I'm getting a message saying "incorrect permissions", what does it mean?'

'Means you shouldn't be noseying in it,' Vernon grumbled.

'Ignore that too, Kit. He's just sulking. It means the file has been locked down.'

'Locked down? Why?'

Nazia perched on the desk next to her. 'There must be something on it that's restricted access. Might be a complaint about a member of staff – those get locked so that the rest of us can't have a gander, especially if it might run on to a disciplinary. Occasionally it might be a staff member's child or relative that's come to our attention and it wouldn't be appropriate for all and sundry to be able to find out about it. You wouldn't want your colleagues to know if there was a safeguarding issue with your own child, would you? So it's on a need-to-know basis, restricted to a certain manager and only they can give individual access if and when needed. There's a procedure around here somewhere. Where is it, Vern?'

'I binned it.'

'Oh, well done. Does that answer your question? I can look at it if you need access to something specific, we can speak to IT.'

'No, it's fine for now. Thanks.' It all fitted perfectly, but it was too soon to mention her suspicions that Tim was covering up a mistake. She didn't want the whole thing taken off her just so that HR could stampede all over it, not until she'd sorted Dylan out. 'So, I can go on with the Merediths for today, then?'

Vernon sighed. 'Oh, all right. But no getting battered on any mountaintops. You've had your time off for this year.'

'I promise.' She left, signing out for Dinas. As she ran down the stairs, she pondered what Nazia had said. She was bound to be right, but that still left the question of how Frankie Freeman had been able to open a restricted file. Not to mention the bigger one of what Tim might be covering up by restricting it in the first place.

Once in the car, Kit pulled out her phone to see whether there was a call or a text from Ben. He'd called her three times but hadn't left a voicemail. No doubt the hospital were keen to shift Rhian. She called him back and while waiting for him to pick up, pondered what excuse she could make to hold them off until she had just a tiny clue about what was going on.

He picked up at last. 'Oh, hi.'

'Go on, what's the bad news?'

He laughed too forcefully. 'It's a bit of a mess, I'm afraid.'

'Spit it out.'

'Dr Del reviewed Dylan yesterday too. He's fit to go.'

'What?'

'They'll be sending him home. The neighbour's agreed to collect them – John Ellis, is it? The mother refused to have you transport them. She's raring to get out, the boy doesn't seem so keen for some reason. He's a closed book, isn't he? I'd be worried about that, if I were you.'

She supposed this was intended to mark the transfer of responsibility back to her. 'Yes, I am. When will they be going?'

'I've managed to persuade the wards to hold off both discharges until teatime today in case you need to organise anything. It really was not easy.'

'Thanks. How did you manage it?'

'Let's just say the charge nurse on the mother's ward owed me a favour.'

That would be Ms Snippy, she assumed. 'What about the one on Dylan's ward?'

'She owed me a favour too.'

'Cracking bit of luck, that.'

'Yeah, I know. Amazing.' He coughed. 'And hey, this is a

good thing, right? We wouldn't want a boy of that age in the psychiatric system, not really.'

'Of course not. Now let's get back to the bad news.'

'Meaning?'

'Ben, you sound like you're about to jump off a cliff, what else is there?'

'Dr Del's not too happy.'

'With you? Well, that's usual, isn't it?' But she already knew the answer.

'With me, yes, but she's pissed off with you now too. I've got her notes here, I'll read the summary to you: *Mother and son, vulnerable and isolated, fearful of the community, some over-valued ideas upon admission, the intensity of these has now diminished. Both guarded but no positive symptoms noted upon examination and none observed since admission. No responding to unseen stimuli. Mother gave an account of unwisely embarking on a walk up the Oer in deteriorating weather to lay flowers for her father, whereupon the pair became disorientated and distressed, police arrived and social worker claimed they were suicidal. The boy is less communicative but does not deny his mother's account.* Basically, there's nothing to justify keeping them. She's fuming. She feels we've wasted her time and landed two people in hospital for no good reason, one of them under detention.' He sounded almost tearful now. Wuss.

'Well, she's obviously gone and given Dylan his mother's story up front. Has she got a clue what she's doing? Of course he wouldn't deny it. Anyway, she's the bloody psychiatrist. She admitted them, not me.'

'Yes, but she admitted them based on what you told me.'

'Well, not entirely. She spoke to them herself, after all.' A suspicion crossed Kit's mind that Ben had tried to pass the blame for all this on to her and omitted mention of his own contribution to the *folie à deux* theory. 'Well, anyway she's not my boss, so she can do one.'

'You tell her that if you like. But she's already saying she's going to make a formal complaint about you.'

Kit laughed to cover up a flash of anger. 'She can speak to Vernon Griffiths. I'm sure he'll give her a quick response.' She had never loved Vernon more than she did in that moment. Nevertheless, once she'd ended the call, she felt a bit of a panic starting up. She'd been enjoying the kudos that had come her way for this, and it was going to be embarrassing to climb down. But more importantly, Dylan and Rhian were going to be put right back where they'd started. She started the car but she couldn't work out where to go next.

CHAPTER 18

'Back again so soon?' Nazia was taking a late lunch, lolling in her chair, her feet in their immaculate Ted Baker suede boots resting on her desk. She didn't look up from her reading of *Closer*.

'Yeah.' Kit took a chair at the desk next to Nazia's, wondering how to break the news about the mess she'd got herself into. Nazia sighed and put the magazine down, carefully turning the corner of her page.

'Tell all, then, I've got five minutes of freedom, his lordship's busy having his final sign-off with occupational health.'

'It's such a muddle. It's gone wrong in about ten different directions.'

'Start with the most urgent bit.'

'I think the psychiatrist's going to make a complaint about me.'

'She can try. Vern doesn't stand for that kind of thing.'

'What don't I stand for?' Vernon was lumbering across the office, a paper bag in hand from the bakery over the road.

'Kit's in trouble with that psychiatrist.'

'Ha! Is she, now? My staff only get in trouble with me. What are you supposed to have done?' He offered the bag around and then went to lean against the door jamb of his office, selecting a doughnut as he went.

Kit explained quickly. No need to take up everyone's time with this; she'd known Vernon would stand by her and the business with Dr Carver was the least important part of the whole thing. When she reached the end, Vernon gave her a quick nod. 'Right, no problem. If she rings me, I'll tell her where to get off.'

'Thanks, Vern.'

'No worries, she can keep her beak out. I'll schedule it for your next supervision, then, don't let me forget.'

'Schedule what?'

'The Meredith case, of course. I mean, don't start worrying over it, we all make mistakes.'

'I didn't make a mistake.'

'Hate to contradict you, but it appears you did. I don't know this Carver woman and I don't like the sound of her either, but she's a consultant psychiatrist. We have to accept what she says. Seems to me that you and this junior doctor of hers got a bit carried away. Too clever by half, the pair of you. Put it down to experience, learn the lesson and move on, OK? Now I'm going to get cracking on the files, see how badly you lot have cocked up while I've been away. I'm not likely to end up in a good mood so don't disturb me for at least two hours, right?' He picked out an eclair and backed into his office, pushing the door shut with his foot.

Kit was crushed. Not because he'd said she was wrong; Vernon said that to everyone in the team on a regular basis, but because he had looked disappointed in her. To top it off, Nazia's expression was not dissimilar.

'You think I screwed it up too, do you?'

'No need to be so hard on yourself. Like Vernon said, we all make mistakes. Now, shall we see what we can do about it?'

'Actually, I think I'll go for my lunch now, if that's all right? I'll catch you later.'

Nazia put out her hand, trying to catch hold of Kit's arm. 'Don't. We can sort it, I'm sure. Don't run away.'

'It's fine.' Run away, indeed. She left without signing out, pounding down the stairs and out of the building, and was already in her car before she stopped to think that she still had no idea where she was going. She felt like hiding for a bit, and she didn't want to talk, but she didn't fancy being completely alone either. If only she could have had Jess to live with her. She'd been with Kit through all of her most difficult times, right up until she left Huw and Menna's. She would have been all the company Kit needed right now, but she wasn't allowed a dog in her flat.

Half an hour later, she arrived in Rock. Getting out of the car outside John's, she realised she only had her hoody. But the weather was mild and quite sunny and the Oer was looking fresh and inviting. Almost verdant, in places. She'd be fine. All she needed to do was to get the dogs from John, resist his Welsh cakes and his gossip, and get herself up there in the fresh air.

He opened the door as she started up the path, bent double trying to hold the dogs back as they barked and leapt behind him. 'Hello, Kit, I wondered if you'd be up. Have you heard? They're discharging them. I'm to pick them up teatime today. Does it seem too soon to you?'

'I'm not sure, John. They're the experts, not me, apparently. Could I borrow the dogs? I fancy a walk.'

'Well, see, they've already been out this morning. I've walked the legs off them. The two old boys, I think it's enough for them for one day.' He'd managed to force Griff and Tomos back from the door now and they'd wandered off, but Bella was still struggling to get past him, her nose appearing now and again to one or the other side of his knees.

'Just Bella, then?'

'Yes, all right. I'll be leaving in an hour so drop her back before then. Or no, you may as well take the key and drop her back at Rhian's, they'll be home in a bit.'

'Will do.'

He shut the door and disappeared for a few minutes, returning with Bella, who was modelling a smart red tartan collar and matching lead.

'I bought them some bits, plus food and treats and so on, it seemed easier than going up the house.' Judging by Bella's size, the treats had far outweighed the exercise over the past ten days. Kit took the lead from John, and he handed her an old-fashioned mortise key too.

'Perhaps I'll see you later. Call in if you see my light on, we can have a chat, get our heads together about what to do next.'

'I will.' No chance. She'd already decided she was going straight from the mountain to her sofa. Sod the bloody lot of them.

She began to walk, letting Bella off the lead as soon as they got to the mountain path. Her mood wasn't lifting as quickly as she'd expected. In fact, she was feeling more and more dejected. She pulled out her phone, wanting to shout at someone, but that was just going to result in someone shouting back, or worse, wanting a discussion about it. She brought up Alex's last message and started tapping out a text, meaning only to tell him that Christine had died. Finding it quite cathartic, she added more of her grievances, including being in trouble at work for things that were definitely not her fault, but omitting the whole topic of Ben James and her doubts about whether he had helped to land her in it. She was about to press Send when she realised that there was something else she needed to say. She missed him, that was the truth. She added it quickly and sent the text before she could change her mind.

Feeling slightly better, she started to take in more of her surroundings. She'd drawn level with the place where she'd spotted the den in the trees when she'd been walking with Dylan. It was probably Aled and Joe's booze and weed den, she realised, based on Aled's habitual scent. The memory of his terrified expression when she had threatened to mention the topic to his mother cheered her as she moved on, Bella trotting happily beside her, and she didn't stop again until they reached the viewing point.

She gasped as she stepped out onto the ledge. She had completely forgotten what it was like up here in good weather. The brightness of the day was softening as the sun started to go down across the distant sea. She left Bella snuffling about in the gorse and wandered over to the bench, where she sat down to enjoy the sight of Rock, laid out below her like a model village.

But as soon as she settled, her mind strayed back to that scene on the mountain. What was it that was still bothering her? She replayed it from the beginning. She saw herself arriving, unsure why she was even there and full of trepidation. Then spotting the two older dogs, searching for Bella and finding her too. Her first sight of the two dark figures, the realisation that it was Dylan and Rhian, standing together on the ledge, holding each other. Hanging back, watching their movements, taking in their body language, finding herself able to read it as if they were speaking their intentions out loud. She'd seen what they were about to do and she'd called to Dylan and then watched as the two of them swung round and Rhian nearly went over the other side. Dylan, finally, filled with the rage he'd suppressed, flinging his mother away from danger. She'd understood at last why it was that Dylan never retaliated. He wasn't afraid to do it; he was afraid he wouldn't be able to stop.

But there was a gap. What had she missed? She hovered over

the scene again and saw the two head movements Dylan had made, the first as if he thought someone was calling him from the far end of the ledge, and the second as if he was checking the same direction for instructions. Was that what psychiatrists meant when they talked about responding to unseen stimuli? Had Dylan been hearing a voice, a command maybe? Ben had talked about that, and about how people could know it was best not to let on that they were hearing voices. He'd said that Dylan was guarded and she'd thought exactly the same. Maybe they'd missed something in the hospital? And maybe she'd missed it too, because she hadn't wanted to admit it all along.

She got up to call Bella to her. She didn't come so Kit followed the sound of scrabbling until she found her deep in the gorse, nose to the ground, tracking some scent or other.

'What are you doing there, girl? Come on.' Leaning forward to catch Bella's collar and drag her out, Kit saw that the dog's digging had pushed back a patch of undergrowth and uncovered a rocky path that lay beneath it. She put Bella on her lead and then straightened up to get her bearings. Memories of her grandad came flooding back. 'The grockles don't know about it, see, or they're scared of it. But it's a safe enough way down, as long as you know your way.' Of course, this was the entrance to the stairway. Or used to be, although it didn't look at all accessible now. It was the exact direction Dylan had been looking in when he had seemed to be casting around for instructions that night, just before he finally changed tack and made up his mind not to jump. And it was the direction Bella had been looking in too, the place where she'd been directing her aggression.

She needed to get off the Oer, and quickly. She started to weigh up which way to go, but it was obvious that she should take the stairway. Not because it was quicker, but as a means to check her burgeoning understanding. The path looked impassable after the first few feet, but she was determined to push through it. If her mind could still find the light switches in Christine's house, surely it had retained her grandad's repeated instructions about how to negotiate the hidden way down his beloved Oer?

And although it was even more overgrown than she'd feared, her familiarity with the twists and turns of it did kick in. She slipped and slid some of the way, and once or twice it was Bella who picked up the path where she had lost it, but the most dangerous bits stood out to her as if illuminated, bringing her grandad's voice back. 'Slowly here, cariad, small steps and you'll be safe.' As she reached the lower levels, the way got easier and she could concentrate on her next move.

She assembled what she knew, starting not with Fflur, or even with Rhian and Dylan, but with the boring-looking journal of psychiatry that John had photocopied for her a couple of weeks ago, which she had glanced at and chucked in the recycling bin. She'd been interested in the young couple. Whereas she now saw that the answer might lie in the other case, the one she'd skipped over. The family.

She slid the last few feet and arrived at the bottom of the mountain. She crossed the lowest slopes easily and found her way to the entrance to Sunnyside. She was suddenly very glad to have Bella with her. She had no idea what awaited her at Ty Olaf and she was suddenly quite squeamish about finding out. But she had to get there before Rhian got back, that was for sure. And there was something else she needed to take care of too. All along, she'd felt that Tim was working against her. Now the feeling gathered strength, and although she couldn't yet put together what he'd done or why, she knew that he must have played a part in Fflur's disappearance from Snowdrop Court.

By some miracle, Ben answered his phone immediately. 'Hiya, how's things?'

'Are you at the CMHT?'

'Yes, why? Have you missed me?'

'I haven't got time for that now. Is Tim still in the office?'

'Charming. Yes, I think I've seen him slithering about.'

'I need you to keep him there.'

'You what?'

'For Christ's sake, it's not hard. Make sure he doesn't go home.'

'How am I meant to do that? It's gone five now.'

'Ask him to meet you in the pub in a bit.'

'Kit, I really don't think—'

'Please, Ben?'

He sighed. 'Oh, OK. I'll see if I can catch Tim now, send him off to the pub.'

'Great. Once you've done that, wait where you are. Do not move. I'll call you back.'

She was running out of time now. John couldn't be much longer getting Rhian and Dylan. But she had to think ahead, and she needed Tim's ID number. Could she remember it? In her mind, she put herself back into the office, where she'd borrowed the badge from him that day. She couldn't pull the number itself back to mind, though. She'd entered it into her computer and swiped the badge in the printer and then she had stood with Tim watching the sheets churning out. The same ones she'd thrown in the shredding bin just that morning. Each one marked with the crucial six-digit code she needed.

She rang Ricky's work extension. It was just after five now, though; he might easily have gone home.

'First Response Team. Maisie Parfitt.'

The universe must hate her. That was the only possible conclusion. 'Hiya, Maze, is Ricky there?'

'Well, no, obviously, or he'd have picked up his own phone. He's gone home, sorry.'

'Of course. Look, I need a favour. It's going to sound a bit unusual.'

'I'm not getting involved in anything dodgy. I have my career to think about.'

'No, it's not dodgy. Could you just go into the shredding bin and find some print-outs? I dropped them in there this morning by mistake. Evans, a couple of others. One sheet will do.'

'Whatever for?'

'I need the ID number off the top.'

'I'll have a look now.' Maise was back after a few seconds. 'They're not in there,' she announced.

'What? They must be.'

'No, you see, the bin gets collected on a Thursday. If you put them in there this morning, they'll be long gone. But Kit? Why don't you know your own ID number? You'll find it on your badge.'

'It's not mine I'm after. It's Tim's.'

'What on earth for?'

'I haven't got time to explain. Can you get it for me?'

'Me? How can I do that without telling him why?'

'You're going to have to lie. Make up a reason, just be casual about it. Say yours isn't working and you need to access the system or something. Please, Maisie, I'm sorry to ask but it's really important. I know it's awkward for you.'

'Not really. I'm not sure things are working out between me and Tim. I'm thinking of ending it. I haven't told him yet but it's for the best.'

'You OK ? I meant to give you a text before but I didn't get round to it, with everything else.'

'I'm all right. Let's just say Tim's not the person I thought he was. Intense. I think he could be quite obsessed with me.'

'Do you reckon? Really? But you are all right, aren't you?'

'Yeah, kind of. Anyway, I'll tell you another time. Five minutes, I'll get it out of him and text it to you.'

As soon as the text arrived, Kit rang Ben's number again. He answered within two rings.

'About bloody time. I've sent Tim to the pub to wait for me. I'm in danger of him thinking we're mates or something. What's with all the mystery?'

'Never mind. I need you to take the ID number I'm going to give you and use it to open Fflur Meredith's file. Go to the placements section and tell me what's in it.' She read him the number.

'OK, doing it now. Got it.'

'Anything look odd to you?'

'Umm, not really. Well, only that it's not very clear who was responsible for her right at the end. We usually transfer people over to the team in the new area three months after discharge. I can't quite see whether that had happened or not, looks like she might have fallen between the two and no one picked it up, but she died around that time anyway, didn't she? Actually, it seems she died on 14th February, the same day the transfer was meant to happen. So I guess it never went ahead and it wouldn't have been clear who was responsible on the day itself. Talk about the right hand not knowing what the left was doing.'

'Yeah, maybe. One more thing. Did anyone visit her while she was in Snowdrop Court? Professionally, I mean.'

'Well, yes, they would have. The care manager always does a review after the first week and again at six weeks.'

'And that was who?'

'I'll take a look.' After a couple of seconds he was back on the phone, his voice uncertain. 'Kit. It looks like it was Tim.'

'Looks like?'

'I mean, it definitely was Tim. But if he had the case all along—'

'Then he knew exactly where she'd died.'

'So why did he say she died in Penlan? She definitely didn't. It's right here in front of me. What the fuck is he up to?'

'That's what I'm trying to work out. Right, go to the pub and stay there until I text you.'

'You aren't going back up the mountain again or anything soft like that, are you?'

'Not the mountain, no.' But he had a point. She should at least let someone know. She needed Ben to stay put. Vernon would throw a hissy fit, Nazia would say something clever to talk her out of it. Ricky would flap. She needed the calmest, steadiest person she knew. 'Ben, one more thing. Call the Public Protection Unit and ask for Dai Davies. Have him rung at home if he's not in the station. Tell him I'm going to the Merediths' house in Rock, the address is on Fflur's file. Ask him to follow me up there.' She ended the call, before he could argue.

She'd lost more than half an hour faffing about on the phone. But it had been necessary. For once, she had pulled herself back and laid a proper foundation for what she was about to do. Bella was pulling at the lead now, fed up with all the standing about and picking up the stress in Kit's voice too, no doubt. She reassured the dog with a rub to her ears and then set off, the last light of the evening helping her out by showing her the way without the need for her torch.

CHAPTER 19

The house stood in total darkness, as she'd expected. She went straight to the front door and tried the key, holding her breath as she attempted to turn it, fully expecting a creaking noise from the old lock. But it wouldn't budge. It definitely wasn't the right key. Of course, John had said that Fflur had passed this key on. How long ago had that been, for God's sake? The lock had probably been changed at least a couple of times since then. So much for her newly hatched planning skills.

She tiptoed to the back of the house, where she picked her way very carefully into the porch, but she saw that the pile of logs was stacked in its place, the axe lying neatly on top. The hairs on her arms rose; again, it was what she'd been expecting, but the confirmation still ratcheted her nerves up several levels. She held Bella's lead in one hand, sliding the key into the lock with the other, and felt it turn smoothly. She hesitated for one last moment; entering a client's home without permission, using a key she shouldn't have had in the first place, was totally unethical. She'd be lucky to get away with it if she was right, and if she was wrong, she'd be back waitressing at Alex's café in short order, and for good. But then she glanced again at the pile of logs and her resolve returned. No one would have been near the house since she'd knocked the logs over on the day Dylan and Rhian went into hospital.

She pushed the door open and slipped into the kitchen. The familiar smell hit her, the dust and trapped air, together with something new. Something fishy. Tinned pilchards or mackerel, maybe. She sniffed hard and looked about, but it was getting properly dark now. Could she risk a quick flash of her torch? She took her phone out and swept the beam across the kitchen, picking up a plate on the table with the remnants of a meal on it. She couldn't risk leaving the torch on long enough to try to ascertain how long the dirty plate might have sat there. The flash of light had startled Bella, who began to growl and suddenly let out a ringing bark, making Kit's heart jump so violently she thought she might be sick. From somewhere above her head came a creak. An old house shifting and settling? Or the sound of someone moving upstairs?

She soothed Bella and then let her off the lead. The dog trotted off into the shadows and flopped down with a satisfied grunt. Pushing open the door that her mapping of the house told her must lead to the hall, Kit could just make out the staircase; she fumbled her way over to it and started up, hardly able to see the uneven steps, feeling for each one with her foot as she went. At the top stood four doors, two to the front of the house and two to the back. Which one to choose? She thought back to Dylan's face at the front left-hand window of the house, and the awful screams that had rung out from there. She flipped the scene in her mind and selected the door on the front and to the right.

Inky darkness and total silence met her as the door yielded to her slow push. If anyone was in this room, they weren't breathing. Only a wait would show her why that was. Seconds ticked by before the sound of someone desperately sucking in a mouthful of air told Kit that she was not alone. It had come from over to her right, and as her eyes adjusted, she made out a large bed frame standing in roughly the same spot.

'Hello?'

Nothing, then another small suck inwards, then silence again.

'Hello?' Moving towards the bed, Kit was more frightened than she had ever been. The breathing sound started up again as she drew closer to the source of it, becoming fast and rasping now. They were both of them terrified of each other, she realised. But she was the one who had to get control. 'You must be very scared. I'm not here to hurt you. I'm only here to help.'

A shift and a creak in the centre of the bed. She took another step and reached it. There was a shape in the middle of the mattress, huddled under some covers. Definitely a person, but very small, turned on their side, facing away from Kit, with what looked like a tiny shoulder jutting a few inches up into the air. Momentarily, she thought it was a child. Then she remembered Rhian's delicate build. It clearly ran in the family; on the female side, at least.

'Fflur? Can I talk to you?'

From outside came the sound of a car pulling up. John must have driven right up to the gate. In a few seconds they'd all be in the house, but it didn't matter. She had what she needed now. She knew who the real primary had been all along. She understood why Dylan and Rhian had been so reluctant to let her into the house. They'd been told not to. And it explained so many other things, too. Why Dylan had insisted she keep so quiet that one time she'd managed to wangle her way in; he'd been rebelling against Fflur just a little, but still afraid she would hear.

Most of all, it explained why they had both got better in hospital. Exactly as Ben had said, their delusions had run out of steam once they were removed from the source. Delusions which had been building since Fflur had somehow managed to get herself out of Snowdrop Court and into hiding in Ty Olaf. At some point she'd resumed her obsessive walking of the Oer, going out at night so as not to be seen, taking her daughter and grandson with her, looking for her husband, and finally finding a way for the family to be reunited. Until Kit had interrupted them on the mountain. Then she'd headed off down the stairway and hidden in Ty Olaf, huddling away on her own while Dylan and Rhian went to hospital, both of them determined to keep their secret. She must have been terrified, tortured by her delusions and hallucinations, unable to go out or summon help, wondering whether they would ever come back. The sheer torment of Fflur's troubled life brought tears flooding into Kit's eyes and without a second thought, she sat down on the bed and placed her hand lightly on the bony shoulder, meaning only to pat it reassuringly.

The figure flew out of the bed and onto its feet, emitting that unforgettable shrill scream just inches from Kit's face. Kit knew she had let out a scream of her own, but it was only from the surprise of it. She understood now that Fflur wouldn't hurt her, hadn't ever meant to hurt anybody. Seconds later, the sound of footsteps hammered on the stairs and Dylan burst into the room, followed by Rhian, her face changing from fear to anger as she hit the light switch and Kit was revealed, still sitting on the bed.

'Get out,' Rhian spat, moving towards Kit, her furious eyes on her face, her tone gathering force as she came. 'Get out of my house. Get out, get out, get out—'

'Stop it, Mam. That's not going to help us,' Dylan yelled. Fflur had run to him and he had hold of her now, just as Kit had seen him hold his mother so many times, securing her in his arms. 'It's all right.' He held out an arm to Rhian and she ran to him too; he gathered them both close and turned to Kit. 'Just tell us what to do.'

There was only one thing she could say but she had no idea how Fflur and Rhian might react and she couldn't rely on Dylan to protect her. 'Dylan, your grandmother needs treatment.'

'Grandmother? What are you talking ... ?' John's voice trailed away as he appeared from behind Dylan and took in the scene. 'Mrs Meredith?' John looked, for a moment, really frightened. Perhaps the stories of ghostly Fflur walking the Oer had got to him more than he'd admitted. But Kit saw him regain his equilibrium almost at once, the unruffled prison officer taking over. 'I'm not sure what's happened here but what can I do to help, Kit?'

'I've got something else I need to see to. A police officer's going to be here any minute. DS Dai Davies. Please tell Dai that I said Fflur needs to be assessed by a psychiatrist.'

Fflur started to whimper, clinging to Dylan. It was heart-rending; the sound of pure fear. Dylan looked at Kit again, uncertain now.

'I'm sorry, Dyl, but you know I'm right. You can't go on like this. It's no way to live. For any of you. I think your gran was better than this when she first came home, and your mother was well back then too. Things have changed and we need to get the two of them back to how they were. That's all I want to do, so you three can have a good life together again.'

He nodded, and she could see that he had finally decided. Somehow, she had won him round. 'John, Dylan will help you with the details. Just tell Dai that Fflur was in Snowdrop Court residential home and she ... well, she kind of went missing. She's got a long psychiatric history and she's been living up here untreated for several years. I can explain it all later but he needs to get her seen. There's a psychiatrist, Dr Carver, she's going to kick off big time, but tell Dai not to take any notice, she's the best person to assess Fflur.'

'Right, I'll let the officer know.' John was one hundred per cent in professional mode now, busy taking mental notes for his handover. 'In case DS Davies asks, how did Mrs Meredith manage to go missing for all these years without anyone knowing?'

He'd certainly gone straight to the heart of it. 'Well, let's just say I think she had some help.'

'Who would do a thing like that? And why?'

'The who, I can't tell you and the why, I don't know yet.' Glancing at Dylan, she saw that his expression was just as curious as John's. But Rhian's body language had changed. She'd pulled away from Dylan and straightened up; she looked directly into Kit's eyes and didn't drop her gaze. She was silently pleading. Begging Kit not to push any further as to exactly why someone would have helped Fflur to leave Snowdrop Court. Disgust rose in Kit's throat as she saw the final bit of the picture fall into place. The part that was now sitting in a pub, making polite conversation with Ben James.

After answering a few more of John's questions, Kit headed off to her car, texting Ben as she went. The roads were clear and dry and she was back in Sandbeach and had parked her car in the CMHT car park within forty minutes. As she approached the main doors, she was relieved to see that there were lights on; Ben must have done what she'd asked and found a pretext to bring Tim back to the office.

The door was unlocked and as she let herself in and slipped

the latch down behind her she heard voices towards the back of the building. She followed the sound through a short corridor that opened into the staff room, where she found Ben and Tim sitting at the kitchen table drinking coffee.

'Kit, I didn't know you'd be joining us. So, where have you been until this hour? Not working, I hope?' Tim looked like he'd had a few. His nose and upper cheeks were flushed and his speech was slightly slurred. All the better to get the truth out of him.

Kit took a chair opposite Tim. To her right-hand side, she felt Ben tense in anticipation. 'I have been working, Tim, yes.'

'Good, good, very dedicated.'

'I've been to see the Merediths.' She didn't intend to drag this out. She shouldn't really be there at all. Strictly speaking, she should have handed the whole thing over to Cole or to Gail Wilson and left it to take its course. She had no business involving herself in disciplinary matters. But Tim Page was sly. He had evaded detection for so long and now she needed someone to witness the whole story through just the once, so that he had no way out later on. No opportunity to fiddle with the records, that being his MO.

'What? Why would you be doing that? Gail specifically agreed with Vernon that the case would be closed.'

'Yeah. Vernon lied about that.' She paused, watching him flail, hating him for what he'd done to the family, to Dylan and Fflur, but most of all to Rhian. 'So, Tim, I guess it's been stressful keeping the secret but you certainly had a few lucky breaks along the way, didn't you? Seventeen years' worth. But they ran out in the end.'

Tim's face displayed something that could have been taken for incomprehension, but for his Adam's apple bobbing as he swallowed repetitively.

'So how did you manage it, Tim? Let's see. I guess Frankie Freeman accessed Fflur's file right at the start, before you even knew the referral had come in on Dylan. It turned out fine for you, because Georgia wouldn't allocate the case anyway, so you were off the hook. You closed Fflur's file down, though, just in case. I guess you didn't know at that point that Frankie had already taken a look. You wanted to be doubly sure it wouldn't get spotted that no one had management of Fflur when she died and that the only confirmation that she'd died at all had come from you. And you definitely didn't want anyone getting wind that she'd been in Snowdrop Court and had been allowed to just go home.'

She noticed that Tim's teeth were working at his lip. Could something like that be inherited?

'So,' she continued, 'you'd managed to keep Fflur locked away in Penlan all those years. Must have been easy enough, sounds like she was really ill. Did you set it up? Did you plan on getting her into hospital, or did you just spot an opportunity once her mental health finally failed and she was off the scene? You'd never have got close to Rhian while Fflur was there, for sure. You went up there as Fflur's social worker,

I assume, and Rhian caught your eye. But Fflur was quite a character, I've heard. An overprotective, domineering mother. She'd have seen you off. And I'm guessing when Rhian got pregnant, she didn't tell Fflur the truth about the father, not at that point, anyway. Fflur was probably too ill, too distressed to stand it. Then Fflur gets a new psychiatrist, she starts to get better and she works it out, perhaps? Or maybe Rhian told her in the end. Either way, you must have thought your number was up. Fflur knew the truth about you and Rhian, and what was worse, she was doing quite well, so she wasn't looking so unreliable anymore. It must have been touch and go whether Fflur might tell someone that you'd had a . . . what shall we call it . . . an *inappropriate* relationship with her vulnerable daughter, got her pregnant and abandoned her, and whether anyone might just believe it.'

'*What?*' Ben's mouth was hanging open. Tim's face had taken on a contemptuous sneer, but the glare from the strip lights was picking up a film of sweat on his upper lip. She should leave it right there; enough had been said, but he disgusted her with his salivating and sweating and his using of women and she wanted to press on.

'Well, you see, Ben, Fflur wasn't completely well at the end, too well to be in hospital, not well enough to be at home, but just about all right to go somewhere supervised. Except that Snowdrop Court weren't so hot on the supervision, were they, Tim? Or on anything, especially not the procedure for assessing capacity. So, you made a reappearance in Rhian's life, just long enough to do a deal with the family. Fflur wanted to go home and Rhian wanted her back, too. It wasn't the best thing for either of them but they have an enmeshed relationship, I think that's what it's called, Ben? So Tim here arranged for Fflur to go, told Snowdrop Court he'd assessed her as capable of making the decision, and Snowdrop Court didn't question it. Or not enough to make a difference. But once she was home, he had her right where he wanted her, because more than anything Fflur feared getting sent back into Penlan. And she thought he could do that to her. She'd walked right into his trap. If she did decide to tell, or if any of them let slip she was there, she thought she'd be sectioned and institutionalised for what was left of her life.'

Ben was fidgeting irritably. 'Hang on a minute. What about her meds? What about her care plan?'

'She didn't have any meds, that's the point. She went home and she got worse and worse. You must have known that would happen, Tim, but you just left Rhian and Dylan to contain it. Except they didn't. They started to slide down with her. Rhian had got herself together before then. I guess you left her to it once you knew she was pregnant, but she's strong like her mother and they did OK, her and Dylan. Once Fflur came home, though, they had to live a secret life, with no one and nothing to act as a touchstone. Rhian just couldn't keep track of reality once she was around Fflur's untreated illness 24/7. Neither could Dylan, in the end.'

'That still doesn't explain the care plan. She was a detained patient, we have to follow them up by law, how could she just disappear? Also, she'd have had a GP, they'd have a record on her.' Ben was still not quite there. Kit decided to leave the bit about the GP. She had a suspicion, but the last thing she wanted was to be the one to get Rhian into trouble if she'd been interfering with records too. No doubt it would come out in time. The rest was easy, though.

'She didn't disappear, Ben. Think about it. She goes to Snowdrop Court, she lasts three months. As far as the home are concerned, she's discharged home on 14th February. As far as the two community teams are concerned, she's all settled down in a permanent bed in Snowdrop Court awaiting transfer to the Dinas patch; Tim's got an eye on her, he's keeping everyone informed. He's holding all the cards. No one's got their eye on the ball when Tim reports to both community teams that sadly Fflur's died in Snowdrop Court on the very day case responsibility was due to transfer across. He marks the death down on the system, case closed. Rhian tells the few people she still talks to in Rock that her mother's finally died after years away in nursing care with an illness. Did anyone in the CMHT check any of this? No, they bloody didn't. They trusted old Tim here. Why wouldn't they? He's a manager, after all. Have I got it right, Tim?'

'I did not take advantage of Rhian Meredith. Just the opposite. She pursued me, she was obsessed with me. The woman's quite mad, like her mother.'

Kit had to laugh. 'That's not going to wash anymore, I'm

afraid. She was the daughter of a client, Tim. She was lonely and vulnerable, she'd only ever had her mum and she'd been taken away. You fathered a child with her and then made sure she didn't tell anyone. What did you threaten her with? Never mind. I'd save it for the disciplinary if I were you. Not to mention the professional registration hearing. You thought it was all done and dusted, didn't you? Until someone spotted something was wrong and referred Dylan in.'

Tim's head was down now, his eyes fixed on the table. Glancing at Ben, Kit could see that he was still full of questions, but they'd have to wait. She needed to get this wrapped up and get to Dylan. Tim looked as if he was going to sit there until someone gave him instructions.

'I think you'd best go home, Tim. Don't think about trying to alter the records or any of that caper and don't go near the Merediths. I'll be calling Gail Wilson this evening to run through the whole thing so no doubt she'll want to see you first thing tomorrow.'

Tim stood, a little unsteadily, and started for the door. 'And I will be speaking to Cole Jackson,' he slurred. 'The whole thing is ridiculous, outrageous. You think you're clever but you're just a cocky madam. Maisie told me no one in the team likes you and I can perfectly well see why.' He stumbled out, weaving and rebounding off the corridor walls as he went.

'Who's Maisie?' Ben asked.

'A colleague. Tim's girlfriend. Sort of. What are you laughing at?'

'Well, I mean – do you care that no one likes you?'

'Not much. They're twats anyway, the lot of them. Right, I need to go and see Dylan.'

'I think you'd better tell me the rest.'

But before she could start, his phone rang. She waited while he took the call, picking up that it was Dr Del on the other end, issuing orders. He didn't even get to speak before she ended the call. He jumped straight to his feet.

'We need to go. Dr Del wants us at the hospital. Apparently, the whole Meredith clan have turned up there; it's something to do with you?'

'She can hang on five minutes. I haven't told you everything yet, and anyway, she doesn't tell me what to do.'

'Well, she does me. Come on, I'll drive and you can tell me in the car.' He was pulling his jacket on now, rushing so much that he got in a tangle with the sleeves and knocked his glasses off his nose. She couldn't decide whether she found it pathetic or appealing.

'I'm assuming she sounded cross, then?' Kit picked his glasses up from the floor and handed them to him.

'Incandescent. What do you call it round here?'

'Tamping?'

'Yeah, that's it. Tamping.'

She could tamp away for all Kit cared. All she was interested in was Dylan, whose world had just crumbled, and who was soon enough going to find out exactly who his father was. She pulled her rucksack out from under the table and followed Ben, laughing at the sight of him falling over his own feet in his haste.

CHAPTER 20

In the car, Kit shot through the whole story again for Ben's benefit. It took a huge effort. She had run and run all day, and suddenly she was on empty: shivery, nauseous and bone-tired to the point that she could barely be bothered to speak. But she had one more lap to get through.

Ben parked the car in an ambulance bay at the back of the psychiatric unit, then led her to a small door, swiping his card to open it. He had hardly spoken himself, and she could see he was entirely preoccupied with what Dr Del was going to say. It must be horrible to feel so afraid of someone all the time. She teetered on the brink of forgiving him for dropping her in it to save his own neck.

They arrived in the lobby to find Dai Davies, John, and Rhian all sitting in a row.

'Ah, here you are, Kit,' Dai said. 'I was hoping you'd turn up. Well, we got it sorted, didn't we, Rhian?'

Rhian nodded. She seemed perfectly calm. The Dai effect, Kit supposed.

'Where's Dylan?' Kit felt worried, although it hardly seemed likely that Dai would have lost him along the way.

'He's in with Dr Carver. She's seen Rhian already and Mrs Meredith is in another room with a nurse, waiting for Dr Carver to get to her. I've explained it all to the doctor; she isn't completely in agreement with your analysis but we had a frank exchange of views. You may as well sit down, I expect she'll be a while.'

Kit sat next to Dai and Ben took the next seat along. He was almost visibly quaking now.

'Don't worry, I'll deal with her.'

He looked at her gratefully. 'Are you ever afraid of anyone?'

'Not really. It's the upside of being spiky.'

'Yeah . . . about that . . .'

'It's fine. We need to talk about "only a social worker", though.'

'Ah, right. All I meant was—'

'Ms Goddard?' The door to the assessment unit swung open and Dr Del appeared, in her knee-high boots and black trousers once again, but looking especially like a dominatrix today due to her blood-red shirt and matching lipstick. Her eyes passed over Ben, her face closing up into a brief expression of distaste, and then moved on to find Kit.

'Would you join me, please?'

Kit did as she was asked, wondering whether they were about to have a stand-up row in the middle of the assessment unit. But when the door closed behind them, Dr Carver's expression was more conciliatory than she'd expected.

'The mother's given me quite a lot of information. DS Davies seems to have a way with her; she was quite forthcoming and opened up far more than she did last time we saw her. She's agreed to be readmitted.'

'That's good. What about Dylan?'

'I can't get a word out of the boy. He will only speak to you. I'd be grateful if you'd give it a try. I'll sit in with you, of course.'

'No. That won't work at all. I'll see him, but it has to be alone.' Of course Dylan would be struggling. He'd kept the secret without fail and now he was being asked to give it up. His loyalty to his gran and his mother ran deep and the last person he was going to talk to was the very one who had the power to put his gran back in hospital. That was exactly what had been held over him as a threat for the last four years.

Dr Del hesitated, wanting to keep her control, but Kit set her face firm.

'Very well. He's in there, please report back to me.' Dr Del stretched out her arm to open the door and let Kit into the room.

'Dylan? Are you OK?'

'I'm not, no.' He was relieved to see her, she could tell at once. He looked so lost and helpless that she almost wanted to hug him, as she might have a much younger child. But she had to remember that no matter how he looked right now, he was a young man. She sat down opposite him and leant forward on her chair. He dropped his head down, away from her gaze.

'Dr Carver said you wouldn't speak to her. You can tell me, though, can't you?'

He nodded. 'I think so, but it's hard.'

'You're very muddled?'

He looked up at her, and his tears overflowed, running down his face and dripping off his chin. She felt in her pocket for a clean tissue and handed it to him, thinking about how to help him begin. He dabbed at the torrent of tears with the flimsy square of paper, making no impression at all on his glistening face.

'Let's start with what I already know,' she said. He nodded slightly and took a juddering breath. 'I talked to you about it a bit on the mountain, do you remember? About how your mum had changed and you couldn't always tell what was real and what wasn't? And I think I had that partly right, but maybe not all of it. Who was the person who got you all mixed up about what was real, Dylan?'

'My nan.'

'You love your nan, right? And you love your mum. So it's not hard to see why you got confused. You were only thirteen, I think, when your nan came back?'

He nodded again. 'We used to go to see her every week, in the hospital and then in that place. My mother used to cry every time we had to leave her there. So when she came home, we were happy.'

'Yes, I can see that. But you had to keep it a secret?'

'Yes, because she said they'd take her back.'

'I'm thinking that at first it was fine, having her home, then it got harder? She started to say she was hearing things? Am I right?'

'Well, she was hearing things. She could hear voices coming out of the radio. So could my mother after a bit. They told her all about how everyone in Rock hated us. Well, that bit's true, I know it is.'

'I'm not sure that's quite right, but go on.'

He shrugged. 'No one ever bothered with us much, anyway. So I think she was right about that. The voices were right, I mean. Then the signs started. One morning, we got up and someone had written on the garden wall, next to the gate.'

'What did it say?'

'Psycho family.'

Aled and Joe's handiwork, no doubt. 'What else?'

'Loads of stuff. People were coming into the house, trying to get her put back in the hospital again, and us with her. They'd move things around, to leave a sign, you'd put something down in one place, it'd turn up somewhere else.'

'That happens to everyone, Dylan. It just means you've forgotten where you put it, or someone else in the family has moved it without you knowing.'

'Does it?' He looked into her eyes, but then he frowned. 'I see what you mean but I don't know.'

'All right, leave that for now. What else?'

'Sometimes we'd find things in the garden. Like that day we saw the money. You saw that yourself so you know it's right.'

'I did, but . . . well, never mind. Anything else?'

'We had to be careful what we ate. They could poison our food, like they tried to do to my gran in the hospital. We could buy food from Rowena, because my mother knew her, but not anyone else.'

'Is that why you wouldn't eat the burger?'

He nodded. 'I wanted to, I really did, it smelt beautiful, but I was afraid.'

She sat back, thinking this was enough for now. But he was biting at his lip.

'Is there something you want to tell me, Dylan?'

'I can see your face, the way you're looking at me. I know it sounds mad when I say it. But it's like, at first, I thought she was definitely wrong, but when my mother started to say it too, and it was the two of them showing me one sign after another, proving the point over and over every day, I got mixed up and I just didn't know anymore. I'm still not sure on some of it.'

'I can see that.'

'But then my nan started making us go up the mountain with her at night, she wanted us all to be close to my grandad, and that night you came up there – we were all going to jump. She kept trying to get us to do it, said it was the only way. My mother agreed with her. It seemed easier to do what they said, they just wouldn't leave it alone. But when you came, I changed my mind, I went back to thinking you could help us. I wanted to tell you, I nearly did, but I was afraid we'd get put in the hospital. Like she'd always said we would. Well, that is what happened, isn't it? So she was right on that, too.'

'I'm sorry. I know it seems that way but I didn't know how else to keep you safe. I can see why it made you think she must be right. Is that why you didn't say anything about all this in the hospital last time?'

'Yeah. I just wanted to get home to her, and to my mother. I knew if I said it, they'd keep me there longer.'

'All right – just one more thing? Is that OK?'

'Yes, it's OK.'

'Did your gran ever hit you?'

He fidgeted, looking over towards the door.

'She can't hear you, Dylan. Did she hit you?'

He nodded. 'She did, once. She slapped my face, it was after we'd been up the mountain at night the first time, I didn't want to jump off and I ran away. On that rocky bit where you and I stopped that time, when you were looking in those trees, remember? I fell there on the way down and they caught up with me somehow, her and my mother, and she hit me. I don't know why she did it.'

The last piece of the puzzle clicked into place, finally filling the gap that had been niggling at Kit's mind for weeks. She understood now who had seen that slap, and how. Aled had been in his drug den having a night-time smoke, and Dylan had fallen right in his line of vision. Dylan was sniffling slightly now. 'I don't know why she did it,' he repeated, more insistently this time.

'She wasn't herself. She wouldn't deliberately hurt you, but she'd lost track of what was real and what wasn't – even more than you and your mum had. I know it's hard but hopefully she can get better again and maybe in time you'll be able to forgive her?'

He nodded. 'What will happen now?'

'I'm afraid you're going to have to go through all this again with Dr Carver.'

He made a face. 'I don't like her.'

'No, nor me. But she's the one to sort it. Sorry, I know she's awful.'

He smiled for the first time. 'All right then.'

She left him and crossed the room to open the door, finding Dr Carver leaning against the wall just outside, suspiciously close to the door.

'Oh, Dr Carver, hi.'

'And how did you get on?'

'I think he'll speak to you now.' She held the door open and after seeing Dr Carver in and giving Dylan a quick wink from behind her back, headed back to the lobby to find Rhian.

She found everyone sitting exactly where she'd left them. From somewhere deep inside, she had to pull up the energy to keep going. Every time she was sure she was on the last lap, there turned out to be another one.

'Rhian? Can I have a word? Alone?'

Rhian got up at once and followed Kit out into the main corridor. It was deserted. Kit leant her side up against the wall. Rhian stood facing her, her hands twisting and knotting around each other.

'Is Dylan all right?'

'Yes, I didn't mean to worry you. He's fine.'

'Are you going to take Dylan away from me?'

She'd answered Kit's question before it was even asked. 'No. Dylan's old enough to decide where he wants to be for himself now anyway. Did Tim Page tell you that could happen?'

Rhian's eyes darted away for a split second, but then she nodded. 'All the time he was growing up, I was afraid the social workers would take him. Because I know you can do that kind of thing, you see. Look at what happened to my mother.'

'I know it's what he told you, but no one is going to take Dylan away.' That was how Rhian's silence had been secured. What with that, and the threats to put Fflur back into hospital, Tim Page had certainly made the optimum use of every last little bit of power he had. 'Was that how he persuaded you to do it, Rhian? Did he say your mother would never get out if you didn't sleep with him?'

'No, that wasn't it. It was worse than that. He was nice to me. My mother was gone and I thought he liked me. Then afterwards he said she'd never come home if I told.'

'Why do you say it's worse? It was just as bad that he did that, either way.'

'No, I meant – it was worse on me. Because it was my fault, wasn't it? He didn't make me do it, so it was my fault.'

'Oh, Rhian, it wasn't.'

'What do you mean?'

'It was his fault, not yours. You've got a lot to sort out and I know you're confused about what's real and what's not, but that one thing you have to believe me on. You did nothing wrong. It was all him. Please just try to keep hold of that.'

'I will try. But what if he comes looking for me?'

'He won't. I've seen to it. You're safe now.'

'Are you sure?' A half-smile appeared, her face becoming almost pretty as a little of the tension drained away.

'Certain. That's the end of it now.'

'Can I ask you another question, Kit?'

'Yes, go on.'

'Who sent you to us?'

But that was for Dylan to hear about first. He needed to know that Aled still cared about him, had looked out for him, even if he couldn't admit it to the other boys. That he'd kept the secret Dylan had shared with him, about his nan coming home. Kept it to himself for years. Until he'd been lurking on the mountain one night, and he'd seen Fflur slap Dylan's face. That he'd done his clumsy best to get Dylan some help but had panicked when Frankie tried to get more information out of him. It would mean a lot to Dylan to know that. He was going to need friends, after all, because he was certainly not going to have any kind of a father.

'It was probably the school, Rhian. Don't worry over it.' She led Rhian back into the waiting area, and they both settled into their places on the row of chairs, to await Dr Carver's verdict.

When she eventually came to summon Kit and then to tell her that she'd probably been right, and that this did indeed look like a case of *folie à famille*, Kit was almost past caring. She'd done what was needed to persuade Rhian and Dylan to accept another admission, waited while Fflur was placed under section, and after firmly refusing a lift from Ben, had called a taxi to take her to the CMHT to pick up her car. She told herself she had done everything she needed to, but when a text told her the taxi was running late, she couldn't make herself settle down to wait. Vernon's scales theory kept popping back into her mind, along with the telling-off he'd given her for othering people with mental health problems. It had been easy to avoid doing that with Dylan; she'd seen the confused, stigmatised boy in him from the start. And she'd even got there with Rhian in the end, understanding at last how she'd been used and how hard she'd struggled to protect her son and keep him close to her. But there was one person she still hadn't connected with.

Dr Del didn't break her stride when Kit caught up with her in the corridor.

'Can I have a word?'

'Walk with me. I need to get these admissions organised.'

'Could I get five minutes with Fflur?'

'I'm not sure that's wise. She's in the ambulance waiting to be transferred to Dinas. She's much calmer now and I don't want her destabilised.'

'I'll be careful, I promise. Just five minutes. I just want to let her know that I understand.'

'I don't suppose you understand at all. Her psychiatric history is complex.'

'You talk as if that's all there is to her. It's part of her life, but it's not Fflur. What about her husband and her family, the personality she is, all the things she's lived through? Don't they matter?'

'Impressive.'

'What is?'

'Your ability to stand up for yourself. Your point is a reasonable one – you can have five minutes with her and no more, and if she becomes upset you are to leave her alone. I've taken your view on board, now I ask that you respect mine. Yes, she has a life history but right now she's a terrified, vulnerable woman who thinks she's going to be incarcerated for life. I don't want this poor lady anymore distressed than she already is. Understood?'

'Understood.'

'I'm not quite the uncaring harridan you seem to have been told I am. I wouldn't rely on Ben James too much if I were you. For anything.'

'Also understood.'

Kit found the ambulance parked outside the unit, doors open, two staff chatting outside while awaiting their instructions. Once she had explained why she was there, they stood back to allow her to jump in.

Fflur sat rigid on a seat at the farthest end from the doors, staring straight ahead. She didn't turn her head as Kit sat down on the seat next to hers.

'Fflur? I've come to have a quick chat. Is that all right?'

She didn't respond; Kit took her hand gently in her own, feeling the loose, thin skin sliding over the fine bones. Fflur turned then, her pale-blue eyes sharp under their hooded lids, examining Kit's face. Her lip was trembling.

'Are they sending me back to Penlan?'

'No. They're not.'

'I don't want to go to Snowdrop Court.'

'No. Not there either.'

'It wasn't a bad place, I made a good friend there, but I want to go home.'

'Of course.'

'I want to be with my family. My husband's there, you see. And my daughter and her son. I love the boy. I hurt him once, I know I shouldn't have, but he's a good boy and he doesn't bear a grudge. Will they let me go home?'

'I'm not sure. But you're going to go to a different hospital first and then we can see.'

'I prefer it in Rock. Did you know everyone calls it that?'

'I did.'

'Mind, we were alone up there. But I was never one to care about that. I have always made my own way in life. Will of iron, my husband says. They did me a favour then they expected it to be repaid. But that's not a favour at all then, is it? It's a debt.'

'I suppose it is.'

'My daughter's different to me. She takes after my husband, and they take advantage of her. That's why I had to look after her, when they were trying to get in.'

'What do you mean? Who was trying to get in, Fflur?'

Fflur snatched her hand out of Kit's grasp and her mouth tightened. 'People up there, in Rock. They're not good people. We have to keep the door locked. We always keep the chain on. I'd like you to go now, please.'

'I will. It's going to be all right now.'

'Yes. But I will need to go home. She can't manage without me, you see. It's a mother's job to protect her child.' She resumed staring out of the ambulance window, chin upward, unyielding.

That night and the next day passed in a blur. Gail Wilson had been Kit's first port of call, listening in horrified silence as the tale was poured out to her. Having parked it all with someone who got paid enough to deal with it, Kit had fallen into bed and slept straight through her alarm and on until late morning, arriving at work near lunchtime and in a panic to find Cole, Vernon and Nazia all waiting to speak to her and numerous messages on her desk from Dr Carver, Ben and Maxine. By the end of the day, she'd repeated the whole thing another four times, given a written statement, ducked questions from almost every social worker in the building and viewed the video that popped up on her phone of Tim Page angrily packing up the contents of his desk in the CMHT office. She called Ben back at once.

'I hope he didn't see you recording that.'

'He did, but who cares? He was straight off home to await the knock on the door. Police, disciplinary, professional misconduct, they'll be queuing up outside his house by now. He's looking at losing his job and his registration at a minimum, but he's put Fflur at risk by altering records, he's kept her away from the help she needed; it's gotta add up to ill-treatment of a vulnerable adult. He could go down for that, mind, and that's before we even get to what went on with Rhian. The prospect of a few months inside is probably bothering him more right now than me recording his departure, to be honest. I doubt social workers have a very good time of it in prison.'

'Fair point. Update me on the Merediths, then.'

'They're all in, Dylan and Rhian in Sandbeach, separate wards just in case, Fflur in Dinas. Psychology referrals have been done, so hopefully it shouldn't take too long before we can get it worked through with them and Dylan and Rhian can go home. Rhian's holding on a bit but Dylan's easing up on the delusional beliefs already.'

'That's great.'

'Yeah. What are you doing tonight?'

'Sleeping.'

'OK, what about tomorrow?'

'I've got a day off.'

'Really? I'm owed some time back myself.'

'Maybe. No, actually, it's my mother's funeral.' Not that she'd forgotten, as such. It was more that she'd tried to block it out.

'God, sorry, of course. Another time?'

'Sure.' She ended the call.

'You don't sound sure to me.' Nazia had appeared to be engrossed in *Closer*, but clearly that had not been altogether the case.

'No, I'm not.'

'I'd give him a miss if I were you, then. We've talked it over in the team . . .'

'What?'

'Yeah, we have. He sounds like a bit of a . . . type, if you know what I mean. We all agree you're too good to waste yourself on someone you're not sure about.'

'That's not what Maisie reckons.'

'I keep telling you, no one ever said that. It's just Maisie stirring.'

Vernon emerged from his office. 'Yeah. And she didn't turn out to be the best judge of character, did she?'

They all laughed, then stopped themselves, feeling a bit mean. Vernon was zipping up his threadbare coat. 'I'm off. I meant to tell you, it's been agreed that once the boy's home you can keep the case on. Mental health will have the mum and the gran. Let's see if we can get the lad back to school, eh? Nice piece of work, Kit. Don't ever go off on a frolic like that again, though, or I'll sack you myself.'

'I won't. Right, I'm going home as well.' She realised that she had just one evening to steel herself for the following day. The last funeral she'd been to had been Danny's, and she couldn't let the memory of that slip back in.

Kit got through the funeral by putting her mind elsewhere. Bits and pieces of the last few weeks floated past her easily enough, all resolved. The American family was the image that caught at her attention. She'd got John's journal out of the recycling bin the night before, congratulating herself on her total lack of household routine, which had prevented it from long since departing for the depths of a bin lorry. She'd reread the part about the young couple first. But it was the other story she'd really wanted to get to. The mum, dad and three teenagers who had gone missing. She felt so sorry for them all, especially the kids. What must it be like if the adults you trusted most in the world told you things that didn't seem right? She could see how you might start to accept it. The family's faces continued to circulate in her mind throughout the perfunctory funeral that Gino had organised and were still churning away by the time everyone had arrived with obvious relief at the pub.

'Thank fuck that's over, yeah?' Tyler slid into the seat next to her.

She dropped her head onto his shoulder. She felt like she

336

hadn't seen him for ages. 'That's it for good, though, isn't it? I mean, we're stuck with how she was, she's never going to get any better at being our mother.'

'Well, no. Not like that was ever going to happen anyway. You're the one always telling me that.'

'I know. And only the one parent we've got left now, then.'

'Oh, I see, here we go again.'

'You seriously need to tell him.'

'I seriously don't. Why should I? He's never cared.'

'I don't know, Ty. That was Christine's version of events, and we mimicked what she said because she wanted us to and we wanted to please her. We didn't even question whether it was true.'

'You reckon?'

'You know it. She was our mother, no matter what. We were just kids. We took it all on board.' She thought about Dylan, how he had accepted his mother's version of events, and how Rhian in her turn had accepted Fflur's. About how much kids wanted to believe that their parents could be trusted, how they would distort their own understanding of reality just to make their parents right.

'He's not exactly dad of the year, though, is he?'

'No. He's pretty useless. But maybe not quite as bad as she made out. Just tell him what happened to you. About the abuse, and about Danny. Gino came through in the end with Christine and the funeral, didn't he? I'm going to need his help with Amber. And you know Josie's a mess too, right? We've got to try and bring him and Mal into the family now. To help me, if nothing else. Just give him a chance.'

'I don't know. Want a vodka?'

'Coke, I'm driving, remember?'

'Boring.'

'Someone has to be.' She'd wanted to keep her self-control, since it was pretty certain that no one else present would. Battle lines criss-crossed the room like tripwires: Christine's siblings against Gino, Gino's cousins against them, Amber against Josie, Josie against nearly everyone present.

After Tyler had gone to the bar, Kit picked up her phone and started putting together a group text. How did people phrase these things? In the end she headed it 'dinner at mine' and added a date and time. She sent it to Dai and Martin, and Ricky and Meg. Her finger hovered over Ben James's name. What was holding her back? She thought about what Gino had said, about realising in the end that he didn't want drama. And about Ben and his slipperiness, that feeling of not quite trusting him to always have her back, the women who owed him unspecified favours, the mention of which made him cough and move on too quickly, the way he had been looking down at the pretty, dark-haired doctor that day in the hospital. She'd had so much of that with Jem, she was hypervigilant now. She was building a life for herself and she didn't need the distraction. How had Gino put it? She wanted to know what she was coming home to.

'Good luck, mate, that's all I can say.' She looked up, not understanding Tyler's words, and saw that he had put a vodka down in front of her and moved away, talking to someone else as he went. Alex. Sunburnt, unshaven, his red hair long and a bit knotted in places.

'Jesus, you look a mess.'

'Thanks very much. I've been travelling for nearly two days straight.' He sat down next to her and took her vodka. 'Do you mind?'

'Go ahead. How come you're here?'

He knocked back the drink 'You sounded a bit upset. In your text.'

'Did I?'

'Yeah. Plus, you said you missed me.'

'Did I?'

'Quit it. You know you did. You want me to be straightforward with you, clear about what I want, no complications, I get that and I'm all ready to sign up for it. But you've got to be the same.'

'That's me told.'

'Yep.' He looked around the room. 'Full of your family, isn't it?'

'Yeah, it's a bit of a tradition at funerals.' On the other side of the pub, Tyler and Gino were deep in conversation.

'Fancy getting out of here? We could go down to Cliffside, open up the café, stay in the flat for the weekend. Should be warm enough for a swim now.'

'Uh-huh.'

'Is that a yes, then?'

'Yeah. But there's something I need to do first.'

'Go on.'

'I need to make a visit. I'll drive, we can stop at the flat for my clothes and we also need to call at a shop.'

'For what?'

'A box of Turkish delight.'

His face broke into his easy-going grin. 'OK then, fine with me. I like a mystery.'

Their visit to Deri took twice as long as Kit had allowed for. They finally got back to the car to find it filled with a repeated buzzing. Alex popped open the glove compartment to investigate. 'Kit, your phone's going mad.'

'I can hear it. It'll be my family. Josie's slapped someone, most probably.'

'I'd better pick it up, then?'

She hesitated, thinking back to Tyler and Gino in the pub. The way Gino had started rubbing at his eyes while Tyler was talking. Gino crying, a sight never seen. Then his arm had come up and gone across Tyler's shoulders, and had lain there stiff as a length of wood. It was one of the most awkward moments she'd ever witnessed; even at a distance it was obvious that neither of them had a clue what to say or do next. But it was enough; every time she thought about it, she had to breathe in hard through her mouth to hold back her own tears.

'Well?' Alex asked. 'Do I answer it or not?'

She'd reached the turning for the coast road now. She pushed her indicator down. 'No. Switch it off. Let's go and get that swim.'

ACKNOWLEDGEMENTS

A huge thanks to Richard Arcus, who persuaded me to do this story, and was quite right. Thanks also to my agent Laetitia Rutherford, for believing in me, for helping me to see this through and for her commitment to Kit and her stories.

Thanks to Jon Riley and the team at Quercus for making this happen, and to Celine Kelly for her thoughtful, insightful editing.

Thanks to my sister and my brother and the whole of my wider family for being so positive about all this and for enjoying Kit's adventures so much.

As always, thanks to all my friends from school, uni courses, many and various jobs and elsewhere for all your support and encouragement. Special thanks and love to Geoff, Gavin, Gary, Cate, Judy and Gareth, Maxine, Kate, Allie, Susan and Sian – you lot are great and you keep me going.

To Nazia, Helen, and Emma, thanks for the farm shop brunches and the laughs, and for always being so excited on my behalf.

Thanks to Dr Ben Curtis for his advice on the practical points of Fflur's story. I am grateful also for Dr David Selway's excellent research on mining accidents and memory in south Wales, which helped me to understand Fflur's life.

Thank you to Alex, who generously gave me so much help and advice with the psychiatric aspects of the book, especially *folie à deux*.

Thank you to Jonathan for all the guidance and support over the past thirty-five years.

And as always, the deepest love and thanks to my husband and my children for always being there to support me and distract me, both of which are vital to my sanity.